Her
Daughter

BOOKS BY JEN CRAVEN

The Baby Left Behind

Best Years of Your Life

All That Shines and Whispers

Her Daughter

Jen Craven

bookouture

Published by Bookouture in 2024

An imprint of Storyfire Ltd.
Carmelite House
50 Victoria Embankment
London EC4Y 0DZ

www.bookouture.com

ISBN: 978-1-83790-732-8
eBook ISBN: 978-1-83790-731-1

For my cousins, my very first friends

ONE

RACHEL

November

If life hadn't thrown her a curveball, maybe she wouldn't be passing off Walmart cookies as her own.

Rachel lined the iced circles on a small tray, then buried the plastic container in the bottom of the garbage can as though it were evidence of her financial shortcomings. No one ever commented on her store-bought offerings, but she couldn't help imagining her best friend silently judging. When it was Monica's turn to host, she always splurged on two dozen delectable gourmet treats from Prantl's bakery.

Rachel covered the tray in plastic cling wrap at the same time her husband entered the kitchen, wearing gym shorts and an old T-shirt.

"Why aren't you changed?" Rachel asked, giving him a once-over. "We needed to leave like five minutes ago."

Chris pulled a Pepsi from the fridge. "I was thinking I'd stay home and get the yard raked. It's supposed to rain tomorrow, and those leaves will be a soggy mess if—"

"What? No. It's family night." Rachel stared at him with a

disapproving look. "Us, Monica, Roman, all the kids. Why wouldn't you come?"

"It doesn't always have to be couples, you know. You and Monica hang out all the time without us husbands."

"Yes, but what's the point of family night if the dads aren't included?"

"I just don't feel like it." He pulled back the cover from the cookies and snatched one before Rachel playfully smacked his hand away.

"Hey, those are for later." But she was only partially scolding—the other half secretly grateful for Chris's indifference when it came to food. Fancy cuisine was as foreign as first-class plane seats or an Ivy League education. "C'mon. Since when don't you want to hang out with Roman and Monica? Oh, shoot—that reminds me. I told Mon I'd pick up the boys for practice tomorrow." She opened her phone calendar to add a note to the already overflowing schedule.

Chris folded his arms across his broad chest. "That's exactly why."

Rachel looked back up; tucked a loose piece of brown hair behind her ear. Her eyebrows pulled together.

"You're always doing everything for them," Chris said. "Pick-ups, drop-offs. You shouldn't let them take advantage of you."

"They're not taking advantage of me. I'm happy to help. Monica's boys are like extensions of our own. And besides, I'm already doing all those things with our kids anyways. What's the difference?"

"I'm just saying."

"Saying what?"

"Monica and Roman should remember that they're parents sometimes."

"Chris." Rachel's eyes widened. She'd never heard him talk this way about their friends. Well, her friend really. The two men were cordial, and they'd watched plenty of sports between their two houses when the families got together, but Rachel and Monica's friendship was the bedrock of the family pairing. They knew each other's ringtones, how to operate each other's thermostats. Their spouses were merely along for the ride.

Rachel also recognized the unsaid part of his jab: There was more to life than being workaholics. But that was a conversation for another day. No time to get into *that* when they were supposed to be out the door already.

"Please come with us," Rachel said, laying a hand on Chris's arm. Touching him still made her skin come alive, even after twenty years. "Even Chloe's coming." If she could get their nineteen-year-old to tag along, surely she could convince her husband.

He let out a breath. "Fine."

Rachel got on her tiptoes to plant a peck on his lips. "Thank you. Now go change. Maybe something nicer than Wranglers?"

He winked at her as he left, clearly finding her request a joke. Only Rachel knew it wasn't. She sometimes daydreamed of sipping an Aperol spritz at the country club pool while he golfed. Sometimes, she dreamed of an entirely different life.

The adults gathered around Monica's kitchen island after finishing the chicken parmesan Monica had catered. Roman, her husband, still in his sleek suit and tie from work, poured his third glass of Cabernet. Somewhere on the floor above, four kids —two of Monica's and two of Rachel's—played "The Floor is Lava," a surprisingly simple imaginative game, but one that involved much jumping and leaping on furniture.

"I swear they're going to fall through the ceiling one of these days," Monica said, shaking her head, her platinum-blonde locks dusting the tops of her shoulders. The sound of stampeding feet spread warmth through Rachel's chest. There'd been a time she and Monica weren't sure they'd have children the same age. Not when Rachel had started so early—an unexpected kickoff to motherhood.

"It was never so noisy when you were little," Rachel said to Chloe, who, although physically with them at the island, had been largely absorbed in her phone.

"That's because there was only one of me," Chloe responded sarcastically.

Monica reached out and gently brushed a stray eyelash off Chloe's cheek. "Why have more when the first is so perfect?" She smiled, even when Chloe rolled her eyes.

"Listen," Monica said, changing the subject, "we really need to decide if we're going to pull the trigger on the beach trip. If we want to try for January, before Chloe's spring semester starts, we should have booked the house months ago."

Rachel nodded. "I know, I know. It's just... things are crazy and—"

Chloe cut her off. "You're *so* busy. We know."

"Hey, be nice to your mom," Monica said. Then to Rachel, "I get it, Rach. The kids are in a gazillion activities, but Chloe's right. You can never be too busy to take a vacation. I'm dying to get away. Roman's campaign is twenty-four-seven. God, I miss his faculty schedule. Plus, it gives us all an excuse to get out of the winter weather. We need to spend some quality time with the boys before the campaign really kicks up. And we just love doing it with you guys. This will be, what, our eighth year?"

"Give or take." Rachel was grateful Monica didn't mention the one year they simply couldn't scrounge up the money.

"We can't let time just slip by. And if you're too busy to look up places, then I can do it. In fact, I'll do some searching tonight."

"I'll help," Chloe said.

Monica patted the girl's back. "See? Leave it up to a Gen Zer to be our tech-savvy house hunter. At least someone's on board."

"I'm always on board for a little vacay," Roman said. "I'm sure I can figure out a way to make it a work expense." He winked to no one in particular then pulled a stool to the other side of Chloe, who recoiled when his breath hit her face. Rachel could smell the alcohol from feet away. Rachel met eyes with Monica, and the two shared a look of understanding that didn't need words. As quickly as it passed, they looked away.

Roman swirled his wine with an air of sophistication that matched his jet-black hair, always parted and combed into a neat business cut. "But can you manage to tear yourself away from that boyfriend of yours—what's his name again?"

"Preston."

"Ah, Preston, right. Don't forget to leave a little time for academics too."

Chloe blushed, responding to his chide with an equally witty, "I'll let my 4.0 speak for itself."

Chris eyed Rachel, and she gave a minuscule shake of the head. *Not now. Just be nice.*

"Speaking of," Monica said to Chloe, "did you end up talking to your history professor about that group grade?"

Rachel frowned. "What group grade?"

"Oh, just this stupid group project that I ended up doing all the work for," Chloe said. "He gave everyone the same grade, which was totally unfair."

"Completely," Monica interjected. "People shouldn't get rewarded for doing nothing."

"Right? But he said he had no way of knowing who did what, and blah, blah, blah."

"Well, I hope you said something to Toni."

Rachel leaned forward. "Toni?"

"One of the group members," Chloe said, eyebrows raised. *Duh.*

Rachel sat back, a prickling feeling coming over her. How did Monica know about Chloe's school assignments? And more than that, how did she know a specific classmate's name? Monica and Chloe's lifelong closeness had always been a source of joy for Rachel. But special "aunts" weren't supposed to replace moms. In that moment, Rachel felt a bitter stab of jealousy for Monica being privy to the inner workings of Chloe's world.

"I can call your teacher if you want," Rachel offered, to which Chloe's expression turned horrified.

"No way. That's so embarrassing, Mom."

"Yeah, Rach. That's borderline helicopter parent," Monica added.

Rachel's tongue swelled. "Okay."

"No offense," Chloe said. "It's just that I don't want to be treated like the little kids. I'm not in elementary school anymore, remember?"

Monica took a sip of her cucumber water; turned to Chloe. "Can you just imagine your mom calling up to argue your grade?"

The two cackled, bumping shoulders.

But across from them, Rachel's cheeks burned. The conversation felt less good-natured and more like poking fun, in an unsettling sort of way. Like she didn't know the rules of motherhood. She wasn't an idiot or an outlier. So why did it feel like her best friend and her daughter were ganging up on her?

TWO

MONICA

THE NAME PLATE ON MONICA'S OFFICE READ, DR. MONICA *Cross, MD,* and it gave her a swell of pride every time she walked through the door. Reproductive endocrinology hadn't been her original goal, but after a fellowship in obstetrics, she knew bringing babies into the world was where she was meant to be. Ten years and thousands of clinical hours later, she was one of the top fertility specialists in Pittsburgh.

But all the tireless work and dedication to her professional life didn't come without a cost of course, as Monica was reminded when her phone lit up on a Tuesday afternoon.

Lucas's game starts in half an hour. Do you just want me to take him?

Monica whipped her head to the clock on the wall and sighed. She'd never make it home in time to get Lucas to Cranberry Township. Or was it Beaver? Her brain rattled. She didn't even know where the game was.

One eye to the computer, the other to her phone, she typed a response to Jessica, their nanny.

Yes please. So sorry. Will be there ASAP.

She hit send then fired off another text to Roman.

Are you going to Lucas's game? Need to relieve Jessica. I'm running late.

It was a lie. She wasn't running late; she was simply working. These were her normal hours, and there was still a final patient to see. Monica prided herself on keeping her office open past five o'clock to accommodate as many people as possible; even if it meant she didn't get home until seven or later most days. Her boys understood, she rationalized. It's all they'd ever known.

When Roman didn't immediately respond, Monica went back to her computer, working on charts and taking notes. It wasn't unusual for her and her husband to go the entire day without contact. They were both busy people with important jobs. It had been her dream to go to med school—or so she thought. The extra fuel from her overachieving parents didn't hurt and was probably the final push toward a career of importance. Still, there were days when she yawned through the whole commute and needed a third cup of coffee to get through the afternoon slog. But it was worth it. She was living proof that women could have both—a career and a family.

Sometimes Monica envied Rachel and her easy job at the preschool. Looking after fifteen toddlers couldn't be *that* mentally taxing. Rachel could clock in and clock out and not have to worry about things like publishing research or dashing people's dreams when another round of IVF was unsuccessful. The weight on Monica's shoulders felt like a hammer drilling her into the ground, and now with the boys and a husband in the picture, she was often pulled in so many directions she thought she might break into pieces.

Forget the earlier sentiment. It was impossible to do it all. Her phone dinged with a response from Roman.

Taking clients to dinner.

Her shoulders slumped forward. Of course the campaign came first. Monica's mind drifted back to the time before Roman's political ambitions took over his life—when teaching political science at the university was enough to appease his interests. The idea of running for mayor was a job in and of itself, and once it became clear he was serious, he'd resigned from teaching—along with the flexible schedule that came with it. Monica hadn't exactly anticipated politics when she married him, but as the saying goes: Sometimes life is unexpected.

So he wouldn't be able to meet Jessica at the game. Monica did a mental calculation. If she finished her final appointment and packed right up, it would still take a good forty minutes to get to wherever the game was—and that was assuming there'd be no traffic.

It was tempting to ask Jessica to stay on for the rest of the evening. She'd pay her overtime. Or she could ask Rachel to pick her son up. But Lucas's face flashed in Monica's conscious. The sweet boy who'd made her a mama eight years ago. She couldn't let him be the only kid without parents in the stands.

Decision made, she left her office and entered the exam room down the hall, where a thirty-something couple sat together holding hands. She'd seen faces like these before—full of desperation and longing—putting all their hope in her. It filled her with the utmost honor to be the person that could help make their dreams come true. It didn't always happen—there was a sad story for every few happy ones—but Monica wouldn't have traded her job for anything in the world.

Even a youth basketball game.

. . .

The 376 out of the city was backed up to a crawl, exactly like she'd feared. Monica checked the time. The game started ten minutes ago and she still had who knew how long to drive. "Come on, come on," she said to herself. After about three miles —which felt like thirty—the traffic cleared like magic, and Monica pressed a heeled foot to the gas.

She pulled into the elementary school parking lot a little after six thirty, flung the Mercedes into park and hurried inside just as the last two minutes ticked off on the scoreboard. Not wanting to miss another second, she forwent a seat and stood by the entrance to the gymnasium instead. A group of moms bunched together several rows up the bleachers— Monica couldn't remember their names—wearing matching shirts made from a Cricut machine, featuring each of their kids' numbers.

Monica scanned the players. Lucas wasn't on the court. Her eyes trailed the bench and found him third from the end in a sea of second-graders. She checked the clock—one minute left in the game. Damn! Hopefully Lucas would get in so she could say she'd seen him play.

He didn't.

The buzzer sounded, and both teams took to the center of the court to shake hands. Monica watched as her son peered into the stands to where Jessica sat clapping, Logan—Monica's youngest and her husband's mini-me—beside her. Jessica gave Lucas a thumbs up and a loving smile. He smiled back. Monica's heart broke.

The game now over, she made her way through the crowd to them.

"Mom, you're here!" Lucas said. His face brightened. "Did you see me score?" Sweat drenched his dark bangs, exertion leaving his cheeks flushed, hands clammy.

Monica pulled him into her so he wouldn't see the guilt on her face. His forehead dampened her blouse. "You did awesome," she said, an indirect response to his question. She hoped it would be enough. "I'm *so* proud of you."

Lucas beamed. It wasn't complicated to fool a child, but Jessica's expression registered the truth. Monica couldn't help but feel the young woman judged her parenting, despite not having children of her own. Still, she'd kept Jessica past her scheduled time, and that made her feel bad. *I'm sorry*, Monica mouthed to her, to which Jessica replied, *It's okay*. She should have just asked Rachel, the friend who never judged.

"Mommy, can we stop for ice cream on the way home?" Logan asked.

Monica picked him up. Even at five, he'd forever be her baby. She trailed a finger down his ear—the attached lobes like a ski slope running into his jawline, a trait from Roman. "That sounds like a great idea."

They left the school and said goodbye to Jessica in the parking lot. The boys jabbered away in the back seat, with an intermittent "Lucas touched me" or "Logan won't stop staring at me," but Monica was too distracted to intervene. Her thoughts were elsewhere. Not just elsewhere but a murky place that felt an awful lot like failure. She'd only made it to two minutes of her son's basketball season, which was already half over. Rachel would never miss one of her kid's activities. In fact, she was the one organizing the boosters, running the concession stand, and sending out reminder emails to parents. Rachel was so involved it was practically her livelihood, and Monica often found herself drawing comparisons. Was she doing something wrong in this whole motherhood thing? Was she a bad mom for not volunteering for every activity? What did it say about her that while her boys were running up and down fields and courts, she was behind a desk in a tall building in downtown Pittsburgh?

Things would have been a lot different if she'd chosen a less demanding career path. But then... would she have been fulfilled? She tried to picture herself as a stay-at-home mom, the type who put her kids on and off the bus and had dinner ready for when her husband walked through the door. Tried to imagine caring about the domestic things Rachel talked about. But there was nothing clear about that picture. It was blurry and out of focus. She was the breadwinner and had made her choice—a choice she loved. Even so, it didn't help the deep sense of guilt that settled in the pit of her stomach.

At the ice cream shop, she got the boys a scoop of mint chocolate chip—a cone for Lucas and dish for Logan, which he still managed to get all over himself. He looked up at her with his raven eyes, the ones he got from his father. "Aren't you getting anything, Mommy?"

"Not tonight," she said, not due to a dislike of the frozen treat, but because her belly had soured.

Monica watched the boys devour theirs with such innocent satisfaction, all the while her mind drifting to the one person missing from the equation. She texted Roman.

Getting ice cream with the boys. Want anything for later?

By the time they finished, there was still no response. She left empty-handed.

THREE

CHLOE

CHLOE OFTEN WONDERED IF SHE WOULD HAVE MET Preston if she'd lived at home instead of the dorms, which she'd initially considered. Room and board at Pitt was expensive, and her parents' salaries—her mom at the preschool and her dad at the tool and die plant—meant they weren't rolling in dough. But Rachel and Chris had both been adamant: You have to live on campus if you want to get the true college experience. Whatever that meant.

Now, Chloe was so glad she'd listened. If not, she wouldn't have roomed with Ava and may have never even met Preston, her two favorite people at Pitt. Commuting to and from Wexford would have been not only boring but excluding. Everyone knew commuters were treated differently—they never quite fit into the social circles as quickly because they missed out on all those after-hour activities. Immediate outcasts. Chloe thanked *God* she wasn't in that category.

"I'm meeting Preston at The Eatery. Wanna come?" Chloe pulled a Reformation top from Ava's side of the closet and tugged it over her head.

"Nah, I'm good. I have a Cliff bar," Ava said. "That looks so good on you, by the way. Not that looks are a measure of a woman's worth."

"A Cliff bar is hardly lunch." Chloe turned in the mirror, grateful for the girls' similar sizes, which allowed for one giant, shareable wardrobe. It was finally like having a sister her own age, a sister who worshiped Gloria Steinem and whose laptop proudly sported a "crush the patriarchy" sticker.

"Well, I don't want to interrupt a romantic date or something."

"Oh please," Chloe said with heavy sarcasm, reaching to grab her backpack from her lofted bed.

But Ava's quip was on point. Chloe and Preston were still very much in the honeymoon phase—everything puppy-dog eyes and sunshine. Both freshmen, they slept in each other's rooms as often as possible without letting the RAs know. Ava and Chloe had made an agreement about visitors: As long as one of the girls was in the room, all clothes stayed on.

The velocity with which she'd fallen in love with Preston had surprised even Chloe. It was so unlike any high school relationship she'd had. This was different, more intense, more serious. They walked each other to classes, and Chloe had been the first to say "I love you" after only a month. The first night they spent together, he'd played connect-the-dots with the constellation of freckles on her cheeks, ending with the mole under her eye. "The North Star—my favorite," he'd said then kissed her deeply.

So absorbing was her love, she'd almost had his name tattooed on her hip one drunken weekend. She'd texted Monica a shaky selfie from outside the tattoo parlor, to which Monica had replied, "Don't you dare! Your mother will kill you." Chloe would have gone through with it if she didn't hold Monica's opinion so highly. In the end, Chloe and Ava got little matching hearts on the insides of their wrists and stumbled back to campus with enough giggles to last the rest of the night.

Her other friends didn't hold a candle to Ava. Something about the two of them just clicked, even if their personalities differed. Ava's focused, matter-of-fact tendencies made Chloe's free spirit and undeclared major seem all the more fickle. And yet the friendship worked.

"You girls remind me so much of Monica and me in college," Rachel once said when she and Chris came into the city and took Chloe to lunch. "Those were the best years of my life."

An awkward silence followed the comment, one in which everyone at the table understood: Rachel and Chris's college career had been cut short with the arrival of Chloe. Her very existence meant her parents didn't get to finish what they started. But as if reading the sudden mood shift, Rachel clarified, "It's when I met Monica, started dating your dad, and then boom—along came you, the cherry on top."

Chloe wanted to believe it but struggled to see how getting pregnant at twenty-one and not completing her degree could be considered the best years of anyone's life.

The Eatery was packed with students, but Chloe and Preston found a small table near a window. She swiped her meal card for a grilled chicken salad, and Preston got two slices of pizza plus fries. She snickered at his ability to eat the way he did, but like all the student athletes, Preston's training schedule meant that he burned so many calories, he could consume whatever he wanted.

"What time's your practice tonight?" she asked.

Preston shoveled three fries into his mouth at once. "Six to eight I think."

"Want to come over after? Ava has a late study group. We could... hang out?" She gave him a sly smile at the same time she walked her fingers up his forearm.

"I'm probably going to be beat."

"We don't have to *just* hang out." She said it as a joke, because there was no world in which Preston could keep his hands off her when they were alone. She'd learned enough in high school to know what to do, but mostly let Preston take the lead. Sex made her feel powerful in a way that pleased him, even if it didn't last long enough for her to reap much benefit. The idea of watching a show without at least a make-out session was laughable.

Then again, they did get through an entire movie last weekend sitting side by side on her bed. It hadn't occurred to her until now. Her fork suspended above the bed of lettuce as her brain whirred. When was the last time they'd slept together?

"Maybe tomorrow," he said. Then, "Fuck. No, can't. We're on the road Thursday through Saturday."

Her bottom lip protruded into a pout. "I'll miss you."

Preston finished chewing his bite then offered a quick smile, though it seemed strained. He finished off the first piece of pizza and went immediately onto the next. A couple of girls walked by in jeans and cropped tops, hair twisted up into claw clips with strategic pieces falling free. Chloe detected Preston noticing them, something he'd never done before. For the past two months, he'd only had eyes for her. A weird sensation came over her, like a blast of heat mixed with nausea. She took a drink of water, letting the cold liquid coat her tongue.

"I'll miss you when you're gone," she said again, locking eyes with Preston. The deliberate address meant he couldn't smile his way out of it. She wanted the security of a response.

"Yeah... I'll miss you too." He guzzled half his bottle of blue Gatorade.

That was better. Chloe's muscles relaxed, and she popped a cherry tomato into her mouth. Preston must be preoccupied with the upcoming games. He took football seriously. She'd have to find a way to distract him. She didn't like this weird mood.

Their relationship had always been effortless—as it should be in such early days. They didn't fight, and Preston always opened doors for her when they walked between buildings. When her parents came to visit, he'd shaken her dad's hand and said, "Nice to meet you, Mr. Moreland," to which Chloe had beamed. *See,* she'd thought, *isn't my boyfriend amazing?* All the girls agreed, Chloe and Preston were the *cutest* couple. All-American, boy-and-girl-next-door young lovebirds. Even though they were only freshmen, she regularly imagined them being together through graduation, and even a wedding someday down the road. They'd make the most adorable babies.

Preston wiped his mouth with a napkin. "I better get going. Economics at one," he said as though Chloe didn't have his schedule memorized.

"I'll walk with you," she said, and despite the briefest pause, he agreed. She reached for his hand and took it.

Preston was uncharacteristically quiet as they left The Eatery, as though he was drifting on an invisible cord. Chloe repeatedly snuck glances his way, giving a giggly smile when he caught her the third time. Something was up, and whatever it was, she didn't want to intensify it by being anything less than the perfect girlfriend. Preston stared straight ahead. Her uncomfortable queasiness was coming back.

"Is everything okay?" Chloe finally asked as they turned up Bouquet Street.

"Why wouldn't it be?" he replied without looking at her.

"You just seem... off, that's all. Did I do something?"

"My mind's on the game. WVU is our biggest rival."

Chloe nodded, trying to convince herself that's all it was.

He did tend to get a little revved up before games, falling into his superstitions like eating the same two-egg omelet every morning and wearing a particular pair of underwear inside out. The Backyard Brawl, as the match-up between the Panthers and Mountaineers was known, always sent mild hysteria over the campus as one of the biggest games of the year.

She wished she could help ease his nerves with a little alone time, but Preston had clearly taken that off the table for the day. So much for shaving her legs that morning.

When they reached his building, Preston went for the door handle. "See you later," he said, seeming content to leave with not so much as a hug. *Uh-uh*, Chloe thought and yanked him back, planting a deep kiss on his lips.

"Love you," she said.

"Love you too." He said it to her mouth, not her eyes. And then he was gone, leaving Chloe with a plastic smile and twisted gut.

Later that day, Chloe lay on her bed with a rerun of *Euphoria* on in the background. She scrolled TikTok but couldn't quite muster the cheer the app usually gave her. She wished Ava was there to help sort out the puzzle in her head—Ava was always one for investigating. Despite what she felt was a profound connection, her relationship with Preston was newish. Did college guys operate differently than high school boys? With Ava covering the women's basketball game for the school paper, Chloe was left to her vulnerability.

Who else could she talk to? The other girls she'd befriended were fun to go out with and made decent study partners, but it wasn't the same. She couldn't shake the dread no matter how much she tried to connect Preston's distance to the pressure of football. And if she sat alone long enough, it would only get worse.

Her fingers moved across the phone to her contacts as if on autopilot, and before she knew it, she was dialing her mom. Warmth crept up her core, like the feeling of coming home after a long day, knowing you're safe and secure. They'd once been so close, two peas in a pod, but when Savannah and Jacob came along, the dynamic shifted. Chloe was a big kid, and they were babies who needed her mom's attention more. Her siblings' needs soon trumped her own, which made sense—shouldn't a mother be more attentive to a toddler than a pre-teen? Only, it didn't make sense to Chloe, who'd never stopped needing her mom. Her high school years came with a natural pulling away, a search for more independence. But Rachel was always there at the end of the day, even if it was in another room of the same house. Now, she couldn't remember the last time they'd gone shopping together let alone had a serious heart-to-heart. Their relationship was more about passing texts and preoccupied dinners on the occasion Chloe went home.

Maybe she'd catch her mom at a good time. *Was there ever a good time?* The phone rang long enough that Chloe was about to hang up, but then her mom was there. "Hey, Chlo."

"Hey." Suddenly, her voice felt small, catching her off guard, as though just hearing her mother on the other line was enough to bring up emotions she didn't want to bear. Part of her wanted to give herself a swift slap across the face. Why was she being all mopey about one weird lunch with Preston? Pull it together, dammit. Everything was fine; she was being overly dramatic. And yet, something tugged at her, and she craved comfort from the most organic place.

Chloe picked at a thread on her comforter. "I'm just bored. Everyone's out doing stuff and—"

"Is it an emergency?" Rachel cut her off. "I'm right in the middle of carpool and these kids make it impossible to hear anything. Jacob, knock it off! Savannah has a dentist appointment, so I'm dropping her off there and then running Jacob to practice before turning around to get Sav again. It's a little nuts right now."

"Oh. No, that's okay. It wasn't important." She swallowed hard.

"Okay, good. I mean, I wish we could talk, but— Jacob! I said knock it off!"

Chloe pulled the phone away from her ear to put distance between herself and the screaming. She could picture the scene perfectly, having spent her high school years riding shotgun with the lunatics in the back. Their bickering drove her mad. Then again, sometimes she wished she'd had a sibling close to her age with whom to fight just because she could.

"It's fine," Chloe said, a sharpness clipping the ends of her words.

"Alright, honey, I'm gonna have to jump off—we're pulling into the dentist."

"Okay."

"Talk to you later. Jacob—" *Click.* The call ended.

Chloe clamped her teeth down and held. Those two always got the best of her mom, and what was left for her? Scraps. She tossed her phone so hard that it bounced off the bed and hit the wall.

Feeling no better about the Preston situation, and even more annoyed with her mother, Chloe stared at the ceiling, trying not to let her mind spiral. When her phone beeped minutes later, she jumped, thinking it must be her mom calling back, now in a quiet spot, ready to talk. Hope swelled then popped. It wasn't her mom. But it was the next best thing.

Hey, chickadee, are you free to babysit Saturday? Some sort of campaign dinner... blah!

Chloe smiled at Monica's childhood nickname for her.

She'd been babysitting Lucas and Logan their whole lives—at least when their nanny wasn't available. The boys were almost like two bonus siblings. Logan, the youngest of all the kids, loved to play with Chloe's hair, often asking her to lie with him at bedtime and rubbing a lock between his fingers until sleep stole him away.

Chloe thought for a moment. She didn't like going home every weekend—too much social stuff to miss—but since Preston would be out of town, she might as well make a few extra bucks. Maybe being off campus would get her mind away from him a little, instead of smelling his cologne on her pillow every night.

She typed back.

Sure!

You're awesome.

Monica added a heart-eyed emoji. It was almost enough to lift Chloe's spirits.

Then, a few seconds later, another text came through, this one with a photo attached.

Need your opinion—black or red?

There were two shirts laid out on Monica's bed—a red blouse that tied at the neck and a black V-neck with a ruffled hem.

Definitely black, Chloe responded, feeling proud that a professional woman like Monica would value a teenager's fashion sense.

Thank you! Mwah!

Chloe sent back an emoji blowing a kiss. The light turn of conversation revitalized her and was enough to put the tension with Preston and the disappointment with her mom to the backburner... at least temporarily.

FOUR

RACHEL

A CHAUFFEUR, THAT'S WHAT RACHEL FELT LIKE MOST days. When she wasn't schlepping one of the kids to an activity, she spent her time waiting in the car for them to be finished. It was constant go here, go there, a million places to be, doctor's appointments, and scrimmages, and rehearsals, and playdates. A tornado disguised as a minivan. By the end of the day, she'd give her head a shake like *what just happened?*

But every once in a while, she'd find a small pocket of time where she wasn't rushing to the next thing. When everyone was where they needed to be and she could remember for a split second that she was a person before she had children, that she had interests outside of being a mom. Like this current minute, when Rachel found herself lingering outside Savannah's piano lesson while Jacob was occupied at the neighbor's. The car made not a sound—a rare phenomenon—and Rachel took advantage of the ten minutes she had by doing what she'd been secretly thinking of doing for months. She opened an internet tab on her phone and typed in the words: FINISH YOUR DEGREE.

The itch had never gone away completely, but once Chloe

started at Pitt, Rachel's yearning had multiplied. The admissions packets, the campus visits, the dorm room shopping had all taken her back to another life when she was wide-eyed and carefree. In a weird way, it felt like Chloe was replacing Rachel, a fresh coed ready to start a new phase of life. Watching Chloe immerse herself into college life gave Rachel a thirst to complete what she'd started. She was only thirty credits shy. Sometimes she envisioned what it would have been like to walk across the stage alongside her friends—alongside Monica—to get her diploma. But by that time, she'd had a baby to take care of. While her counterparts were picking out the perfect heels to go with their caps and gowns, Rachel was on the other side of the shoe department buying sneakers for Chloe, who was just learning to walk.

If the pregnancy took her by surprise, it was her own fault. After going off birth control following a scary blood clot, Rachel had resigned herself to non-hormonal methods, but lo and behold, the pull-out technique wasn't quite as effective.

Their families had held a meeting to discuss what to do. Rachel should stay in school; Chris should work to provide for them. No, Chris should stay in school to improve his chances at a better job, and Rachel would take on the motherly responsibilities and care for the baby. As if they were in the 1950s instead of 2004. It became a tug-of-war between who deserved the degree more, an unspoken blame for whose fault the pregnancy was. Chris should have known better. Rachel should have been on something. All the while, two terrified barely adults clasped hands and held on to the only thing they could—each other.

It didn't take long for Chris and Rachel to thrust a stiff arm in both their parents' faces. *Screw you, this is our decision.* They'd both drop out, both work and take care of their child. Picking sides would only cause resentment. If one thing was true about them, it was that they were a united front. They agreed then and there that they'd put a pause on college to do what needed to be done. School would always be there. They'd go back eventually; this was just a blip in the road. Temporary. A pivot.

Only they didn't go back. One year turned into five, then ten, and now their baby was nineteen and in college herself.

Rachel scrolled the search results and clicked links for several of the local colleges around Pittsburgh. Many offered online classes, and her brow furrowed trying to map out the feasibility. Could she heap college courses onto her already overflowing plate? The homepage for the education department contained three embedded videos, and Rachel clicked on one, listening as a fresh-faced kid talked about how he "just knew" this was the school for him. The video ended with big block words across the screen: YOUR FUTURE STARTS HERE.

But wasn't her future already decided long ago? She enjoyed her job at the preschool, but she'd always envisioned working in a different setting—middle school or maybe even high school. A job with strong benefits and security backed by a teacher's union. Those required the degree she'd never finished. And the feeling—she couldn't quite call it regret—had followed her for years, a quiet shadow of what could have been.

She read through a program description and reached the bottom where a luring button screamed GET MORE INFO. She clicked. It couldn't hurt to be curious. She'd review the digital files once the kids went to bed.

Rachel closed her phone and tucked it back into her purse. Savannah would be done with her lesson any minute and would come bounding out of the instructor's house hankering to go on to the next thing. They'd probably have to swing by the drive-through for dinner. She hated that her kids ate McDonald's twice a week, but it was easy and cheap.

Rachel stretched in her seat, catching a glimpse of herself in the rear-view mirror. Her hair, parted in the middle and pulled into a low ponytail, made her look even younger than usual.

When she visited Chloe at college, a professor had asked, quite genuinely, whether the two were sisters. Rachel still got carded regularly at the liquor store. It didn't help that she was built like a teenager herself—waif-like with zero curves. She was the type who didn't have to wear a bra if she didn't want, much to the annoyance of Monica, who lamented about "life over size two."

With her arms above her head, she caught a whiff of something zesty coming from her underarm (had she showered this morning?), just as Savannah flung the car door open. Rachel righted herself.

"How was your lesson? Should we sign you up for the Philharmonic?" she joked.

"Mrs. Linden made me do scales." Savannah rolled her eyes like it was the worst thing in the world.

Rachel waved at the sixty-something woman on the porch then put the car in reverse. Onward they went. "Scales are important."

"They're boring. I want to play *Moonlight Sonata.*"

Rachel laughed. "I think you're a little ways away from that, Beethoven. But I like your ambition." She noticed her hands on the steering wheel, nails chewed down to the skin. She really should get a manicure. Monica's nails, like everything else about her, always looked presentable. A reflection of a professional, put-together woman, not some frazzled maniac who put everyone before herself. But, like renting massive inflatable jump castles for the kids' birthdays, nails were a luxury not a necessity.

"Where are we going now?" Savannah asked from behind. She wove her fingers in and out of a looped cord to make cat's cradle like Rachel had taught her.

"Home—is that okay?" She said it on an exhale, like *hasn't there been enough today? Must you people cram anything else into twenty-four hours?* even though it had been Rachel who'd signed them up for most things.

"Will Dad be there?"

Rachel checked the time. Chris got off an hour ago. "Should be. Maybe he'll have made us dinner. What do you think?"

When the smell of pizza hit her nose, Rachel smiled. Her husband's meal of choice. She hadn't instructed Chris to make dinner, but she didn't have to. His natural capability gave Rachel comfort, knowing that if something were to happen to her, the kids would be fine. Still, it was only frozen pizza. Rachel didn't care, glad solely for the fact that someone else had taken the initiative. If only her husband were as ambitious in other parts of his life beyond preheating an oven.

The four of them ate together around the table in their eat-in kitchen. Dehydrated from the day, Rachel slammed two glasses of water, which she'd later regret in the middle of the night. Her mind drifted to the one member of their family who was missing. She wondered what Chloe was having for dinner on campus.

"Brody said the SH word in art class today," Jacob said animatedly, popping Rachel's daydream.

"Oh yeah?" Chris said.

"What's the SH word?" Rachel said, because even though she didn't condone regular swearing, there was nothing cuter than a little kid saying a bad word.

Jacob eyed her like it was a trick.

"It's okay, you can say it and you won't get in trouble. Go ahead."

He looked around the table then quietly said, "Shut up."

"That's not the SH word, bozo," Savannah said.

"Yuh-huh!"

"No, the SH word is 'shit.'" Savannah said it with authority, like at the ripe age of ten she held barrels of wisdom over her younger brother.

Rachel and Chris looked at each other and hid smiles behind their napkins.

"Oh," Jacob said. "Shit." He tossed the word around in his head, trying it out for the first time.

"Yeah, you say shit when—"

"Okay, that's enough," Rachel cut her off. They'd had their dose of cuteness; no need to overdo it. The last thing she wanted was a call from the school that Jacob was teaching his classmates some new vocabulary.

When dinner was finished, Rachel cleared the table and stood at the sink loading plates into the dishwasher. Chris pulled a Coke from the fridge then leaned against the counter. Rachel noticed his calloused hands. His floppy hair that needed trimming at the back of his neck. When he'd been studying engineering, a machine operator hadn't exactly been the goal, but here they were. Rachel would be lying if she said she didn't envy Roman's career aspirations, his social standing. When side by side with Chris, Rachel often wondered what it would be like for Chris to match Roman's level of social class. It felt pathetic, but she couldn't help it.

Rachel closed the dishwasher door and wiped her hands on the waffle-cloth towel. This time of the evening, before bed, was one of the only chances they got each day to catch up. She thought about the college websites she'd been looking at in the car. The desire felt so strong, she couldn't comprehend how her husband never had the same thoughts. Didn't he want more for himself? For them? A degree would mean a better job, and a better job would come with more financial freedom.

She'd tried to drop hints over the years, but it never seemed to work. And she didn't want to push too hard, because after all, it took two to tango. But with the thought of finishing her degree wriggling to the front of her mind, it felt like she needed to bring it up again. She'd start with a wide net.

"Isn't it awesome how Roman's made this career change?"

Chris's face scrunched. "Sure, I guess?"

"I just mean, he's following his dream, you know? He said he always envisioned a career in politics, and so he took a leap and is doing it." This was cheesy, and she knew it, but cheesy went hand in hand with the angle she was pushing.

"Yeah, good for him."

"It just shows that you can do something even if it seems like a risk."

Chris dropped his drink to the counter. "I feel like you're trying to say something here and you're beating around the bush. What are you getting at?"

Rachel felt her face flush. She didn't want an argument. She'd have to tread gently; pull that net in slowly. "It makes me think of us, that's all." She was careful to use the word "us" instead of "you."

"Us?"

"Going back to school, getting the jobs we always wanted."

"I thought we were happy with our jobs."

"We are. I mean, I think we are. I like my job, but you know it's not what I would have picked. It was sort of the closest thing I could get. And you—I'm sure you didn't plan to be casting molds and running machinery on your feet all day. Look at these hands." She took his hand and turned it palm up.

"What's wrong with my hands?"

Rachel dropped her grip. "You're missing the point." But it didn't seem like he was. She could tell on his face he understood... and that he didn't exactly agree.

"Does my job not provide enough for this family?" His nostrils flared a little, a sign of his defenses rising.

"That's not what I'm saying. I just mean that there are bigger things out there."

"Like becoming a politician?"

She groaned. "Of course not a politician."

"Because it sounds like you're comparing me to Roman. I'm

sorry if I don't wear a fancy suit and take you out to two-hundred-dollar dinners."

"You know that's not what I meant." Rachel wrung her hands. Maybe this wasn't a good idea. But it's exactly what she'd meant. It would be nice to have more of a safety net in the bank, and for her husband to not come home with grease under his nails every day.

"Listen," Chris said, "I work hard, and I'm content with our life. I wouldn't go back and change a thing. I'm sorry if you can't say the same."

He walked away, and Rachel tried to stop him with, "Chris, wait..." but he was out of the room. She let out a long sigh. It wasn't how she'd envisioned the conversation going. Maybe she shouldn't have led with Roman. Maybe she should have kept the focus on herself, told him about requesting information packets from a few schools. So many maybes, but none of them mattered as she stood by the sink alone.

Footsteps above reminded her there were two small humans who needed her attention for bedtime. Rachel folded the dishtowel, returned it to the handle of the oven, and climbed the stairs with heavy legs.

FIVE

MONICA

December

Monica looked forward to her Friday wine nights
with Rachel. They'd each pick up a bottle they hadn't tried
before, or sometimes flip the script with fresh-fruit sangria or
margaritas rimmed with salt. It depended on their moods—
times of less stress called for lighter, livelier drinks, while darker
stretches only felt right with the deepest, driest red. Like when
Monica's dad passed. Or when Rachel miscarried before Savannah's birth. Or when one of the kids was going through a particularly rough patch that couldn't be solved with extra kisses.

On the occasion either of them had to cancel for one reason
or another, Monica felt herself deflate. Rachel wasn't only her
best friend but practically her only friend. She didn't click with
the other school moms like Rachel did—not for lack of trying
but simply because she wasn't around as much. But with
Rachel, she had a history, one that spanned all the way back to
being paired up to room together freshman year at Duquesne.

They'd been given each other's contact information from

Duquesne weeks before classes began freshman year. It was Rachel who'd reached out first, commenting on the coincidence of their names: Monica and Rachel, just like the beloved *Friends* characters.

"I swear I'm not neurotic about cleaning," Monica had said over email, to which Rachel replied, "And I promise not to sleep with your brother." When they met face to face on move-in day, it was like they'd known each other since childhood. A hug and laughter and plenty of chitchat as they unpacked tubs of clothes and a beaded door curtain bought to replicate Britney Spears' album cover, their parents could barely get their attention long enough to say goodbye.

Rachel and Monica's friendship solidified that instant, and to do their namesakes justice, they held *Friends* viewing parties in their room every Thursday night, complete with popcorn from the communal microwave down the hall. Their friends called their room Central Perk, and for a short stint they even had an illegal goldfish they named Gunther. Registering for the same electives meant the girls were able to spend even more time together. They were two of the most popular girls on campus, and even when Chris entered the picture, their friendship never wavered. Their lives were a continual conversation via text which they'd pop in and out of on a daily basis.

Now, in Rachel's living room, the pair eased onto the couch, stemless wine glasses in hand. Of the two, Rachel was usually the first one to catch a buzz thanks to her birdlike frame, but having forgotten to eat lunch that day due to back-to-back patients, it was Monica who felt the alcohol peel back an edge within the first two sips.

"How's the campaign?" Rachel asked, sitting cross-legged, the hem of her boyfriend jeans rolled up to her ankles.

"I'm not going to lie, it's a lot. Roman's gone all the time. I'm surprised I got him to stay home with the boys tonight. It feels like every weekend there's some sort of event. Tomorrow it's a dinner. I don't know what for exactly, just that I can't wear jeans and sneakers." She stared off. "I miss our family nights at home—the four of us all together."

"A nice dinner sounds fun."

"Not when you have to be *on* the whole time. My cheeks end up hurting from forced smiling. I don't really know these people; they're his crowd. I feel like I fit in more with his academic friends." Monica took a sip from her glass, letting the woody aftertaste seep into her tongue. Tonight was a 19 Crimes red blend with Snoop Dogg on the label because Rachel couldn't help herself. "Plus, I have to dress so stuffy. I need to go shopping. Maybe tomorrow morning. Want to come?"

"I can just see you with a rainbow of skirt suits. You'll have to open a loyalty card at Talbots or something."

Monica jabbed her friend's arm. "Eff off. Don't make me feel any older than I am. Turning forty was bad enough. See these lines?" She gestured at the skin around her eyes.

"Please." Rachel scooted closer. "Look at these." And then the two women, barely in their forties, conducted a competition as to whose face had aged worse. Rachel, with her olive skin tone, always had pockets of darkness under her eyes. In contrast, Monica's fairness seemed to almost glow. There would never be a clear winner—the two of them so different in many ways—but picking at their flaws was what they'd done since their roommate days. If they couldn't be brutally honest with each other, then with whom could they?

"Chloe's going to babysit tomorrow," Monica said.

"She is?" Rachel cocked her head.

"She didn't tell you? Yeah, she said she'd come watch the boys for me. Preston's going to be out of town for an away game."

"Oh." Rachel's cheeks burned, maybe from the wine, maybe from embarrassment. But then she rebounded with, "Great!"

Whoops, Monica thought when her brain caught up to her

mouth. Maybe she shouldn't have said anything? But why wouldn't Chloe have told her mom she'd be home?

The garage door opened, and Chris came through with the kids in tow. "Hey, Mon," he said before Jacob and Savannah came barreling past, the younger one somehow outrunning his sister. They sprinted through the room, shedding coats and hats as they headed to the stairs, yelling:

"Don't you dare!"

"I'm gonna find it!"

"Jacob, *stop!*"

"Ha ha, you can't catch me!"

And as quickly as they'd come, the kids were gone, leaving the women with whiplash.

"What was that all about?" Rachel asked Chris.

He gave a humored shrug. "Something about Jacob reading Sav's diary."

The adults all chuckled. Oh, to be young again.

Chris topped off the women's glasses then went to the small sunroom in the back to put on a football game, giving them their privacy. Rachel resumed her story about a crazy PTO mom, and Monica detailed good news about a patient who'd finally gotten pregnant after seven years of trying. Their evenings were always a chance to go deeper than they could in the dozen or so daily text messages they shared. Catching up in person far exceeded communication behind a screen.

But not fifteen minutes later, a crash upstairs sliced through the ease of the evening. Rachel jumped to her feet. "What the...? Savannah?" she yelled. "Everything alright?"

The sound of crying answered the question, and within seconds, a bloody Jacob was coming down the stairs, hand to his face.

"What happened?" Chris asked, pulled from the game after hearing the thump.

"I was... hide Savannah's diary... fell," Jacob managed between sobs. Blood dripped into his cupped hand.

"Oh, Jacob," Rachel cried.

"Jesus Christ," Chris muttered, leading them both into the kitchen.

"That's why we shouldn't be sneaky with other people's things," Rachel said, reprimand hidden within concern.

Monica stood awkwardly in the center of the living room, wine glass in hand, unsure what to do. "Can I help?"

"It's never dull," Rachel said. "We're good. Just give me a minute."

Even with a quick fly-by inspection, Monica could tell the cut didn't look deep enough to need stitches. A good wipe and a Band-Aid would probably be enough to get Jacob patched up.

"Good thing you already took your Christmas card pictures!" Monica called, aiming for levity. From the other room, she heard rummaging and running water followed by Jacob yelping. That would be the hydrogen peroxide, she thought. Her boys weren't fans of the stinging either.

Chris came back through, dust broom in hand, shaking his head. "Guess I'm on clean-up duty." He trod upstairs.

While Rachel tended to her son, Monica used the interlude from girls' night to text Roman.

How are the boys?

Happy with their movie and popcorn, he replied, which made her smile. She was glad they were together, even if a little pang of jealousy lingered near the edge of her cheer. She'd like to be there too—the four of them hadn't spent much time together in what felt like forever. But girls' night was essential. A wind-down at the end of her week. Maybe she could convince Roman to stay home tomorrow, to cancel the dinner, and they could make gingerbread houses with Lucas and Logan.

The front door opening made her jump, and Monica was surprised when Chloe came through, arms wrapped tight around herself. Right away, Monica knew something was wrong. She lowered her phone and studied Chloe's face. Her eyes were redder than a tomato. Her face looked puffy and not in the way that could be blamed on allergies. This was something else. A cold chill traveled to Monica's toes.

"Chloe," she said, getting up from the couch and taking a few steps toward the girl. "What's wrong? Are you okay?"

Chloe sniffled. Water pooled in her eyes before cresting over, falling and landing on her gray Pitt sweatshirt. "Is my mom here?"

"She's in the kitchen. Jacob cut his chin." What was going on? Had she been in an accident? Monica scanned Chloe for signs of blood.

Chloe showed no reaction to her brother's dilemma. She passed by Monica toward the kitchen with stifled sobs.

"What happened?" Monica tried again, following.

The noise level in the kitchen was rampant, with Jacob still crying and Rachel trying to clean him up.

"Mom," Chloe said, clogged with emotion.

Monica stood beside her. But Rachel was busy inspecting the cut, repeating things like *stop wiping your hands on your shirt* and *would you hold still?*

Chloe put her hands to her temples. "Mom," she repeated.

It took her saying it again before Rachel, who probably thought it was Savannah in the doorway, whipped her head in their direction. Her eyes narrowed. "Chloe? What are you doing here?"

"Last I checked I still call this place home," Chloe said.

"No, I mean, I thought you weren't babysitting until tomorrow. I didn't expect you tonight, that's all." A beat, then, "What's wrong? Are you crying?" She hadn't taken her hand from Jacob's chin.

Chloe's shoulders shook. "Preston broke up with me." She squeezed her eyes shut, but somehow the tears still managed to leak with impressive force.

"Oh, honey," Monica said, putting an arm around Chloe's shoulders.

"Oh, Chlo, I'm so sorry," Rachel said. She was mid-wipe of Jacob's chin and must have pressed a little too hard because Jacob let out another yelp. "Sorry, bud," she said, returning her attention to him.

It was a chaotic moment with too much happening at once. Chloe standing there crying, Jacob bleeding, Chris upstairs picking up shards of glass. Finally, Chloe burst. "Aren't you going to hug me or anything?"

Rachel gaped, her words fumbled. "Yes, of course," she said, scrambling to unwrap a Band-Aid. "Let me get this on here..."

Chloe let out a groan. "Ugh, forget it!" She swiveled and retreated to the living room.

Monica watched her leave, looked back to her friend, then toward Chloe once more. *What do you want me to do here?* she said to herself. But instead of asking, she instinctively followed Chloe and sat next to her on the couch, where the teen had buried her head in several throw pillows.

"I'm so sorry, sweetie," she said, lightly rubbing a swirl pattern on Chloe's back. She could feel the heat radiating through the girl's shirt. The nape of Chloe's neck was sweaty, and little hairs curled where they'd fallen from her ponytail.

"I thought he loved me," Chloe voice came muffled through the pillows.

Monica's heart broke. It wasn't Chloe's first boyfriend, but this one seemed different, and she imagined it must have felt different too. High school relationships and college relationships were on two separate levels. But heartbreak was heartbreak no matter what.

"Come here," Monica said, giving Chloe's elbow a gentle

tug. Chloe sat up and fell into Monica's arms, resting her head on Monica's collarbone. "I thought he was away this weekend."

Chloe sniffed. "He is. He didn't even have the decency to wait till he got back. He texted me from their hotel. The whole team probably saw it."

A lump formed in Monica's throat. What a jerk. She wished she could find Preston and tear into him for hurting Chloe. If one of her sons ever did such a thing, she'd be horrified.

"He broke up with you over text?" Rachel was there now.

"He said he still wanted to be friends," Chloe choked. "Friends? Really?"

Rachel kneeled on the floor in front of them, hugging her daughter's waist, not far from where her half-drunk glass of wine sat. The way they were positioned, Rachel was the third wheel, the add-on of the embrace.

"What can I do?" she asked. "Do you want me to make you hot chocolate?" It was always Chloe's favorite, a drink for celebrations and bereavements.

"No," Chloe said, her voice still shaky. She didn't let go of Monica. Rachel didn't let go of Chloe. The three of them were stuck in this clumsy triangle.

After a long minute, it was Monica who gently pressed back, letting Chloe sit up again. The poor girl's eyelids hung like crescent moons, heavy and tired. As much as Monica would have loved to stay there and comfort Chloe, she slid back, making room for Rachel to take her place on the couch. It felt like the right thing to do.

Rachel reached out and ran a hand along her daughter's silky hair. "I'm sorry," she said again because what else do you say to a girl with a broken heart?

Chloe shook her head with a sense of defeat. "I just want to go to bed." She stood lethargically and looked to Monica. "I'll still babysit tomorrow." And with that, Chloe trudged up the stairs to her bedroom.

The women exchanged looks—sympathy, hopelessness, exhaustion. Monica held up the wine bottle. "Refill?"

SIX

RACHEL

CHLOE HUNG AROUND ON SUNDAY, MUCH TO RACHEL'S delight. It was like her daughter was in high school again—home for breakfast, lunch, and dinner. Rachel would have liked to curl onto the couch and watch movies for hours, but Jacob had a birthday party and Savannah needed help completing a science project for the next day. Rachel had volunteered to put together "build a snowman" kits for the elementary school, and she didn't have nearly enough cotton balls, which meant another run to the store. It was impossible to divide her attention three ways—someone was always getting the short end of the stick. And that was just the kids. Rachel still needed to save a part of herself for Chris, her work, and whatever morsels were left over for reading the latest Reese's Book Club pick each evening.

If Sundays were supposed to be the day of rest, she'd missed the punchline. What a joke. Still, when she wasn't driving someone somewhere, Rachel popped her head into Chloe's bedroom to check on her oldest.

"I'm fine," Chloe kept saying, though her demeanor proved anything but. Chloe didn't want to eat and even fell asleep midway through *The Greatest Showman*, which Rachel had turned on while cutting orange felt triangles for snowmen noses. They say first loves are the sweetest, but the same is true on the flipside: The first cut is the deepest.

When three o'clock came, Rachel left to pick up Jacob from the birthday party. She ran through the list of things she still needed to accomplish on her typical Sunday schedule—laundry, cleaning. She didn't know when Chloe planned to head back to campus. Maybe she'd stay for dinner. Then they could spend some time together after the day wound down.

Something nagged at Rachel's gut like a warning. Chloe's sad eyes, the girl chained to her bedroom all day. It made Rachel rethink. The laundry could wait. So could the groceries; she could give the kids cash to buy lunch at school. When she got home, she'd go straight to Chloe's room and devote the rest of the day to some quality time.

Feeling a lightness with her decision, Rachel loaded Jacob into the car.

"Dad duty when we get home," she told him, using the term she'd coined when they were younger and she couldn't handle another moment of parenting. The days when she was so touched out by the time Chris got home, she'd look at him and beg, *Please take over*.

And yet, the kids still came to her first. She was, as they call it, the default parent.

But she'd try again today. When they got home, Rachel was going to be in Chloe-mode. Inside, she dropped her purse on the counter, gave Savannah's project one final inspection, and climbed the stairs to her daughter's room. She missed her big girl. A passing memory of the years when it was just Chloe floated through her brain. Those were sweet times, easier in a way. They'd gone everywhere together.

Light snuck out from under Chloe's door. She was awake. Rachel smiled. This would be so nice to just sit and talk and be in each other's company without distraction.

A soft knock on the door and Rachel eased it open. But then her smile dropped. "Oh," she said. "Are you—"

Chloe was fully dressed in jeans and a baggy sweater, back-pack slung over her shoulder. "Yeah, I'm gonna head back to campus."

Rachel couldn't hide her disappointment. It must have been plastered across her face because Chloe gave her a look and said, "What?"

"I was coming to hang out. I thought we could talk or watch a movie or, I don't know, whatever you wanted to do."

Chloe's eyebrows rose. "I've been here all weekend." The tension was thick, the message evident. Chloe didn't have to add the words *why'd you wait so long?* for Rachel to read between the lines.

"Okay," Rachel said, clasping her hands in front of her body submissively. She gave a pinched smile. Her daughter was an adult now, and as hard as it was, Rachel had to cut the strings. She couldn't force Chloe to stay if she didn't want to.

Chloe gathered a few last items into her backpack. Note-books. A bulky textbook. Rachel's eyes grazed the room for other pieces of Chloe's new college existence. The things that weren't here half a year ago and now marked a world Rachel wasn't privileged to. And that's when she noticed a mint-green gift bag on the dresser, tufts of tissue paper poking from the top. "What's that?" she asked.

Chloe followed her mom's pointing finger. "Oh, Monica dropped it off when you were gone."

"What is it?" Rachel stepped into the room and toward the dresser.

"A Stanley cup. All the girls have them." She yanked out the tissue paper and removed a pale pink travel mug with handle and chunky straw. Admired it like a trophy. "I've been wanting one."

Rachel's expression darkened. She picked up the card that was next to the bag. "She bought it for you?"

"Hello? Privacy?" Chloe said, but Rachel was already reading.

Just a little something to cheer you up. Big hugs. Love you! Monica x

Chloe ran a hand along the oversized cup. "She said she was going to get me chocolate, but this was better."

Rachel's throat burned. Why hadn't *she* thought to get her daughter a cheer-up gift? This would have been the perfect time for a surprise. She'd seen the trendy, must-have accessory all over social media, but when Chloe had mentioned wanting one, Rachel had balked at the price tag. "Seventy dollars for a cup?" she'd said. They had Yetis—wasn't that enough? She couldn't keep up with all the teen essentials. But here was Monica, swooping in with not only the right gift but at the right time.

Rachel swallowed and forced a gracious tone. "That is so thoughtful." She replaced the card on the dresser. She knew her friend had only good intentions—Monica clearly loved Chloe like her own—so why did she feel threatened?

Chloe zipped her backpack and slung it over her shoulder. She started toward her bedroom door, and at that moment, Rachel found herself reaching for her daughter with urgency. *Don't leave.* "Wa— wait," she fumbled. "I mean, how are you feeling?"

"Mom, I just don't want to talk about it, okay? I've literally cried for three days and just want to get back to my routine. Final exams start Tuesday, and I really need to study."

Rachel nodded, an ache growing under her skin like a bruise. "I understand. Just want to make sure you're okay."

"I'm fine. I'll be home for break before you know it."

"And Florida?" Rachel raised her eyebrows, hopeful. She needed Chloe to go. Reassurance that her family was still a tight, complete unit. No fractures. No scattering.

Chloe let out a breath, and Rachel held hers. Expectations floated between them before Chloe's response. "I'll still go. But if the little kids annoy me, I'm locking myself in a room for the week."

Rachel's chest expanded, and she gave a knowing laugh. "Deal." She'd agree to anything to ensure Chloe joined them.

The two went downstairs, where Chloe hugged her dad goodbye in the kitchen. "See you soon, Sweets," he said with a kiss to her head. "Remember to carry your pepper spray."

"Got it, Dad."

At the counter, Savannah let out a groan. "*Moooom,* Saturn's rings keep bumping into Jupiter. I need heeeeeelp."

She flung a glue stick to the floor, and Rachel knew this meant the girl was on the verge of a complete meltdown. Rachel closed her eyes. This was why they didn't wait to do school projects on Sunday evenings. If she didn't open her eyes, could she pretend there wasn't always chaos around her?

"Mooooom," Savannah griped again. And so Rachel went to calm Savannah, ensuring they could restore proper order to the solar system. When she turned back to say goodbye to her teen, Chloe was gone.

Rachel removed her contacts at their double-sink vanity while Chris brushed his teeth. A blanket of lethargy had hit her as the evening wore on, and she felt like she could fall asleep right there on the cool, marbled surface. She replaced the contact solution in the medicine cabinet heavy-handedly.

"It's just a cup," Chris said, mouth full of lather. He spit then rinsed his toothbrush. "I don't know why you're letting it bother you."

"It's not the cup itself."

"What then?"

She turned to face him. "It's just that if I'm being honest, I wish I'd thought of it." There, the truth. Only it didn't feel any better to voice it. She sounded callow, whiny.

Chris placed both hands on the sides of his wife's face and kissed her forehead, his whiskers tickling her skin. "You're her mother. You don't need to buy her love."

"Well, it sure wouldn't hurt." Now she really sounded whiny.

"You're being ridiculous. Chloe loves you—you know that. Kids go through phases. She's a teenager. Don't be so hard on yourself."

Rachel considered his words, but they fell short of easing her discomfort. He didn't get it. Mother–daughter relationships could never compare to anything he'd experienced with the kids. Looking at Chloe was like looking at her own reflection, a piece of herself outside her body, fragile and beautiful and tied with so much emotion. Chloe was her greatest achievement and also her biggest challenge. Allies at war with one another. Raising her had brought Rachel to her knees more times than she could count.

And yet, Chloe hadn't chosen a school on the other side of the country. She hadn't packed up with a swift goodbye never to return. She still needed them. Last night was proof. And that said something, didn't it?

Rachel clung to this truth, trying to lift her mood. It wasn't fair to drag everyone down with her. "At least she agreed to go on vacation." One upside of their earlier conversation.

Chris chortled. "Of course she did. Who wouldn't take a free beach trip? She can grumble all she wants, but you know she'd never miss a chance to sit by a pool for a week. Isn't sunbathing some sort of sacred ritual in college?"

Chris always managed to make her smile, his optimism

finding a way even when unwarranted. Sometimes she thought it was part of why he was so complacent about things. Never a lot of fire behind his mindset.

Rachel applied her under-eye cream—which claimed to decrease bags but probably did nothing—then brushed her teeth.

"Speaking of vacation," Chris said, "we need to get a check to Monica and Roman for our share."

"How much is it again?" She was already calculating where they could skimp to save. She could probably shave off a few dollars from her weekly grocery list if she bought frozen veggies instead of fresh.

"Fourteen hundred."

Rachel bristled. "Okay."

"Relax," Chris said, coming up behind her. He wrapped his arms around her, their bodies curving together like nesting dolls. "We deserve a vacation. Let's just enjoy it."

"Okay," she said again, pushing away the thoughts of money and jobs and ambition and bitterness. Fine. They deserved a vacation. It would be good family time, and wasn't that exactly what she'd been craving? Monica's crew would be the icing on top.

Chris drew a string of butterfly kisses along Rachel's neck. "I know something else we can enjoy right now that doesn't cost a thing."

The corner of Rachel's lips pulled up into a grin. Whatever faults she might find with her husband, their connection wasn't one. She let him carry her to the bed, where everything else melted away.

SEVEN

CHLOE

January

CHRISTMAS BREAK FELT EXTRA LONG TO SOMEONE WITH A heavy heart. So when Ava and some friends suggested a ski weekend at Seven Springs, located just an hour away, Chloe jumped on the chance to shake the dust off before next week's family vacation. The friends pooled their meager part-time job earnings for a small lodge on the slopes. It was intended to fit six, but college students had a keen ability to stretch the limits, and Chloe was sure there'd be at least double that squeezing in for the two-night stay. Couches and floors weren't so uncomfortable after half a dozen beers.

The bitter air bit her skin as she cut down the slopes, making a wave of tracks behind her. She let the wind wash away the funk she'd felt since the breakup. On the ride up the lifts, Ava chatted her ear off about wanting to chop her hair as a symbolic act of feminism, while Chloe and a friend named Marcus discussed which classes they were taking in spring semester. When they huddled around the fireplace at the end of the day, she propped her toes on the hearth to defrost, a cup of cocoa in hand.

Being with friends again was good for her soul. The weekend was the perfect escape.

Until Preston walked through the door.

Chloe's body stiffened like a board the instant she saw him gliding in, bookended by two other guys. "What's he doing here?" she whispered to Ava out the corner of her mouth.

"Shit! I don't know. They must have caught wind. You know how word travels." And it did—news of parties and hangouts always managed to spread like wildfire, people showing up uninvited, friends of friends tacking on until the crowd grew into more than originally intended. "Do you want to leave? We can go."

Chloe thought about it. Her instinct told her to pack up and head home. She'd had one full day of skiing; did she really need two? She balled her fists at her sides. She shouldn't have to leave just because Preston had shown up. "No," she said. "It's fine."

Chloe watched him from the corner of her eye as he made his way into the room, smacking friends on the back, grabbing a beer and snapping it open. Her belly burned, hands turning damp. Longing made her feel like a wet noodle, all wobbly and soft, and she wondered if being in the same house as Preston would prolong her healing. She reassured herself. There were plenty enough people there—it's not like she'd even have to talk to him.

They talked all night.

It started after about two hours of avoiding each other, skirting the outsides of the room and catching glances when they didn't think the other was watching. But like magnets, a force bigger than them drew the two together by ten o'clock, and before she knew it, Chloe was standing opposite him at a long table, ping-pong ball in hand, taking the winning shot in beer pong. The crowd of friends whooped and chanted, *Chloe, Chloe, Chloe*. Preston smirked at her, a flirty challenge, which only made the butterflies inside her flutter more. Those eyes. Those lips. The way his gaze was glued to her. She didn't care if it was the alcohol talking. She was back in his orbit, and it felt fucking amazing.

Chloe lifted the ball, did a slow practice shot for aim, then released. It soared through the air and landed with a wet plop in the last remaining cup.

The room erupted, everyone slamming together like a drunken mosh pit. Chloe bounced off chests and shoulders, until finally the crowd settled, people dispersing from the game, back to the counter for drinks, or to huddle in amiable groups. And then Preston was at her side.

"Nice shot," he said, and the way he leaned toward her made Chloe melt. "You wanna go somewhere quiet?"

It was exactly what she'd hoped he'd say. "Sure."

He clasped her hand in his, and she led them upstairs to an empty bedroom. Preston locked the door behind them. Her heart thumped to the bass of the music downstairs.

When his mouth met hers, it was as familiar as one's own neighborhood. How she'd missed the way he cradled her head, the herbal scent of his body wash.

Preston guided her onto the bed, and it didn't take long for their clothes to hit the floor.

"I missed you so much," she breathed, and he kissed her lips so hard she wanted to cry tears of joy. This whole breakup had been a mistake, a blip in their relationship. Clearly Preston agreed. Obviously, he regretted it. How else could two bodies fit like jigsaw pieces?

They fell into a well-known rhythm, only this time with greater hunger, and afterwards passed out, limbs intertwined. Chloe only momentarily worried about someone coming in—

Ava, after all, had shared the bed with her the previous night. Knowing her friend, Ava would take one for the team and find another place to crash. Chloe dropped off to sleep with the relief of knowing they were firmly back together. Because that's surely what this meant, right?

When her eyes peeled open, a blinding early-morning light filled the room. She was naked. Her head hurt. And then it came back to her—Preston's surprise arrival, the flirting. The sex.

Chloe rolled over, expecting to find him snoring away—she loved the way he slept with one arm up, the other by his side. These little intricacies were things only she knew about him.

But when she flipped over, the far side of the bed was empty. Disappointment hit like an arrow, but Chloe told herself Preston may have just gotten up early. Maybe he was downstairs already, cooking up breakfast before they hit the slopes again.

She pulled on a fresh pair of underwear, sweatpants, and a hoodie. Wiped the leftover mascara from under her eyes. Looking back at the rumpled sheets, she felt a sense of warmth remembering their rendezvous, and a broad smile stretched across her face.

Downstairs, the place showed the remnants of last night's festivities. One guy was already going around with a trash bag, collecting empty cups. Two girls sat at the table sipping bottled water, looking less than fresh. A bedroom door opened and Ava emerged.

"Well, hey," she said knowingly.

Chloe flushed. "Morning." She couldn't wipe the grin from her face. But the more she glanced around the house, the more the smile faded. Preston wasn't in the kitchen. He wasn't in the living room. She even checked the bathroom. At last, she scoured the shoes by the door, looking for his familiar Nikes.

Nothing.

"Anyone seen Preston?" she said to no one in particular.

The guy with the garbage bag replied. "He and a few people peaced out an hour or so ago."

Chloe's throat tightened. She clenched her toes in her wool socks, trying not to let her disappointment show. "Oh. No biggie." But Ava was watching her and gave her a serious look. Chloe quickly shook her head. *It's fine.*

It was anything but fine. They'd just hooked up after weeks apart and he'd left without a word? How was she supposed to interpret that? She'd gone to bed fully certain they were back together, but now a knot settled in her stomach that made her question everything. Were they a couple again? And if not... what the hell was last night all about?

Chloe couldn't wait to find out. The swirling thoughts drove her back upstairs to her room, and she flung clothes aside until she found her phone. She prayed there'd be a message from him. Some sort of explanation. There had to be.

The blank screen made her eyes well up. Chloe opened her texts and drafted a new message to Preston.

Where are y—

She deleted it.

About last ni—

She deleted again.

Nothing sounded right. She didn't want to say the wrong thing. So, in the end, she simply wrote **Hey**. Three dots appeared, and her body buzzed with anticipation.

Hey. Sorry we cut out so early.

She steadied her breathing. At least he'd acknowledged it.

No worries. Last night was fun.

She thought for a second then typed more.

When can we see each other again?

There was a long pause, during which Chloe stood, sat back down, stood, paced the room, and sat again. Finally his response came.

I hope you didn't get the wrong idea. Like I said before, I hope we can still be friends.

Chloe's blood rushed to her toes. Friends... with benefits? Is that what he meant? The visions she'd had of a reconciliation wiped angrily from her mind. This wasn't at all what she'd thought it was.

And with that, she tossed the phone to the floor, buried her head in the pillow, and cried.

EIGHT

MONICA

SHE HADN'T MADE A DRIBBLE CASTLE SINCE SHE WAS A KID, but Monica let every ounce of those childhood memories flood back sitting there on the beach with her boys. Logan kept building his too close to the surf, sniveling each time it washed away when a wave came in.

"Move back a little," Monica said. "Come here—build it next to mine."

They were right where the sand turned wet and firm. Monica sat cross-legged in her black Calvin Klein one-piece. Its plunging neckline accented her breasts, the padding giving them a boost to pre-kids placement. When she bent forward, they flopped freely in the molded cups. She didn't love her thighs, which were pasty and dimpled with cellulite, and looked utterly massive next to Rachel's spindle legs even though she recently bought a pair of size-eight jeans. But it was one of those in-the-moment situations, and when your five-year-old asks you to make a dribble castle, you make a dribble castle. Lucas had joined in on the fun, and now the three of them competed to see whose drippy sand tower was the tallest.

Monica couldn't remember the last time she'd played—actually played—with the boys. A few minutes here, a few minutes there. Rushing to finish up dinner before baths and bedtime. Maybe a quick monster battle or helping Logan convert his Transformer from car to robot. But mostly the kids only needed her help with batteries or setup or Lego instructions, and then they were on their own. Or they had their faces in their tablets, where Minecraft reigned supreme. This vacation felt like she'd won a jackpot of time. Even though work was the first thing she thought of each morning, she'd promised herself she'd disconnect from it all just for the duration. And miraculously, she had.

"Are you taking me to camp next weekend?" Lucas asked.

Monica had to think for a second, switching her brain from vacation mode to calendar mode. Camp. *Oh yes*, they'd signed Lucas up for a weekend camp through the school. And then the satisfaction she'd felt connecting with her boys on the beach burst.

"I can't, honey. But Jessica will take you." She hoped that would be enough. But Lucas was frowning, and that made her feel even worse. She scrambled. "Maybe one day, Chloe could even take you. She has another week of break, I think. Wouldn't that be fun?"

"Yay, Chloe!"

Monica warmed again. All was well. If she couldn't be there, at least she had a slew of substitutes, including the teenager who was like the boys' older sister. Monica had been so happy Chloe decided to come along on the trip. The group wouldn't have felt complete without her. And it seemed like the getaway had been good for Chloe too. Despite being the odd middleman between the kids and the adults, she'd still managed to smile. It had been nearly a month since the breakup, and nothing cured heartache like time and distraction. And sunshine.

At that thought, Monica glanced back up the beach to where they'd set up a large blanket, umbrella, and chairs. Rachel was reading a book, an open-front cover-up draped over her shoulders, while Chloe lay flat on a towel, earbuds in, Stanley cup to her right. Monica had been so pleased to see her using it.

She returned to face the vast ocean. Chris and Roman had Savannah and Jacob out in the water, one in each set of arms. They jumped to crest waves, squealing when white foam splashed their faces.

"Mommy's going to go sit with Aunt Rachel for a bit, okay?" she said to her boys, who were going on an hour of letting wet sand drip off their fingertips. She was all for quality time but could only stand the gritty texture against her bottom for so long. Her fingers were pruning.

Back at their area—"home base" Chris called it, so the kids could always find them among the busy beach—Monica took the chair next to Rachel, who lowered her book and smiled.

"They're having a blast," she said.

Monica agreed. There was a certain serenity that came with having her favorite people all together in one place. Here with her best friend, close enough to watch her boys play. No phone dinging with emails. It felt like heaven.

"Chloe seems good," Monica said, and Rachel nodded.

"She's hanging in there. Breakups are no fun."

Monica gave a burst of laughter. "And you would know how? You and Chris have been together since the dawn of man."

"It's not like he was my first boyfriend," Rachel chided. "I had experiences before him, don't forget."

"Oh, right. That guy with the weird throat clearing freshman year."

"Hey, he was hot. You just had to block out the noises."

They laughed so hard their faces hurt. Rachel grabbed two mango seltzers from the cooler and gave one to Monica.

"Do you think Preston was Chloe's first?" Monica said, leaning close and eyeing Chloe a few feet away. She appeared to be asleep, and even with earbuds pumping music into her brain, Monica didn't want to risk being overheard.

"No," Rachel said. "Remember Max who took her to junior prom?"

"Wait, she slept with him?"

"I'm pretty sure they were a 'thing' for a hot minute. I'm just glad I got her on birth control when I did. Not like some of those other parents who think their kids are angelic virgins."

Monica sipped her seltzer, the bubbles sparkling like fireworks in her mouth. She remembered the day Rachel had called freaking out shortly after Chloe's fifteenth birthday.

"She's hanging out in mixed company more often," Rachel had said. "I think I should talk to her about birth control."

Monica knew Rachel was more paranoid and careful than the rest, given the surprise pregnancy that had changed her life. She'd made it very clear she didn't want Chloe to follow in those footsteps.

At the time of that call, Monica's boys were mere toddlers, and the issue of teenage sex had felt like a lifetime away. Something to worry about far, far down the road. And even then, she had boys, not girls. Part of her was glad she didn't have to concern herself with a daughter getting pregnant. But then she gave herself a mental slap—boys were the ones who *got* the girls pregnant. Lucas and Logan could be on the other end of the equation. She'd shuddered then cleared her head. Parenting was all so overwhelming sometimes.

"I hope she moves on fast," Monica said, returning to the conversation. "I hate seeing her heartbroken."

"I know. All those teenage hormones."

Something nagged at Monica like a pesky mosquito bite.

Something she knew that Rachel didn't. Should she bring it up? It made sense in the context of their discussion. Monica teetered. Chloe hadn't sworn her to secrecy, so there couldn't be a harm in saying it. What the hell.

"She met up with him again," Monica said.

Rachel gulped the last of her seltzer. "Chloe? Met up with who?"

"Preston."

"She did? When?"

"Like last week. Remember when she went skiing with friends?"

"She told you that?"

Monica gave a little nod, feeling like she'd somehow misstepped. Rachel was quiet for a beat. In profile, Monica saw her jaw tighten. Then just as quickly, it softened, and Rachel dropped her head to one side. "Oh, Chlo. She's only going to make it worse for herself if she drags it out. Why would he string her along like that?"

"I don't know. I told her the same thing. A clean break is better."

"I guess being young makes you do stupid things."

"Mmhmm."

Monica's shoulders relaxed. *See?* It wasn't a big deal to tell Rachel. She'd want to know if it were one of her own kids. Moms had to look out for each other. Chloe was young and still figuring it all out. Hoping a post-breakup hookup would spur a reconciliation was no surprise, even if it hadn't worked. Monica had said as much when Chloe told her.

Now, the women both looked to where Chloe lay. She'd pulled her bikini ties down to avoid getting tan lines. Built like her mom, she was thin and petite, but with delicate curves in the right places. What some girls would call the perfect body. A body Monica had never had, even at that age.

"I'm ready for a drink." The women turned to find Roman

approaching from the water. His color-blocked swim trunks clung to his lean thighs, water glistening off his bare chest. Monica felt a prickle of heat. Her husband and his model good looks, dark and sultry.

Roman took the end seat, and as he lowered himself, he took a quick scan of their area.

"How's the water?" Rachel asked.

"Refreshing. Hand me one of those?" He gestured to the drink in Rachel's hand, and she tossed him a mixed berry flavor from the cooler.

Roman cracked it, took a swig, and exhaled. He ran a hand through his wet hair, slicking it back. When he did, his abs flexed.

The three sat in companionable quiet, watching the kids now filling buckets for a sandcastle on the drier sand, and Chris trying to teach Savannah how to bodyboard. The pleasant sea breeze kept them comfortable despite the heat. All around were sounds of a lively beach day.

A pair of young women walked by in front of them, untied cover-ups blowing open, revealing firm, tanned bodies underneath. Roman watched them as they passed, as though they'd invited him to. As though they weren't twenty years younger than his forty-six. Monica looked away and pretended not to notice—or care. But in that moment, like so many others, she understood something about her husband. Something she didn't want to be true but that she brushed off as typical man behavior. She took another sip of her drink, losing its crispness in the midday warmth. He'd looked at her like that once, hadn't he? Their multi-week sexcapades had trickled down to once a month, but that was normal. Marriage was built on more than just sex.

· · ·

Later, the afternoon sun began to dip into its slow descent and they still held post. After rotating multiple times throughout the day, Chloe finally sat up from her towel, like someone awakening from the dead.

"Well, hello, Sleeping Beauty," Chris joked, to which she rolled her eyes.

Monica and Rachel had commented on it more than once this past year—how Chloe had gone off to school a girl and come back a woman. She looked different somehow, more mature, more worldly, even in the few months she'd been in college. She carried herself differently. Was it the relationship with Preston? Was it immersing herself in diversity and new philosophies? How it was possible their little doe-eyed sidekick had turned into a beautiful young lady was beyond them. Monica often wondered what it would be like to have a daughter, but Chloe was the closest thing she'd know, and she felt many of the same emotions as Rachel when it came to the girl they both loved.

"I'm fried," Chloe said, pressing the skin on her arms, watching a white spot appear and disappear. "I'm heading back to the house. Want me to take anything?"

Rachel handed her a bag of sand toys the kids were done playing with, along with a few soaking-wet towels. "Hang them up; don't leave them in a pile," she instructed. Going to the beach with children was like packing for a month. Bags upon bags of *stuff*, not to mention the cooler and boards and a six-foot umbrella. They'd had just enough hands to carry it all the quarter-mile walk from the house.

Chloe tossed a loose shirt over her bathing suit and departed. Monica was envious—she was ready to go too, but the boys were still having too much fun. Another hour and they'd call it a day. She parked herself under the shade of the umbrella, afraid that despite SPF 75, she'd turn into a lobster if she wasn't careful. Her skin wasn't of the easily tanned variety like Rachel's and Chloe's. She was more of the instant-burn type that required multiple applications of thick, white sunblock. When she'd get back to the house, she'd undress and check her tan lines in the mirror, then take the always-refreshing post-beach shower that somehow felt a hundred times better than a normal one.

Monica returned her attention to the group. "What do you want to do for dinner?"

"Hmmm," Rachel said. "What about fish on the grill? I can make a big, tossed salad."

"That sounds perfect." She checked her phone for the time. "It's already four. Someone will have to run to the store."

"I'll go," Roman offered, sitting up. "I've had my dose of sun for the day—I can call it quits and go pick up the food."

"Are you sure?" Monica asked. She could count on one hand the number of times he'd offered to grocery shop.

"I don't mind. You guys hang here with the kids. They're having a blast. I'll just go change and head to the store. I'll be done by the time you guys get back."

She searched for his eyes, but they were hidden behind his dark sunglasses. "Okay, great," she said tentatively.

"Thanks, Rome," Rachel echoed. "Don't forget the ketchup."

Chris piped in then. "And make sure it's Heinz, not any of that generic crap."

"Got it."

They chuckled. As Yinzers, they were loyal to many things, but Heinz ketchup topped the list. Whenever they were out of town and a restaurant served the condiment, they could tell immediately when it wasn't their hometown brand.

Roman folded his towel longways and tossed it over his shoulder. He carried another bag of stuff back with him, so there'd be less for the rest of the adults. No more than two steps away, he pulled out his phone, typed for several seconds, then replaced it in the pocket of his shorts.

As Roman high stepped through the sand away from them, Monica studied him from behind. Her husband might be an in-demand guy with a full plate, but deep down she felt lucky to have him. Little moments like this served as the perfect reminder. It was a busy time in their lives for sure, but she held on to a thread of hope that it would all be worth it for a future where things leveled out. Someday they'd be connected like they'd been in the beginning.

There'd been a time, with thirty-two on the horizon, when Monica had wondered if she'd find a partner and have a family of her own. And then Roman had swooped in like a prince. Bouquets of peonies delivered to her work just because. Three-hour dinners over candlelight.

"He's perfect," she'd gushed to Rachel.

"He sounds great," Rachel had said, something lingering at the end.

"I sense a 'but' coming."

"Just be careful, that's all. Perfect doesn't exist. And there's no need to rush. I don't want to see you get hurt."

When Monica introduced Roman to Rachel and Chris for the first time, he'd brought a hundred-dollar bottle of wine, along with his infectious personality.

"Nicer than the boxed stuff!" Chris had joked, and the four of them had got to know each other over glasses of Sauvignon Blanc. Monica had been elated that Roman fit right into the mix —mostly. Only it didn't matter. She was the one dating him. He was her choice.

"So?" she'd said to Rachel later. "Any red flags?"

"If you're happy, I'm happy."

They'd married six months later, and, because her clock was

ticking, got right to work on kids. Never did she wonder after that. It wasn't perfect, but she reminded herself that nothing was. And now, she might not see her husband as often as she'd like, and he might be a little more distracted than she'd wish, but in there was a good man who, once in a blue moon, offered to get the groceries for dinner.

NINE

RACHEL

ON THE LAST NIGHT OF VACATION, THE DRINKS FLOWED freely. As she had a couple of times over the last week, Rachel had even let Chloe have one to get her out from behind her phone and join the fun. Besides, she wasn't an idiot—she knew Chloe drank at parties. That's what college kids did. There, around the table playing games like *Pictionary* and *Monopoly*, Chloe was almost one of the adults. Plus, there was supervision involved. And so, Chloe had a beer but declined to play. She sat quietly at the end of the table. It was, Rachel admitted, the best she'd get.

Monica rolled the dice and moved her token. "No, not Boardwalk!"

"That'll be four hundred," Roman said, opening his hand.

"What? No way."

"Two houses, baby. Pay up. I'm king when it comes to sucking people dry."

Monica playfully groaned and counted out four hundred orange Monopoly dollars for her husband. Chloe cracked open another beer.

"Better you than me," Chris said, eyeing his measly funds. "I'd go bankrupt."

Rachel pointed to his silver car token. "Don't speak so soon —you're coming around the corner."

"Stick with me," Roman said haughtily to Chris. "I'll give ya some money tips."

They'd spent the morning at the beach and the afternoon at the pool, soaking up every last ray they could. Rachel was pleased they'd come after all—it had proven a good chance to decompress and reconnect. No severe sunburns, mostly behaved kids, and even a crab-leg feast one night.

Thirty minutes later, in a surprising turn of events, Monica won the game after monopolizing an entire side of the game board with hotels and taking everyone's cash.

"Boom!" she said, doing a mic drop in the air. They laughed with the ease that comes with alcohol, the booze going to their heads and making everything soft around the edges. Cheeks glowed and stress didn't exist. Rachel wished they could stay in this bubble with no worries forever.

As they cleaned up the board, Roman poured a drink. "Chlo, you want another?"

Before she could answer, Rachel spoke up. "I think two is good."

Chloe arched her back. "I'm actually a little sleepy. I think I'll go to bed soon."

"Aw, we're just getting started," Roman said, though it was nearly eleven. The younger kids had fallen asleep on the couch hours ago, exhausted from a full day in the sun, Jacob and Lucas's arms tangled together.

Roman continued, unfazed, not showing any signs of winding down. "Listen, I've got a proposition to share." He pulled up a chair across from Chris and laid his forearms on the table like it was a serious business meeting. "I've been doing some thinking."

"Uh-oh," Monica joked.

"What do you think about joining my campaign?" he said to Chris. "I need some help with management, fundraising, those sorts of things. An assistant, if you will."

"Assistant?" Chris said.

"Manager, whatever you want to call it. Labels don't matter."

It was as though Roman had read Rachel's mind—it felt borderline invasive, like he'd been studying her personal thoughts. And yet, a sudden excitement took over. Finally, someone was presenting exactly what she wanted on a silver platter.

Before Chris could respond, Rachel jumped in. "That's a great idea!"

Chris met his wife's eager face with reservation. "I don't know anything about politics."

"You'll learn fast," Roman said, aloof. "It's not that hard."

"But I have a job."

Rachel put a hand on his arm. "But this sounds really exciting. Who knows? You might love it." Why was he not jumping at such an opportunity? Then she remembered their last conversation around this topic, the one where he'd basically shut her down, saying he was content with their life.

"It's pretty demanding," Monica inserted. Rachel noticed a look of concern on her friend's face. "Not to sway you one way or the other. Just be aware that it's fast and the hours are long. A bit of a dog and pony show."

And her husband couldn't handle it? "Chris is used to long hours—aren't you, hon?"

"You love it," Roman said, giving his wife a tease and making Rachel feel better. Of course Chris would love it. Who wouldn't want a little more influence? Roman regularly used his position to get better reservations in the city. He had connections with important people.

Rachel could read the skepticism all over Chris's face and knew immediately what he was thinking: Wasn't his job enough? But she couldn't help drawing comparisons, and envisioning Chris in a role beside Roman could only mean one thing —prestige. It wasn't fame or riches she was searching for exactly; perhaps just a bit more security. The kind of comfort that came with a little padding in the bank account. Knowing people who scratched each other's backs. If Roman's campaign was successful, who knew where it might lead. Maybe Chris could go along for the ride, their families woven together in the same circles. Rachel let her mind drift to updating their kitchen with new cabinets, not feeling like such an outcast with the cliquey moms at the kids' school.

"There's a salary budgeted for this position," Roman said. "It's not six figures or anything, but it's decent. Plus, you'd get to meet so many people. Doors really open when you network with the right crowd. I guess what I'm saying is you could leave tool and die behind."

Rachel's heart leaped—Roman had said exactly what she was thinking. She gave Chris's arm a little squeeze. Her husband was mute, expressionless, and she worried Roman would take offense.

"That's really generous of you," she said. "Chris, doesn't that sound like an interesting offer?" She could already see him getting ready in the mornings, trimming his beard neatly instead of letting it overgrow. He'd look so handsome in a suit. All this time she'd wished he'd find something more white collar and less blue—after all, that's where the money was. She didn't know what it would be or how it would come about, but here it was, falling into their laps. He'd be crazy not to accept.

"Thanks, man," Chris finally said. "I'll think about it."

Roman gave a nod. "Good. I'd love to have you."

The room seemed a bit tighter then, like some of the oxygen had been sucked out. Rachel and Monica exchanged a look that said, *We'll have to talk more about this later*. She wondered if Monica had known about Roman's proposal in advance.

Next to her, Chloe sat quietly, watching and taking everything in. She tore peeling skin from her bottom lip. Rachel gave her a rehearsed smile to indicate all was good. *This could be great for our future*, she wanted to say, but something in Chloe's eyes gave her pause. Why wasn't everyone as thrilled as she was?

It didn't take long for Roman to drink himself into a stupor. In fact, they were all pretty buzzed—Rachel included—and by the time midnight rolled around, she knew it was time for bed. The kids would be up at the crack of dawn.

Everyone departed to their rooms, and Rachel brought any remaining cups to the sink before joining Chris. She crawled into bed and snuggled next to him, raking her fingers through his chest hair. "I think you should take the job," she said.

"Of course you do."

"It could be awesome. You never know unless you try. Think about how it could change our family." She kissed him, and when their tongues met, she tasted the yeasty flavor of his craft beer. "We're on this journey together. You and me. Don't let fear stop you from a new possibility."

"I'm not afraid. Fear has nothing to do with it."

"Then what's stopping you? Give me five good reasons why you shouldn't take the job."

Chris didn't respond, and Rachel knew she was getting close to the edge of a cliff. Push too hard and they'd both tumble over. It was after midnight and they were drunk. No productive conversation would come out of this, especially not when Chris's hand snaked up her shirt.

She bit her tongue and gave in, telling herself to enjoy the last bits of vacation before they returned to the real world. They'd talk in the morning. Everything would be clearer in the light of a new day.

. . .

The morning did bring perspective, just not exactly what Rachel was expecting. She'd fallen asleep convincing herself that Chris would be too stubborn, too set in his ways to agree. He'd decline Roman's offer. Her dream of moving up in the world would be put on the back-burner again. So when she woke to find Chris and Roman chatting in a corner of the living room, her heart skipped a beat. Chris nodded along, even jotted a few things down on a notepad. And then, right then and there, he extended a hand, which made Rachel gasp.

"Thank you for your offer," Chris said. "I'll take it." He gave Rachel a look, and she knew what it meant: He was doing it for them but mostly for her.

"Good man," Roman said. The two shook on it.

Rachel did a little clap, and the kids chimed in with a chorus of "What's going on? Why is everyone excited? Are we going to Disneyland?"

She couldn't put it into words, but the moment felt momentous, like the turning of a page, the start of a new chapter. Everything had been mundane for so long, their daily routine bleeding into a repetitive cycle of motions. She was ready for something new, something different. Something better.

Chris wore a smile, but it didn't quite make his eyes crinkle the way she knew they would if it was genuine. He must be nervous for change, and she understood, which was why she wrapped her arms around his neck and whispered in his ear, "I'm proud of you."

The men planned a meeting to discuss all the details. The women did a final sweep of the house. It had been another successful family vacation in Rachel's mind. Sun, fun, friends —*what more could she ask for?*

As they departed for the airport, Jacob pressed a clammy

hand against the car window. "Bye, beach house. See you next time."

Rachel grinned, feeling a surge of happiness. Her bucket was filling. A new job for Chris, and now she just needed to figure out the logistics of her own goal. They'd end up exactly where they were meant to be all along.

She looked over her shoulder at Savannah and Jacob in the bucket seats, and Chloe taking up the third row in the back. Chloe leaned her head against the window, hood pulled up, eyes closed.

Teenagers, Rachel thought. Such tricky creatures.

TEN

CHLOE

IT WAS UNFAIR HOW FAST BREAK FLEW BY. CHLOE FELT like she'd just finished finals, and now spring semester was creeping up. Email reminders cluttered her inbox—schedules from the registrar's office, syllabi from professors. She had stacked classes and got into Slavery in America, which checked off her history requirement. Ava got in too—that was a bonus. But school felt miles away. She still had to get through this last, dragging work shift.

Chloe straightened a stack of sweaters, refolding the top one the customers always picked up and tossed back down haphazardly. Working at the mall wasn't the most thrilling, but it got her a little extra cash during breaks, and the employee discount didn't hurt. If there was one takeaway from college jobs, it was that you learned what you *didn't* want to do for the rest of your life. Retail, Chloe had discovered, ranked high on her list.

She yawned. Two more hours left in her six-hour shift. Her arms struggled to function, everything somehow taking more effort than usual, as though the air itself was thicker, harder to move through. She'd felt sluggish for days, slept nearly twelve hours the last two nights, and still wanted nothing more than to close her eyes for more. She recalled when she was younger and her mom had made comments about growth spurts whenever she'd go on long sleep stretches. Could she still get growth spurts at nineteen? Maybe it was the shortened days of winter—dark before five p.m.—kicking that melatonin into gear early.

"Sitting around only makes you more tired," her dad had said last night at dinner. "Go do something. You know, maybe leave your room?"

She'd rolled her eyes, taken another bite of pork chop, and gone to bed. Whatever it was, she wouldn't be able to enjoy it once classes started. So she wanted to lie around—what teenager didn't? Sue her.

Chloe moved onto the next table and tri-folded a pile of jeans. Greeted a customer. Opened another register when the line got long. She went through the motions, but the whole time thought, *Can I just sit for a minute?*

On her fifteen-minute break, she did sit. "Jesus," she said aloud to no one but herself, as though she'd just finished a marathon instead of ringing out customers standing perfectly still. She laid her head on the little table in the back room, unfazed by the layer of grime on its surface.

When her chest pressed against the edge, she winced and shifted. Her breasts were sore. She touched one, realizing it felt heavy in her bra. That pre-period tenderness, the same one that made her wear two sports bras instead of one when she'd go for a jog. That must be it—her period about to start. How lovely. Just in time to go back to school.

"Dude, you were supposed to be back on the floor ten minutes ago."

Chloe startled, lifting her head and blinking to remember where she was. She'd really fallen asleep right there on that gross table?

The sales associate—a girl whose spray tan bordered on

orange—looked at Chloe like she would transmit something if she stood too close. "Are you good?"

It took every ounce of energy for Chloe to stand. Invisible sandbags weighed down her shoulders. "Just tired," she said, passing the girl and returning to the floor, one foot in front of the other.

The feeling didn't go away post-nap either. And the longer she stood at the register ringing up boyfriend jeans and crop tops, the more her mind wandered. She did an internal body scan in a way she hadn't before. Was this really just the onset of her period? Why did it feel so... different?

She tried to calculate her cycle in her head but kept getting interrupted by customers and had to start over. She'd had a period last month. *Hadn't she?* Timelines were blurring. Was it before or after her week at the beach? She must have—the birth control pills kept her regular. A consistent promise, the security of being in the clear. Some of her friends weren't on the pill, and each month they'd freak out and catastrophize until the bleeding finally started. Chloe thanked God she didn't have to worry like that.

But...

There were those few times she didn't take a pill on time or forgot to take it altogether. When she'd slept over at Preston's and left the case on her dresser. Once she'd gone home for the whole weekend and forgotten it on campus. This was rare though, so it couldn't be that big of a deal. How many girls were really completely consistent with birth control? *No*, Chloe thought, it didn't have anything to do with that. Being on semester break, out of her normal routine, it was throwing her body off. Nothing more.

She was sure.

She was fairly sure.

She wasn't sure at all.

The more she thought about it, the more a kernel of dread

planted in her stomach. By the time she clocked out and made it across the parking lot to her car, the kernel had bloomed into a full-blown weed. And if she'd learned anything from her mother, it was that weeds were hard to kill.

Neither of her parents were there when Chloe got home, which was a blessing because she was sure any sort of communication would have made her nausea morph into actual vomit.

Chloe managed a quick "hey" to the babysitter and dashed up the stairs, hollering over her shoulder, "Can you stay for five more minutes? I just need to do something real quick."

It was her responsibility to relieve the babysitter if she got home before her parents. Rachel had made it very clear that Chloe could help look after her siblings, thus lowering the out-of-pocket cost of holiday childcare. What did Chloe care? She'd let them sit in front of the TV all day.

Upstairs, Chloe locked herself in the bathroom and withdrew the plastic bag from her purse. Her hands shook, gut in knots. When she'd left the mall, it was like her car had driven on autopilot to the drugstore. She'd scanned the rows, trying to appear as nonchalant as possible. Do-da-do, nothing to see here.

But that was all on the outside. Inside, she'd been a basket case, nerves stacked on top of nerves. And then she'd found what she was looking for. In the same aisle as the tampons and pads. Only a few hours earlier, it was these things she'd thought she needed. Now, it was something else entirely—a pregnancy test. How rude for them to be right next to the feminine care products. One the clear absence of a baby, the other proof of the opposite. A cruel contradiction.

It had occurred to her that some women actually bought those tests in a state of excitement and hope. They prayed to see that little plus sign, or whatever it was, that told them they were pregnant. For Chloe, the idea was as foreign as offshore currency. Her stomach had rolled like the waves from the beach multiplied by a hundred. She couldn't believe she was buying this.

She'd done a quick check left and right to make sure no one was watching then snatched a test off the shelf—a pink box with bold letters saying, "Triple check! 3x the confirmation!" The bag had sat on her passenger seat like a ticking bomb the whole way home.

Chloe leaned against the bathroom sink and dropped her head, letting a wave of dizziness pass. She pictured that last time with Preston at the ski lodge, when she'd hoped her efforts would show him what he was missing. Their connection had always been so good—maybe one last taste would bring them back together. How wrong she'd been.

She sucked in air and let it out again. The box said results appeared in as quick as ninety seconds, but she should wait up to five minutes to be sure. Impossible. There'd be no way she could wait that long.

On the toilet, she spread her legs and held the stick below. The whole thing felt offensive—peeing on a stick and getting your hand sprayed on. Then to watch the yellow urine soak into a firm little pad. Disgusting. It made her even more nauseous just thinking about the process, as if she were high above on the ceiling looking down at herself. She was supposed to be heading back to school the very next day. *How the hell did she get here?* Well, she knew exactly how. But that no longer mattered. There was no way to go back and take her pill as instructed. Right now, she needed to control her breathing while the test did its job. That and pray for a miracle.

Chloe laid the stick on the counter and waited. She looked away, not wanting to watch a line either form or not form.

On the wall next to the shower hung a triple picture frame, holding pictures of her, Jacob, and Savannah as babies in tubs full of bubbles. Big eyes, toothy smiles, wet eyelashes. Laughing at nothing more than the magical concoction of soap and water. How innocent they looked, not a care in the world. Happy to splash away and be wrapped up in a warm towel later. Not a boyfriend breaking up with them, or an AP exam to cram for, or a pregnancy test computing on a sink ledge.

Chloe checked the timer on her phone. Ninety seconds had passed. The test could be done. She could peek. But what if it wasn't? What if she looked too early and it was a false negative? She used all her might to keep her eyes away. Just a little longer.

Her mind drifted to what she'd tell her parents. At that, her eyes filled with tears. This was her mother's worst nightmare, another too-soon pregnancy. What would she say? Would her mom cry? Would her dad shake his head in that disappointed way that crushed Chloe's heart? Would she have to drop out of school?

The timer reached three minutes and Chloe couldn't wait any longer. She needed to know. Maybe this was all a terrible error. Maybe she'd misjudged everything. Her period could just be off. It could show up tomorrow. And then she'd laugh and laugh at what a big deal she'd made of it all. She'd be one of those paranoid girls she always laughed at. Oh, how she wished for that.

No more questions, no more what ifs. The time was now. Last thing she needed was a curious Savannah coming to check on her. Chloe let her eyes drift to the test. She picked it up and held it in front of her. The room went white.

"No," she whispered.

There it was, clear as day. A vivid pink cross. She didn't have to double-check the instructions or compare to the sample pictures. There was no mistaking those colored lines. No squinting to see. She was pregnant. And at that, Chloe spun off the toilet and gagged into the bowl.

ELEVEN

RACHEL

"I HAVEN'T WORN ONE OF THESE DAMN THINGS SINCE YOUR grandmother's funeral." Chris struggled with the tie, looping and tucking, then yanking it out again when the finished result was comically short.

"Here," Rachel said, coming to stand in front of him. "Let me help you." She draped the tie around his neck and crossed the wide end over the top. With another twist, tuck, and pull, she formed a neat Windsor knot. "There."

Chris stood back, taking in his appearance in the bathroom mirror. "I feel like a bobble head."

"A handsome bobble head." She planted a kiss between his shoulder blades.

Rachel knew Chris had mostly accepted the job to make her happy, even though he hadn't said so aloud, but she hoped once he got started, he'd find aspects he enjoyed. People got stuck in their ways so easily, they missed opportunities just because they were too scared to try something new.

She spent the last two weeks envisioning what his new job would mean for their family, the places it could take him. Starting out as a glorified assistant wasn't much, but this wasn't big city poli-tics—there weren't many positions to be had. According to Roman, Chris would be leveraging his connections to the working class. Chris knew much of the blue-collar set around the area, both from living in Wexford for years and also through the workers' union. These were important votes, and Chris would network to get them.

"I guess I'm getting a headshot taken today," Chris said, using his fingers in place of a hairbrush.

"Oooh, fancy."

"He said something about a shot of us together for marketing purposes. Something about introducing me to the public." Chris tugged on his collar. "This thing is gonna drive me nuts."

"Leave it," Rachel said, smacking his hand away. "You're just not used to wearing dress clothes."

Chris groaned.

"You look very hot, by the way."

He accepted the compliment with a sarcastic pout of the lips.

Rachel couldn't pinpoint the last time she'd seen Chris dressed and groomed so well. Her grandmother's funeral, yes. But other than that? Maybe a cousin's wedding years back? Though even then, chinos usually sufficed. A golf shirt maybe. But this morning, he'd even trimmed his beard, cleaning up the scruff on his neck.

All of it made Rachel tingle.

"You're going to do great," she said, knowing him enough to tell when he was jittery. He'd been restless all night, tossing this way and that, yanking on the covers, which had kept her awake. In response, she'd lain a palm on his chest and he'd settled—at least temporarily. "And maybe this will be a chance for you and Roman to get closer?" She said it like a question, like she wasn't so sure herself.

He wheeled to face her. "Rach, you know this is temporary. The campaign only lasts so long."

"Right, but if he's elected, you could continue." Chris gave her a wary look, and she crossed her arms. "C'mon. You never know."

"Maybe it will lead to other things. But I can't imagine working with Roman for the rest of my life."

"No one said you had to."

"It feels like that's what you want."

"I never said that. And besides, why did you accept if you hate the idea of working with him so much?"

Chris stared at her. His lips twitched like he wanted to say something but was holding back. And so Rachel took the plunge. "I know this wasn't your first choice—not even really your idea at all. I know you're doing it for me, for us, and so I just want to say thank you."

He gave a slight nod. Rachel followed him downstairs.

"Whoa," Savannah said from the table where she shoveled the last bites of breakfast into her mouth. "You look... different."

"Different in a good way, right?" Rachel said with wide, suggestive eyes.

"Yeah! Super good! Like a prince."

"Are you going to meet the president?" Jacob asked excitedly.

Chris chuckled. "Not quite." He grabbed the coffee Rachel had made him from the counter, turned, and lifted his shoulders to his ears. "Well, guess I'm off."

"See ya, Dad!" the kids said, as if the day were the same as any other. As if it wasn't a big moment for their family—a morning that could change their trajectory.

They bounded from the kitchen toward the tiny mud room that housed their backpacks in overflowing cubbies. Rachel watched them go, struck by their indifference. If the kids didn't care so much about Chris's job, should she?

TWELVE

MONICA

After her second consult of the day, Monica opened a bag of salted almonds and sat at her desk, enjoying the midday snack. It had been a good day so far. She'd done an embryo implantation for one of her favorite couples over a week ago—the husband whose eyes sparkled every time his wife smiled—and now this morning they'd received a positive pregnancy test. The husband had choked up while the woman cried freely. The joy never failed to give Monica goosebumps.

Her phone buzzed from her desk, and a Facebook notification popped up on the screen. She swiped it open: A new video post from Roman's official campaign account, *Roman Nash for Mayor*.

A high school senior doing a pre-college internship had set up the page, mostly to post campaign updates, videos of Roman addressing the public, and rebuttals to his opponent. They'd used a headshot of Roman in a suit and tie for the profile picture, but one of the early posts had been a family photo—Roman, Monica, Lucas, and Logan in coordinating blues—to show that not only was he a dedicated public servant, he was also a family man. Aside from that, Monica didn't interact with the page much, and seeing as she hadn't taken his last name when they married, many people didn't even connect the two. She was Dr. Monica Cross, the fertility specialist, not Mrs. Nash, the prospective mayor's wife.

Curiosity made her click to expand the post. A new message to voters, posted less than an hour ago.

"Part of my role as mayor will be to increase transparency to the Wexford community. The citizens deserve to know the ins and outs of their city, and I believe politics has been set up with too much smoke and mirrors. In my tenure, I'll break down those walls. Because I'm here to serve you with honesty and loyalty."

Monica grew taller in her swivel chair. The speech was good. This was the man he presented to the world, one of dignity and poise. A pillar of the community. She'd seen it too, sometimes still did. He'd disappeared a little recently, but seeing this video gave Monica hope that maybe her husband was returning.

She scrolled down to the comment section, and a shiver zoomed down her arms to her fingertips.

Loyalty? Yeah, maybe to his bank account.

Monica stiffened. Heat spread through her chest cavity. She kept reading.

Roman Nash is about as transparent as a closed door.

Somebody better check this guy's financials, that's all I'm gonna say.

Heard he's got slippery fingers when it comes to cash flow. Hmmmm...

Wouldn't vote for him even if the rumors weren't true. Politi-
cians are all dirty.

Monica's temperature went from hot to cold. Chills crawled
over her skin as she scrolled and scrolled. For every one positive
comment, three opposed it. A comment storm barreling in over
the course of the last few minutes. They attacked his character,
his morals. Some could even be considered slander, she thought.
Toeing the line without coming right out and saying what was
clearly implied. And then there were the few that didn't sugar-
coat it. Embezzlement. Theft of public funds. Scam artist.

Monica's heart raced. She picked up the phone and dialed.

"What's up?" Roman asked. "I'm reviewing a report from
the transportation department. Is it important?"

Monica balked. "Yes, actually, it is important. Have you
seen these comments on Facebook? They're attacking you."

"You know I hate social media. That's why I got the intern.
What's his name? Ben."

"Well, you might want to tell Ben to take them down." She
heard typing in the background. "Roman? Are you listening to
me? It doesn't look good, what people are saying."

Why couldn't she just come out and say it? *Are you stealing
money from your campaign?*

"You know, sometimes it's just better to not comment on
things that are unfounded. But sure, I'll have Ben look into it,
okay? I gotta go."

It didn't completely ease her concern, but at least the online
lynching would be gone. Plus, Roman didn't seem overly
concerned, and that gave her some sense of comfort. A guilty
person would surely fly into denial mode.

Monica swiped the screen away. Her phone's background
was set to a picture of the four of them last year at a water park
in the Bahamas. The boys grinned from ear to ear, clunky
goggles sucked to their foreheads. Behind them, Roman and

Monica emanated nothing but happiness. His arm around her waist. Matching twinkling eyes. She remembered that day; how much fun they'd had taking turns going down the slides then floating through the maze of the lazy river.

She studied the picture as though it would contradict what she'd just read. This wasn't the face of a man who'd commit a crime. These rumors simply couldn't be true. Just trolls behind a screen, willing to say anything to destroy someone else's livelihood.

Monica popped another almond in her mouth, trying to convince herself not to worry, but after sucking off the salt, she spit the nut out, unable to chew. Outside, fat snowflakes drifted past her window. She wished they were back at that water park where the only concern was remembering to apply sunscreen.

Monica's pulse racketed. It was her duty to protect her husband. She couldn't let his campaign fail because of unfounded hearsay. None of it was true. They didn't know her husband.

Her ribs tightened. Did *she* know her husband?

Monica brushed away the doubt as quick as it came. She'd chosen well. Worked hard for the family she'd built. These things, they couldn't be true. She said it again to drive home the point: *It's not true*.

Doubt had a funny way of weaseling its way into a brain. Roman didn't get home until after ten, when Monica was already in bed reading—or at least trying to read. She'd told herself she'd let the Facebook comments go. She'd trust her husband. But seeing him in person threw all her faith into question.

"How was your day?" she asked in a quiet voice, even though the boys' rooms were down the hall, separated by layers of drywall. Often she was asleep when he returned, their chance to talk pushed back to the next morning if at all. But she'd had an uneasy stomach ever since their earlier conversation. A nagging poking at her. She didn't know the exact moment things had changed, but the marriage she'd thought she had felt very different from reality. Was it her fault? Maybe greater investment in his daily life would help their connection. She should ask more. Care more. Maybe then he wouldn't feel the need to have secrets.

"Long," Roman said, dropping his shirt in the hamper next to their dresser. "Chris is doing well though."

"He seem to like it?"

"As far as I can tell. I mean, he's a bit of a fish out of water. But I've shown him the ropes. He's taking calls. And we've got that dinner coming up, don't forget."

"That's great." She scooched up against the tufted headboard. Roman slid his pants off so he stood in his boxer briefs and undershirt. Monica felt heat rise to her face. Embarrassment for her physical attraction to a man who might not deserve such reverence.

"It's a little annoying that he has to leave at four most days."

"Oh?"

"Jacob's soccer or something. Rachel has to take Savannah somewhere, so he's in charge of Jacob. I don't know. They need a nanny."

Monica clamped down on her tongue. She knew Rachel and Chris couldn't afford a nanny. Instead, she said, "Maybe."

"I just hope he's taking the job seriously."

"I'm sure he is."

"Who knows? It's not like Chris is known as some glowing big shot."

Monica's defenses flared. Chris was her friend. "He's a good guy."

"Sure. But good guys don't usually make it far in politics."

Monica stiffened, and she almost said, *What?* before Roman quickly backtracked.

"Except me of course." He gave her his most charming smile, the same one that had knocked her off her feet when they first dated. She gave a quiet laugh because it felt somehow appropriate, even though the comment confused her.

"Why'd you offer him the job if you didn't think he'd be good at it?" she asked.

Roman was brushing his teeth now, and she waited for his reply until after he spit, swished, and spit again. "We both know they could use the money, right?"

"True."

"I just wanted to help the guy out. You know me, Mr. Good Samaritan."

She took a second to process this. She'd never have considered Roman the Samaritan type. It sounded so silly she almost laughed, but he spoke again.

"Maybe you can check in with Rachel? See what she says about how things are going?"

Monica nodded. She felt a headache coming on, a tightness behind her eyes. She needed the day to be over. To close her eyelids like curtains and not think anymore.

Roman climbed in beside her in nothing but his underwear like he always did. Oh, to have the confidence of a man, she thought. Her lace-trimmed silk set hid all the bits and pieces she disliked, while still feeling semi-luxurious.

His leg brushed up against hers as he settled, and the touch sent a jolt of electricity through her body. When was the last time they'd been intimate? Something about the day made her ache for attention. She wanted him to see her, to whisper all his inner thoughts in her ear. Sex could prove to herself that everything was fine. The craving thrilled and repulsed her. What kind of woman could read smears about her husband and then want to be close to him? It was ugly desperation. But she couldn't deny the flutter in her belly.

She inched toward him, closing the distance. The heat between them warmed the Egyptian cotton sheets. Roman's eyes were closed; he was already half asleep. She'd always envied his ability to turn off his brain so easily. Her face was inches from his. His breath smelled boozy, despite the teeth brushing, but in the moment she didn't care. She was back in those early days when she'd leave butterfly kisses along his neck, finger the place where he once wore an earring in his twenties to hide the self-consciousness that came from his small ears and attached lobes.

"They're rare," she'd reassured him then. "Part of what makes you special."

Now, Monica slid a hand around his torso and up his strong back. His eyes popped open. She leaned toward his lips, feeling a surge down below, but Roman pulled back.

"Not tonight," he said. "I'm exhausted."

Monica froze there for a beat, mouth stuck in her seductive grin, waiting for him to crack. *Just kidding, baby.* But he didn't, and Monica quickly shrank away, curling in on herself. A lump formed in her throat. The humiliation stung. He'd never turned her down before. Even though their sex life had waned in recent years—especially with the addition of kids—it hadn't dried up completely. Here she was trying to initiate, and he'd slammed the door in her face.

Roman rolled over so his back was to her, and within seconds his breathing slowed to a deep, rhythmic pace. Monica watched his ribcage rise and fall. She bit her lower lip to keep the emotion at bay and wrung the sheet in her fist.

Monica spent the night not sleeping but convincing herself she could fix this. Their connection. Her role as wife.

Monica checked her calendar for an open night she could plan a dinner, just for the two of them. With Valentine's Day coming up, they were due for a date night anyway. All those nasty rumors should be gone by then, and if they weren't, it would be a good time for her to bring it up again.

In the morning, she dialed Chloe, their loyal babysitting backup. Chloe rarely turned her down—the premium rate didn't hurt.

"Hey, Chlo," Monica said when the girl answered. "How's it going?"

"Fine. Why wouldn't it be?" Chloe's words were clipped and fast, like she was on the defense.

Monica's face twisted and she almost laughed in response. "Just asking," she said lightly.

"Oh. Okay."

Weird, Monica thought. *What's up with her?* "I just called to see if you could babysit Saturday."

There was a pause. Monica started to repeat herself, thinking there'd been a break in connection, but Chloe quickly cut her off. "I can't, sorry."

"Oh," Monica said, surprised. It wasn't like Chloe to say no. "Big plans? You're not going to see Preston again, are you?"

"No. I, uh... I promised Mom we'd do a movie night."

"Fun!" She'd felt the tension pulling Rachel and Chloe in different directions recently, and the thought of them spending the evening together made Monica's core warm. But it didn't solve her babysitting dilemma. "What about Friday?" She could reschedule her wine night with Rachel.

Another pause. "I'm busy."

"Okay," Monica said slowly. If she didn't know any better, she'd think Chloe was making excuses to get out of something. Was it her? Did something happen with the boys last time? Logan could be pretty needy. Or worse, maybe Chloe heard the money rumors too. A vision of it tearing their families' friendship apart made her shudder. What would Rachel and Chris say if they learned people were saying Roman's financials weren't above board. Chris might quit. Rachel might question her. *What wife doesn't know when her husband is acting shady?* She thought of Ruth Madoff, wife of scorned Ponzi scheme leader Bernie Madoff, the one who'd ruined so many lives with his greed.

"Sorry," Chloe said again.

"No worries. I'll see if Jessica might be free." She shook the spiraling thoughts from her brain; tried to keep her tone light. "Enjoy the time with your mom. See you soon, okay?"

They hung up, and Monica gave a little *hmmph*. Why was everything so... off?

THIRTEEN

RACHEL

February

HER FINGER HOVERED ABOVE THE BUTTON. RACHEL curled and flexed it, back and forth, as though she were about to touch something dangerous.

Do it.

Don't do it.

"Stop procrastinating," she said to no one but herself. She sat outside Savannah's piano lesson and had taken the few minutes to pull up the college website—the one she'd narrowed her search down to—again.

When the information packets had hit her inbox three months ago, she'd scoured every word in an effort to convince herself it was possible. Phrases like "where bright futures await," and "adult learners," and "fast-track your degree," jumped out in eye-catching colors. She'd read up on night class offerings, what courses she'd need to take to finish what she'd started over twenty years before. The school held classes once or twice a week for two to three hours. That was feasible, wasn't it? She could take a night or two away from everything for herself, right? Then there was distance learning, fully remote thanks to the power of Zoom. She wouldn't even have to leave the house. She could cook dinner while listening to the lecture.

The blue button flashed on the screen with two words in all caps: APPLY NOW. A simple tap could set her on a new path. Chris was on his way—why shouldn't she be? They'd paid their dues; they'd done what was needed. Now it was time to get back the little pieces they'd missed. Re-right the direction.

But then Jacob and Savannah and Chloe flashed through her mind, and Rachel hesitated again. Only selfish women put their desires before their children. The family calendar already overflowed several months out. How would she be able to fit in one more thing—one more very big thing. It felt futile. Vain.

But also essential.

Rachel sucked air in through her teeth. The multitude of hypotheticals threatened to make her balk completely, so she clicked the button before she chickened out. And when she did, a wave of exhilaration swept from her baseball cap down to her worn-in Vans sneakers. She buzzed, emboldened. Yes, this was right. This was feasible. She could do it. And she shouldn't feel guilty.

Savannah bounded out of the house, and Rachel waved to Mrs. Linden. She rolled the window half down to avoid letting in a chill and yelled, "Thank you!" to which the woman smiled and held up a hand.

"Hey, hon," Rachel said, voice an octave higher than usual. As they drove, Rachel turned up the music and sang along. She bopped her head, even did a little drum solo on the steering wheel.

"Why are you so happy?" Savannah asked with a look somewhere between bewilderment and mortification.

"What, I'm not allowed to sing?"

"You haven't stopped smiling since you picked me up."

"Would you rather I drive like this?" Rachel slumped her

shoulders dramatically and put on an exaggerated frown. Savannah laughed. But the girl's sentiment settled on Rachel's mind. Did her kids think her an unhappy person? Was she going through life—the motions of each day—in some state of outward discontent? She resolved to be more aware of her moods.

Savannah's comment was all the more justification for Rachel's decision to apply to school. The idea of starting classes soon buoyed her. Almost like the sun had come out for the first time in a long time. She imagined making a grand announcement on Facebook like high school seniors. *College-bound!* Though as excited as she felt, she decided to keep it to herself for now. Applying was only one step. Who knew if she'd even be accepted. There was no point sharing the news until it was official. No sense causing disruption to the family if their schedule wouldn't be changing after all.

Rachel tucked the secret into the back of her mind, promising to tell Chris once she heard official word from the school. Once accepted, they'd talk out the details, formulate a new order of business for how the family operations would go. That's how she thought of it—a well-oiled machine with herself in the center. The conductor. But every functional plan had a backup. Even captains of a ship rerouted course when needed. They'd be fine. As long as she could get Chris on board. She could start classes that fall alongside Chloe. How new and fun it would be.

She and Savannah were the first ones home. Savannah quickly jumped out, seeing a neighbor friend, and Rachel gathered everything else—purse; Savannah's backpack and coat.

"Don't worry, I got it," she said, only half serious.

Inside, she dumped everything on the floor, planning to tell Savannah to take care of her own things. It was her I'm-not-your-maid speech the kids had heard endless times yet was clearly ineffective. If she did indeed go back to school, things would have to change around here.

Rachel's phone dinged with an incoming text, and Monica's name flashed on the screen.

Have a fun movie night with Chloe! XO

Rachel cocked her head. Movie night? She stood still, trying to conjure plans she'd made but couldn't remember. Had she told Chloe they'd go to the movies? She didn't think there were even any movies she was interested in seeing. Her daughter had been coming home most weekends, even though the semester had just started, but that didn't mean Rachel got any more face time. Chloe spent most of the time in her room. She understood —their home life was still "little kid," but Chloe was an adult now.

Not wanting to sound daft—once again, did Monica know something she didn't?—Rachel put the phone in her pocket. She'd respond in a bit, but first she needed to clarify.

Chloe was on the couch, phone in hand, when Rachel entered the living room.

"You're going to lose brain cells if you watch TikTok all day, you know," Rachel joked.

Chloe didn't respond.

Rachel crossed her arms. "Did we have plans tonight?"

That made Chloe look up. "Plans?"

"Yeah. A movie or something?"

Her daughter's brows furrowed. "I don't think so?" Then, just as quickly, a knowing. Like when a light goes off in your head. Chloe's forehead smoothed, making Rachel's senses pique. Hmmm.

Chloe returned to her phone. She pulled on the neckline of her shirt, drawing it up to her chin. "I was gonna get a jump start on reading for American Lit. Probably head back to campus in the morning."

"Monica sent an odd text about you and I having a movie night."

Chloe shrugged without looking up. "Maybe it's menopause."

Rachel laughed. "Oh, please." She continually liked to remind Chloe that she was only forty-one. There were still people her age having babies, for goodness' sake. But to a teen, forties were a lifetime away. She couldn't blame Chloe for not understanding. What she wished the girl would see, though, was how quick it all went. How it was no more than a blink between college and this middle-of-life stage. How Chloe should enjoy her youth before it was gone.

Rachel found a seat on the couch. "Well, if you want to watch a movie later, I'm game." Amends filled each word. She placed a hand on Chloe's foot, but Chloe recoiled and slid out of Rachel's vicinity, darting her eyes everywhere but her mother's face.

"I really do need to read." And then she got up and left.

Rachel shook her head. "Hormones." Her phone rang, and a picture of Rachel and Monica lit up the screen.

"Hey," Rachel said.

"Oh good. I'm glad I caught you before movie night."

Rachel almost spoke up, almost corrected her friend—there was no movie night; where did you get that?—but decided it only made her sound even more detached from Chloe. She didn't want Monica to know the plans were cancelled, or worse, that they'd never existed in the first place. Instead, she kept her tone light. "What's up?"

"Just checking in. How's Chris liking his job? Everything going okay?"

"As far as I know." She'd called to talk about Chris? Rachel couldn't help herself. "Why?"

"No reason," Monica trilled.

"It doesn't sound like no reason. Is there something I should know, Mon?"

"No, no. Nothing bad. Roman just said he's hard to read. So I thought I'd check to make sure everything was good."

Hard to read? What was that supposed to mean? "I think he likes it. He hasn't said otherwise. We don't talk about work stuff all that much to be honest."

The truth was that Rachel didn't have to hear the words from her husband to know he wasn't loving the job. The deep exhales before heading out the door, the shorter fuse, even his posture, small and hollow—it all told Rachel what she needed to know.

"Okay, well..." Monica trailed off. "I just know it can be demanding. And Roman needs Chris to be all in."

Rachel's face flushed with heat. "Why wouldn't he be all in?"

"No, I just mean like all the after-hours things, the dinners, that stuff. A full workday. It's a lot, but it's important."

"Chris is always committed to whatever he's doing."

"Right, of course. It's just—"

"Just what?" Rachel's heart thundered in her ears. Why was Monica going down this line of questioning?

"Roman said something about Chris needing to leave early for the kids' stuff a lot, and I mean, I know you guys are super busy, and of course the kids come first. I guess he just wanted me to check in, that's all."

"He wanted you to? You just said it was your idea to call."

"Well, both, I guess. Minor detail." She laughed, but it had a nervous timbre.

"If Roman has a problem with Chris, shouldn't he talk to him directly? Why did he need to say anything to you?"

"Oh, well I'm sure he just assumed you and I talk about it a lot. It's not a big deal, Rach. I wouldn't worry about it. Everything's fine."

"Is it?"

"Of course! Why wouldn't it be?"

"You're the one who called me with concerns about my husband."

"Not concerns. Just... interest. Care. You're both my friends."

Rachel counted to ten to slow her breathing. There were so many things implied in the conversation that were going unsaid. Monica didn't need to say it out loud, but the message was clear: Chris wasn't as good as Roman. Chris wasn't as dedicated to his job as Roman. Their family priorities were screwed up.

"Listen, Rachel," Monica said, "I didn't mean to upset you. Honestly. Forget I even said anything. I'm sure Chris is doing awesome at his job."

Rachel's voice clogged. "Okay."

"Sorry I couldn't do girls' night yesterday. Are we still on for next week? I could really use some friend time."

Rachel paused. It was such a 180-turn in the conversation her brain struggled to keep up. She always looked forward to their wine nights, a chance to unwind and catch up. When old stories and current gripes made Rachel laugh so much she would go to bed with a sore jaw. But in this moment, the idea of gossiping with Monica didn't sound appealing. The phone call had put her on edge and left a residue of resentment on her skin. She rubbed her forearm, as though she could remove the nasty feeling. She shouldn't cancel just because of this one exchange. It was Monica, her best friend in the world. They'd never fought. The idea of them being pissed at each other was completely unfamiliar. Was that what this was? A fight?

When she finally spoke, a return to the familiar prevailed. "Sure, I'm still good."

"Perfect. I'll bring a bottle of white."

They disconnected, and Rachel stared at the wall, processing the conversation; the idea that Chris wasn't performing like he should, wasn't meeting expectations. Did Roman want to fire him? She'd be furious. Where would that leave them? And Monica—why insert herself into a situation that clearly should stay between their husbands? She wished Monica had never brought it up. She fiddled with the tassel on a pillow for nearly half an hour, letting her thoughts take over. It wasn't until Chris and Jacob came through the door that she blinked back to life.

"What's for dinner?" Jacob asked without even as much as a hello. Rachel's insides simmered. She'd gone from chauffeur to maid and now was expected to put on her chef hat.

"How was ball?" she asked, but Jacob was already gone.

"He had some good shots," Chris said, hanging his jacket in the closet by the door. "Coach said he needs to work on dribbling." He dropped down next to Rachel and put his feet up on the ottoman. The socks were new—the kind you wear with dress shoes instead of sneakers. Rachel had had to buy him several new professional pieces.

Chris laid his head back against her shoulder, and she instinctively raked her fingers through his hair.

"Do you like your new job?" she asked, bracing herself.

"It's alright."

"Just alright?"

"I mean, it's fine. I'm sure it'll get better once I'm into it longer."

Not the response she'd hoped for. Where were the glowing reviews? The gushing about how much he loved it and how right she'd been to push him for the change? These were the things she wanted him to say.

"And Roman? How's it going with him?"

Chris shrugged. "It's not like we're becoming best friends or anything. Remember, it's just a job."

"Right, but like, you're getting along?"

"Roman's not the first person I'd choose to spend eight hours a day with, but yeah, it's working. The only thing is..." He trailed off.

"What?" Rachel asked, curious.

"It's probably nothing, just a weird quirk."

"Tell me."

"He's on his mobile banking a lot. Like we'll be having a meeting or out to lunch, and I can see him looking at his account."

"Huh."

"I guess the guy's just meticulous about money."

Rachel agreed—lots of people had odd habits. There could be worse things than being aware of one's finances. She brushed the comment aside, concerned more with Chris and his position.

"We can make arrangements for the kids so you don't have to leave, you know. I don't want you to miss out on stuff with Roman just because of Jacob's practices. He can get a ride with one of the other parents, or I'll have someone drop Sav at piano so I can take him."

She was rambling, and Chris sat up to meet her face. "What's this about?"

"I just want you to do well and get the most out of your job. The kids have busy schedules, but we can figure something out."

The college website flashed through her mind. The APPLY NOW button. Her stomach twisted even harder. But right now she needed to encourage her husband. If he didn't do his job, Roman might get upset. Maybe he already was upset. She imagined the men squaring off. It would be a whole calamity. And then what would that mean for her and Monica? She couldn't let something as silly as a job come between her and her friend.

Chris leaned in and kissed his wife on the lips. "Everything's good," he said, and a wash of calm came over her body with just those two simple words. He was always able to make her relax. "Chloe still going back to campus in the morning?"

"Yep."

"Back down to two."

"At least until she comes home again." Rachel exhaled. "I feel like I barely saw her this weekend. It's like she wasn't even here."

"When does the moody phase end and the my-parents-aren't-so-bad phase pick back up?" He smirked.

Rachel simply closed her eyes and shook her head. Sometimes there was too much stuff and not enough brain space. Too many tabs open, the command center about to fry. She'd talk to Chloe next time she was home. She'd figure out if something was wrong.

"Hey," Chris said. "We got this." He put out his hand for a fist bump, and Rachel met his knuckles with hers. A reminder: We're a team.

And while she appreciated the attempt at diversion, a knot twisted in her stomach. An acceptance email might come any day. And when that happened, she'd have a big choice to make. A choice, and then a confession.

FOURTEEN

RACHEL

"Does this dress make me look frumpy?" Rachel rotated in front of Chris, who was buttoning up a dress shirt. The sweater dress had been hanging in the back of her closet for years—she couldn't even remember when or why she'd bought it in the first place—but it was far from her normal rotation of jeans or leggings. She momentarily let her mind drift to what the other school moms would wear in this position. Women like Vienna Scott, the trendiest mom in the school, and her designer wardrobe.

"You could never look frumpy," Chris said.

"Says the man who's barely aged in twenty years." She pressed out a wrinkle in the hem and gave herself one final look over. Whatever. This campaign dinner was about Chris, not her. She and Monica would just be expected to smile along. Roman had arranged a meeting with the president of the contractor's union. This would be Chris's time to shine—he could speak to this demographic far better than Roman ever could.

"I wish we could just get takeout," Chris said.

"Oh, come on. It's not that bad. When was the last time we had a date night?"

He gave her a deadpan look. "I don't consider this a date night."

Rachel turned so he wouldn't see her roll her eyes. His grumpiness was starting to get to her. Why couldn't he at least be open to liking all this?

On their drive, Rachel was preoccupied with her bag. It was one of those imitation styles from Target. Fake "leather" that felt more plasticky than anything, whereas Monica would probably be carrying something designer.

"Would you stop?" Chris said. "This guy works in construction. It's not like we're meeting with the governor of Pennsylvania or something."

She folded her hands in her lap. She just wanted it to go well.

They arrived at Napa Prime Chophouse and pulled into a spot right next to Roman's BMW. When Rachel looked out the window, she noticed Monica and Roman still sitting inside the vehicle. They appeared to be in the middle of a deep discussion. Roman's hands jerked and flew. Even through the tinted glass, Rachel could see a look of disapproval on her friend's face.

"Wonder what that's about," she said to Chris and pointed with her thumb. A second later, Roman turned and waved, a smile on his face. All four got out of the cars. The men shook hands. Monica circled around to give Rachel a hug. Her eyes looked tired. No one said a word about the previous few minutes.

Inside, they sat at a table under a fancy chandelier. Rachel had been to the restaurant only twice before for anniversaries.

"I'm starving," Monica said. She smoothed the lapel of her tweed blazer. Not a hair out of place. It only made Rachel feel dowdy despite her effort. She'd even put on eyeliner.

A waiter took their drink order—an array of wines. "You

know what?" Roman said. "Why don't you just bring the bottles."

When they'd finished their first glasses and the union president still hadn't arrived, Roman grew agitated. "Not a very good first impression if you ask me," he grumbled.

Rachel couldn't disagree. The only reason for this dinner was for campaign purposes. If all it ended up being was a double date, they could have gone somewhere far less expensive. She still wasn't even sure if Chris was expected to pay for his and Rachel's dinners. Was this a business expense?

Roman poured another glass. After twenty more minutes, he pulled out his phone, mumbling. "Damn contractors. Probably don't even know how to use their calendars." He punched a number into the keypad. "Let's hear the excuse." He laid the phone in the middle of the table and pressed to put the call on speaker.

Rachel broke out in nerves. This dinner was going in a weird direction. And Roman had nearly finished a full bottle of red. She eyed Chris, whose face remained stoic, giving nothing away. She wondered if this was par for the course when it came to Roman and business.

The phone rang three times before a man's voice answered.

"Sam," Roman said boisterously. "I'm taking it you forgot about our dinner tonight? I've got Chris Moreland here, and we were looking forward to meeting with you. There's a full glass of Malbec with your name on it." He rolled his eyes, like, *What an idiot.*

"I'm sorry, Roman," Sam said. "But the union decided it was no longer a smart idea."

"Smart idea?"

"To affiliate with your campaign."

Roman scoffed. Under the table, Rachel wrung her napkin. Everyone's eyes bulged, but no one said a word.

"I'm afraid I don't understand," Roman said. He seemed to

be keeping collected despite the tightness in his jaw. The flush from the wine didn't help.

"We've heard some whispers."

"Wha-What kind of whispers?"

Did Roman just stutter? Rachel looked to Monica, whose face had gone whiter than normal.

"Listen, Roman, I'm sure you know exactly what I'm getting at here. And if you don't, you soon will. We're not interested in being associated with any sort of conduct that's not on the up and up."

At that, Roman clenched his fist on the table. "I'm sure you're not accusing me of running a dirty campaign, Sam. Because if you are, you better be careful."

"Is that a threat?"

"No, it's a—"

Monica reached out and hung up the call. Her hand shook as she withdrew it. Rachel glanced around the table, trying to understand. Did Chris know what this was about?

"What the hell is going on?" Chris asked, the first to speak.

That answered Rachel's question. His scrunched forehead paired with a general look of dismay proved he was just as confused.

"Fucking politics," Roman muttered.

Chris leaned forward. "Roman, what was that all about? What conduct is he referring to?"

Roman rolled his neck. He reached for a half-full bottle of wine and gave himself a tall pour. The rest of the table watched and waited for him to speak.

"It's all bullshit," he finally said. "Haverty is running a smear campaign against me. He knows I'm beating him in the polls."

"But what are these whispers?" Rachel asked. Why wasn't Monica grilling him too?

"There's talk of some mismanaged funds." He waved a

hand like it was no big deal. "It's nothing. They're just trying to ruin my campaign."

Chris blinked. "Wait, are you saying extortion?"

"Call it what you want. But like I said, none of it's true."

Rachel thought back to what Chris had said in their earlier conversation, about Roman always being on his banking app. Her fingers went numb. Had Chris been witnessing crimes in action? She stared at Roman as though seeing him for the first time.

"Chris, my man," Roman said. "We can't let these things shake us. This is politics, baby. Mudslinging at its finest. In fact, why don't you do a little digging yourself on Haverty. Make something up if you have to. Two can play this game."

Chris gaped, and Rachel followed suit. Was Roman serious? His suave posture and easy sipping of wine sure said so. And why was Monica so quiet? Did *she* know shady things had been going on?

Roman flagged the waiter, who promptly came to the table. "I think we'll order now," Roman said. "It'll just be the four of us. Our guest is no longer coming."

"You know what," Chris said, suddenly pushing back his chair. "It'll just be the two of you. I've lost my appetite." He gave Rachel a look that said *get up*, and so she did.

Without another word, he led her from the table. She had to take two steps to his one. Before they were completely from the room, Rachel looked back over her shoulder. Monica's head was down.

Chris waited until they were outside to explode. "I never should have taken this job!" He stormed to their car, Rachel following close behind.

"But you didn't know," she said, trying to match his pace. "And who knows if it's even true. Roman said it's all a lie."

"And you believe him?"

"Well, why shouldn't I? He's our friend."

They got in the car and slammed their respective doors. "He's your friend's husband. That doesn't make him our friend."

"What are you talking about? Of course he's our friend. He's been part of our lives for nearly a decade." She knew what Chris meant. But admitting that they weren't really friends with Roman felt like admitting the allegations were true. It felt like she was betraying Monica.

"I knew I should have trusted my instinct," he said. "The banking stuff, constantly checking his account. No one does that. I knew something was shady, and I didn't say anything."

"It could be a complete coincidence," Rachel tried. She didn't know why she was defending Roman. Maybe because it felt like defending Monica. "He's right about politics—it's all one big character assassination until someone finally wins."

Chris continued to grumble under his breath. Rachel caught words like *fucking job* and *fine before*. And that's when her insides started to burn.

"You can just say what you're really thinking. You never wanted this job. I forced you to take it."

"I didn't say that."

"You didn't have to. Your attitude ever since you started has been enough proof."

"Fine then!" he boiled over. "You're right. I didn't want this job. I was perfectly happy with my old one. I did it for you. And it's been nothing but stress. And now this? If my name is yanked into some extortion scheme? Then what? Huh, Rach?"

They both breathed heavy. Rachel's gut twisted into knots. This wasn't how she'd expected the evening to go. And on top of everything, they had to go home and shell out money to the babysitter.

She rested her elbow on the window ledge and dropped her head into her hand. The remainder of the ride was silent.

FIFTEEN

MONICA

Her office phone blinked and let out a single beep, indicating a call from the front desk.

"Yep?" Monica answered.

"There's a girl here to see you?" her receptionist said. "Says her name is Chloe."

Monica perked up. *What's Chloe doing here?* "I'll be right out."

Over the short walk from her office to the lobby, Monica ran through reasons. Had she forgotten a meeting they'd scheduled? Of course not—what reason would Chloe have to come to Monica's work? Which only made her even more curious. Was something wrong with Rachel? One of the kids? Monica's heart rate sped up as she anticipated finding Chloe crying on the other side of the waiting-room door. The awful dinner two weeks ago still lingered in her mind. She couldn't handle any more drama.

When she opened the door, Chloe was sitting in the first row of chairs, back straight, hands crossed, like someone uncomfortable in their surroundings. Half a dozen other women were scattered throughout the room, some with a partner, others alone. They looked up when Monica opened the door.

"Hey," she said to Chloe and gave her head a jerk. When Chloe got closer, Monica whispered, "Is everything okay?"

Chloe nodded and followed Monica past three exam rooms and a small, open nurses' station. Monica had known Chloe all her life, but the girl had never been to this office. It felt like a weird clash of worlds having her there.

The last room in the hallway had a name plate that read Monica's name. "We'll go in here," Monica said.

Framed degrees and certificates decorated the white walls. A plant sat on the windowsill. Chloe took one of the seats opposite a shiny brown desk covered in stacks of folders.

Monica closed the door and turned. "What's going on?" Chloe shifted uncomfortably. When she swallowed, Monica could see the lump travel down her throat. "Are you in trouble?"

Chloe's response came out in a squeak. "I guess? Maybe. I don't know." She blinked in succession, appearing to keep her emotions in check, an attempt to be strong. The same look Monica remembered when Chloe had fallen off the trampoline at eleven and broken her arm. Monica's heart gave an almighty thud.

Chloe twisted her ID lanyard in her lap. She took a breath. "I'm pregnant."

Monica closed her eyes and exhaled. "I was afraid you were going to say that." She took the other chair next to Chloe; put a hand on the girl's knee. "How far along?"

"I took a test four weeks ago, so...?"

"When was your last period?"

"Four weeks before that... I think."

"So that would make you at least eight weeks."

Chloe's brows knitted together.

"It's confusing. They actually calculate it from your last period so— Never mind; that doesn't really matter. Oh, Chloe."

"I fucked up."

"And I'm assuming since you're here, that means you haven't told your parents?"

Chloe shook her head. Monica stood with her hands on her hips and paced the small office. Her throat felt tight, like she couldn't breathe.

"I think I want an abortion," Chloe said.

The words stopped Monica in her tracks. "Really? I mean… okay."

"I can't go through with this." Chloe gestured to her stomach, which was currently flat and toned, but Monica knew would be swelling within the upcoming weeks. "I can't do it to Mom and Dad."

"You haven't even told them yet. How do you know what they'd say?"

Chloe gave her a look. They both knew exactly what Rachel would say, and it wouldn't be pretty.

Monica squared her shoulders. "Just because… I mean, if your mom had… then we wouldn't have you."

Chloe's fingers flexed and curled. "My mom's choice doesn't have to be mine."

"That's not what I'm saying. I just want you to think it through. Don't rush into anything." She sat again, placing her hand on Chloe's. Heat coursed through her. "And what about Preston?"

"What about him?" Chloe was off her chair then. "I'm the one who has to push a baby out of my body. I'm the one whose life will change. Forget about it. I shouldn't have come. I thought you'd be on my side. I thought you'd help me."

"Wait! Of course I'll help you." Monica pulled on Chloe's arm to keep her in the office. "You're like my own daughter. I want nothing more than to see you healthy and happy."

Chloe stood in place, and Monica begged with her eyes. If she let Chloe leave, who knew what would happen. She could never live with the guilt of Chloe thinking Monica had brushed her off.

"Sit," Monica said. "I want to help." She tried to keep her face soft and open. "Weren't you taking your pill?"

Chloe sat. "Not consistently apparently."

"And Preston didn't wear..."

"There were no condoms, no." Chloe wrapped her arms around her chest.

Monica wished they could go back to texting about fashion choices and babysitting schedules.

Chloe's voice turned quiet. "You're not mad at me?"

Monica's shoulders rounded. "Mad's not the right word. I'm a little shocked, that's for sure."

At that, Chloe's chin quivered.

Monica pulled Chloe in against her chest. "I'm not mad at you. I'm sure you've got enough emotions going on—I don't need to add anything to that. There's no sense wishing something were different when it's not." She rubbed Chloe's back in a gentle circular motion, a swathe of maternal affection causing a prickling in her chest. "Whatever you want to do, I'll support you. Just take a minute to consider all options."

"I have been. That's all I've been thinking about for four weeks."

"Well, there's still time. You don't have to decide today." Monica did some quick math in her head. Chloe didn't have to make a choice that moment, but something would need to be decided sooner rather than later.

Chloe nodded. A quiet, "Okay." The room was hot, and Monica stood, walked to the thermostat on the wall, and pressed the down arrow. She pulled a brochure from the holder on her desk and fanned herself before turning it on Chloe, who was also red in the face.

"How are you feeling?" Monica asked. "I mean, have you been sick?"

"Nauseous, but not throwing up every day."

"Lucky you. My pregnancies were rotten. I got sick well into the second trimester." A flashback then: Lying on the couch at fifteen weeks with Lucas, garbage can on the floor beside her. It had been awful. But not awful enough not to do it again two years later. Chloe shifted in her chair. "Don't worry—most women don't have it that bad."

A moment of silence made them both look around awkwardly. Monica opened her mouth and closed it repeatedly, unsure what to say. Did Chloe want her to make the choice? Is that why she was there? Monica wouldn't do it.

Behind them on the double computer monitors, Monica's email dinged. She discreetly checked the clock on the wall. This impromptu visit had come at a very inopportune time. "Listen, sweetheart, I have a patient appointment soon. Do you want to stay here? You can take a nap on the couch if you want. I should have another little break around— Oh, wait. No, I forgot there's a webinar I'm presenting. Shoot. Well, you're still welcome to hang. It's so cold out; you're crazy for walking." She thought ahead to the end of the day. If Chloe hung around, they could finish this conversation. Go grab dinner.

Chloe brushed the tops of her thighs. "I don't want to be in the way. It's fine—the air clears my head. I'll just go back."

"Are you sure? Let me call you an Uber." She couldn't just let Chloe walk all the way back to campus *pregnant*.

"Really, I'm fine."

But she looked anything but fine. Her shoulders curled forward, gaze staring into space through glassy eyes. Monica placed both palms softly on Chloe's cheeks. "Remember what I said—just think about it. Everything will be all right. I'll call you tomorrow, okay? We'll figure out a way to tell your parents."

Chloe yanked away. "No. I'm not telling them. And you can't either." Her voice rose in hysteria. "Promise me you won't say anything. It would crush them. Please. That's why I came to you. I knew I could trust you. Promise me."

Monica's face went slack, terror freezing every muscle.

Chloe backed away. "You're not going to tell Mom, are you?"

Monica pumped her hands slowly. "Chloe, I really don't think you should keep this from them."

"I can't believe it," Chloe cried. "Monica, please." Her shoulders shook, and she dropped her head into her hands.

An uncontrollable shudder swept through Monica's body. What stood in front of her was pure and utter desperation. How could she add to it? She stepped forward and wrapped Chloe in a hug. "Okay, okay. I won't say anything. Don't get upset."

Chloe sniffed. "Promise?"

What was she promising? To keep a secret this gigantic from her best friend? Unimaginable. Wrong. A bitter taste formed on her tongue. But then Chloe squeezed her tighter. Monica could feel Chloe's whole body trembling. All at once, she was a kid again. A scared little girl looking for protection. And so Monica made her lips move. Forced the word out. "Promise."

SIXTEEN

RACHEL

"I want to sit in the middle!"

"No, *I* want to sit in the middle!"

"It's my turn!"

"You sat in the middle last time!"

Rachel spun around. "Guys!" she barked over four high-pitched voices. "It doesn't matter who sits in the middle. We're all going to the same place. It's literally a ten-minute drive, okay? Chill. Get in a seat and buckle up."

She had not only her two kids in the SUV but Monica's as well. She gave them each her *I mean business* look. Lucas and Logan obeyed quicker, taking the window seats quietly.

"Thank you," Rachel said. "Let's not be late for the first game of the season, huh?" She spun forward and put the car in gear.

Indoor soccer had just started, an eight-week circus where kids mostly chased the ball around in a pack while parents yelled from the sidelines: *Spread out! Don't take it from your teammate! Wrong way!*

Lucas and Jacob had been thrilled to be on the same team. It made carpooling easier, even if Monica wasn't able to split it evenly. Rachel didn't mind taking the boys—what was two more anyway? Plus, Chris would meet them there after work, so at least there would be an extra set of hands to yank off sweaty shin guards.

"Why can't my mommy take us?" Logan's little voice carried from the back.

"She's working today, sweetie, remember? You're gonna hang with us. Isn't that fun?" She peered at the kids in the rear-view mirror. Logan and Lucas exchanged a look that made Rachel's heart ping. "Don't worry, she'll come to the next game."

Lucas frowned. "No, she won't."

"Aw, don't say that. You mom tries as best she can to come. She's busy, honey."

"She never comes to our games."

Rachel bit the inside of her lip. There wasn't much rebuttal to the boy's statement. Monica rarely did attend their activities, something Rachel knew was a sore spot for her friend. She tried not to bring their sports up in conversation often.

"What about Daddy?" Logan asked, and his older brother quickly answered: "Dad's busy too."

"He promised to take us to the movies soon though," Logan said with the bright innocence of childhood.

A vision came to Rachel then, seeing Logan on the day he was born, a sweet little thing in Monica's arms.

Rachel smiled. "Won't that be fun!" But Lucas just stared out the window like someone with far too much worry on his young shoulders.

"How about I video the game and send it to them?" she tried.

Lucas shrugged.

After that, Rachel was quiet. She turned up the radio as a distraction, and soon all the kids were singing along to some pop tune they couldn't possibly understand the lyrics to. She felt bad Lucas and Logan missed their mom, but she was glad she could step in as surrogate from time to time. The boys were like extensions of her own kids, and she'd cheer for them as loudly as Monica would.

Between buzzers, Rachel checked her phone. There was a message from Monica, asking how the game was going.

The boys are doing great! she replied then hesitated before adding another sentence.

Lucas misses you though.

Monica's reply came back in a second.

Tell him I love him and I'll be at the next game. Promise!

The text helped, but the feeling still festered in her all through the game.

"What's wrong?" Chris asked at halftime. She told him what Lucas had said in the car, and the sad faces both the boys wore the entire drive.

Chris gave a small shrug. "You should say something. She didn't have a problem bringing up my deficiencies to you."

Rachel gave him a disapproving look. "This isn't about an eye for an eye."

"Well..."

"But I see what you mean. If it's clearly bothering the boys."

"Exactly."

"Maybe I will mention it. I'll wait and see how Lucas is after the game. It could have been a short-lived moment."

But it wasn't. Because as the game concluded, and the boys ran off the field in all their sweaty glory, Lucas sulked at the back. Not even a win had lifted his spirits. It made Rachel's heart hurt as though he were her own son.

"Great game, kiddos!" she said, giving them both a hug. Lucas only half smiled. Rachel showered down the compliments, how well he'd played, but nothing worked. Not even ice cream—a double scoop!—on the way home. The whole time, an itch pestered Rachel. Should she bring it up to Monica? Things had been a little tense since their dinner. She didn't want to meddle in someone else's business, but it wasn't just *someone*— it was Monica. And the boys she loved so much. No eight-year-old should carry around such sadness.

At the same time, she worried about crossing a line; would Monica get defensive? Rachel remembered Monica's comments about Chris's work ethic. Wasn't this sort of like the pot calling the kettle black? Monica wasn't perfect either, and perhaps it was time the Cross-Nash parents were put in their place. Yes, their careers were important, but nothing should outweigh the children. Every mother knew that.

By the time Rachel got home after dropping off Lucas and Logan with the nanny, she was formulating a script in her head of how the conversation would go. She didn't want to offend. Didn't want to stab the sword too deep. Just a little prick at the surface. See how it feels? Just enough for everyone to be on the same page again.

SEVENTEEN

MONICA

When Chloe left the office, Monica took several deep breaths before meeting with her next patients. Her internal temperature had skyrocketed, and despite wanting to remain collected in front of Chloe, she'd felt a bead of sweat drip down her back.

Pregnant?

It was like she was reliving the experience with Rachel. She remembered her friend confiding in her, folding in half with liquid eyes. Saying how her parents were going to kill her. Monica had hugged Rachel then and stood by her friend's side as a beautiful baby girl entered the world. Now that beautiful girl found herself in the same situation as her mother.

Monica put a hand against the wall to brace herself. The ground had felt uneven ever since Chloe stepped foot in her office. She was now in on a secret. A secret she didn't wish to possess. It felt weighted and dangerous. Instinct told her to call Rachel—she was always the first person Monica turned to in times of stress. But that was out of the question... wasn't it? She'd promised Chloe she wouldn't say a word. Only, it felt wrong keeping something so momentous from her best friend. Especially when the secret directly impacted Rachel herself.

And then her phone lit up with a text, as though it could hear Monica thinking—Rachel responding to Monica's earlier message. The boys' game. They missed her. How could she think about basketball at a time like this? She sent off a quick response—she loved them and she'd be there next time.

But her thoughts weren't with the boys or a possibly fraudulent husband. They were with a scared teenager.

"Oh, Chloe," Monica whispered. She silently calculated it all again. It was that last time Chloe met up with Preston that had sealed the girl's fate. A jumble of conflict blocked Monica's airway, making it hard to inhale. How on earth was she supposed to focus for the rest of the day?

Turned out, she didn't. Monica only half listened to her patients, a smartly dressed couple with sad eyes. After a string of sentences from the woman, Monica gave her head a little shake and said, "I'm sorry, can you repeat that?"

It wasn't until the day was wrapping up that she was able to fully grasp what Chloe had confided in her. The mental strain of it, plus her normal everyday pressure, meant that Monica was wound as tight as a corkscrew as she packed up her briefcase to head home.

Just as she was slipping her phone into the side pocket on her purse, it rang, making her jump—Rachel's face, a picture of them lounging on wooden chairs in front of Deep Creek Lake.

Monica felt a sickening drop of dread. *She knows.* Chloe must have decided to tell her mom after all. The tension must have been too much.

Monica glanced around the room, as though there were someone she could reflect this on. Someone who could take the call instead of her. Would she be able to play dumb enough to convince Rachel she didn't already know? Then a new thought: What if Chloe had told Rachel that she'd come to Monica first?

Maybe Rachel was calling from a place of anger. If so, Monica would need to be on the defensive. She hadn't *asked* Chloe to tell her. It wasn't her fault Chloe had come to her first. She'd only done what she thought was right.

Her leg muscles twitched, and Monica stabilized herself by leaning against her desk, in turn knocking off a fountain-pen holder. She bent down to retrieve it. She answered.

"Hi, Rach." The words hitched in her mouth, and Monica cleared her throat. "What's up?"

"Did I catch you at a bad time? I had like two free seconds and figured I'd better use them."

Rachel's light and friendly tone came as a shock. Wasn't she about to drop a bombshell?

"No, now's good. I'm actually wrapping up on time for once."

"Oh, nice!" Then Rachel's inflection dropped. "I actually was calling to talk to you about something."

Here it was. Monica's stomach fell to her feet. "Okay?" She wiped her clammy hands on her thighs. She held her breath, bracing.

"It's about the boys."

The boys? She released the breath. "My boys?"

"Yes," Rachel said. "I had them today for soccer, you know. And Lucas was talking about you a lot. He mentioned how... Well, I don't really know how to say it; I don't want to upset you... He said he wished you could be there more often." Rachel knew she was embellishing—Logan hadn't said those exact words.

Monica was too stunned to talk. Her mouth couldn't form words. She was too busy trying to reel her heart back into her chest.

"Mon?"

"Sorry, I'm here."

"I didn't mean to catch you off guard with this. It's just that he seemed sort of... sad. He made a comment about all the other moms coming except you. And trust me, I tried to explain how busy you are at work. You have an important job. Same with his daddy."

"Uh-huh."

"I wasn't even going to say anything, but it was weighing on me. I just wanted to let you know, in case, I don't know, he seems off or anything. That's probably why. Maybe you could talk to him about it."

Under normal circumstances, Monica would have been defensive. She *was* a good mother. Just because she couldn't attend every single activity didn't mean she wasn't fit to be a parent. But what Rachel had said was so completely opposite what she'd been expecting, Monica barely registered what she was being told. All she felt was intense relief the call wasn't about Chloe. She tilted her head skyward then pulled open the neck of her shirt to let out all the trapped hot air.

"Sure. I'll talk with him," she said, waving her collar back and forth.

"I'm sure it's nothing. You know how kids are."

"Probably right. I appreciate you letting me know." Nothing registered, she simply said what sounded good. This was a conversation for another time.

On the other end of the line, Rachel breathed hard. "Oh, I'm glad. I was a little worried, to be honest. But then I told myself, 'No, if Monica knew something about my child, I would want her to tell me.'"

At that, Monica broke out in a second wave of sweat. The guilt made her skin itch. "Of course," she managed. When had her office become a sauna?

"Hey, anything new with, you know, the campaign stuff?" Rachel was tiptoeing around it, but Monica knew the real question: Have there been any more allegations? Anything beyond rumors they could pin on Haverty's camp?

"Nothing. It's been quiet. Roman's convinced it was all rumors." At least that's what he'd told her. At least that's what she continued to tell herself.

"Oh, good. Such a relief. Okay, well, I've gotta run."

"Me too," Monica said, thrilled to be ending the call. "Talk soon."

And with a quick, "Bye!" Rachel hung up.

Monica's knees buckled, and she slumped into her chair. Her mental state felt like it had taken a wild roller coaster ride, the kind with loop-de-loops and sudden drops. Fear of Rachel's reaction about Chloe, alleviation at the turn of topic, and finishing with a slap of mom guilt. Could the day just be over already? Monica strongly considered spending the night right there on the floor.

She sat for a moment, but it only made her more exhausted. Finally, as she hauled herself out of the office, into the car, and onto the highway heading north out of the city, she made a decision. She'd have to talk to Chloe again. Regardless of what Chloe decided, Monica couldn't keep the knowledge from Rachel. Secrets were dangerous weapons. Harboring this one could backfire.

EIGHTEEN

CHLOE

THE SECRET HAD EATEN A HOLE IN HER STOMACH OVER THE weeks she'd been back on campus. Everywhere she went, it felt like people looked at her differently. As though they *knew*. Chloe hadn't told a soul aside from Monica. But Monica was a busy person. She wasn't available to talk at the drop of a hat. And besides, could she really understand? Chloe didn't know how much longer she could keep it to herself. A decision had to be made. A big one. One that required support and advice from a friend, which was how Chloe found herself perched on the edge of her bed in the morning before class, ready to reveal her news to Ava.

Nausea swirled in her belly like a wicked witch whipping a deadly brew. If she thought about it enough—the feeling, the smell—she'd gag. She couldn't eat to help settle her stomach. Not when she was about to share something so urgent. Part of her worried what Ava would say. Could she trust Ava to keep it quiet? Chloe had kept plenty of Ava's secrets this year, but nothing as big as this.

"Fucking eight a.m.s," Ava said, throwing on a sweatshirt

and pulling her wheat-colored hair into a messy bun on top of her head. "I hate being a freshman."

It was true, the underclassmen always got the worse class times. She and Ava had trudged to plenty of early-morning classes. At least Ava, a journalism major, had creative courses, hands-on topics like writing and reporting. Ava was always conducting mini-interviews with friends and said things like, "You'd make such a great profile piece." Whatever that meant.

"Why are you up so early anyway?" Ava gave Chloe a puzzled look. "Isn't your class not till nine?"

"Couldn't sleep," Chloe said. She hugged her knees. She could leave it at that. Let Ava stroll out of their dorm none the wiser. But then she'd be stuck in the same lonely predicament. And that would be worse. She needed help. She needed someone to tell her what to do—which Monica hadn't done. And so, she swallowed down an acidic burp and mustered the courage. "Actually, there's something I've been meaning to tell you."

Ava rummaged through their snack drawer; chose a granola bar. "Yeah?"

"I'm pregnant." It came out faster than Chloe had anticipated. The words she'd repeated in her head over and over again. *I'm pregnant, I'm pregnant, I'm pregnant.* They felt weird leaving her mouth a second time.

The drawer slammed shut and Ava whipped around. "Shut up. You're lying."

"I'm serious."

"Stop."

"No, for real."

Ava stepped in front of Chloe so mere inches separated them. "But you're on the pill."

"I guess it only works if you take it right."

Ava's eyes grew to the size of saucers. "Holy shit. When did you find out?"

"Few weeks back."

"Does Preston know?"

"No."

"You haven't told him?"

"Only Monica. And now you."

Ava slapped her forehead. "Oh my God, Chlo. What are you going to do? I mean, there are options, right? Are you going to keep it?"

"I don't know. I'm sort of freaking out."

"Um, yeah! As you should be."

Chloe's face burned. "Gee, thanks."

"Sorry, that's not what I meant." She sat next to Chloe, and the two turned to face each other, crossing their legs on the bed like two girls at summer camp about to do a secret handshake. "Is there anything I can do?"

Chloe shook her head. "Give me some of your energy? I feel like I'm moving through quicksand. I'm so tired all the time. Like worse than an all-night study sesh."

"So you haven't even told your parents?"

"Are you kidding? My mom would lose her mind. Getting pregnant in college is literally the worst thing I could do to her."

"So you're not going to keep it?"

"And drop out of school? I'm nineteen; I can't be a mom right now." Tears welled in her eyes then, and Ava leaned in to give Chloe a hug.

"It's okay; it's okay. We'll figure it out."

Chloe sniffed. "Anyway, I just wanted to tell you. It's been killing me, and I'm fucking scared. It feels good not to keep it to myself anymore." She waved a dismissive hand. "But we can talk more later. You have class. You'll be late."

"Screw class. This is more important." Ava clasped Chloe's hands. Their heart tattoos kissed.

Chloe managed to smile through her tears. "Thanks."

"Of course. I'm here for you."

They sat there for a minute, then Ava said, "Are you going to tell Preston?"

"It's my body—don't you think it should be my choice?"

"Well, yeah, clearly. Duh." She poked Chloe's leg. "Look at you being all feminist and shit. I'm so proud." The moment lasted only seconds though—both girls unable to dismiss the gravity of the situation. "It's just..."

Chloe looked down. "I'd rather just deal with it myself."

"Don't you think he's eventually going to put two and two together? You're going to get bigger. And if you leave school? You shouldn't go through this alone."

Maybe it was the slew of questions and scenarios, or maybe it was that single word—alone. Either way, it triggered a flood. Chloe flung her hands into the air. "I don't know what the hell to do."

It was all so much weight on her. Deciding to keep the baby meant telling her family. Choosing another path meant figuring out logistics she didn't even understand. Where would she start? Did you just waltz into an abortion clinic? Did you need a referral? All she knew was that she'd peed on a stick, her boobs hurt like hell, and there was a cluster of cells inside her that were growing into another human. She wished she could go back and make it all go away. Never have sex. Never forget to take her pill on time.

But that was useless thinking. A waste of time and of the small amount of energy she had. This was real. And she needed to make a decision sooner rather than later.

Chloe wiped her eyes. "Listen, Av. Please don't tell anyone."

"I'd never."

They intertwined their pinky fingers in promise.

And then Ava had an idea. They'd play hooky for the whole day. Stay in and watch a marathon of cheesy chick flicks. So that's what they did. Ava only left to grab food and bring it back to their room. It was exactly what Chloe needed—a friend on her side, a diversion from reality. Still, the noodle soup only did so much to quell her unease. Chloe napped halfway through the afternoon, woke up, shifted position, and dozed more. Her dreams were fraught with worst-case scenarios—her parents in tears, an excruciating labor and delivery—so the sleep never felt quite restful.

She and Ava talked more about options—what it would be like to keep the baby; what it would be like to have an abortion. Ava was glued to her phone, typing in detailed Google searches. "Wait, you can't eat deli meat?" she said, aghast. "Or sushi?"

"And no alcohol," Chloe added. "There's a whole list."

"Fuck."

"I'm the one who's going through it, not you."

"Oh, right. In that case, I'll have a beer."

They laughed, and it felt good. Everything had been such turmoil in her brain, every waking thought so serious and heavy, it was nice, even for the briefest interlude, to make light of the situation.

By the time evening rolled around and their back-and-forth got her no closer to making a decision, one thing felt clear: This would be the biggest decision of her life. Instinct willed her to call her mom. That's what most girls her age would have done. But Chloe knew that wasn't an option—not yet. Maybe never. Her mom would fly off the handle, and Chloe couldn't bear to crush her parents with so much disappointment.

When she'd first gotten on birth control at fifteen, her mom had sat her down for a lengthy talk about safe sex and the consequences of actions. By that point, Chloe had done the math—she knew her parents were young when they'd had her. It wasn't a secret in their family. Instead, Rachel and Chris had used their own experience as a lesson for their daughter. They loved her unconditionally and would never wish she hadn't been born—but... the timing wasn't ideal, they'd explained.

Trust us, they'd said. Be careful. You don't want to find yourself in the same situation.

Turned out she was her mother's daughter.

She hadn't listened. She'd been careless. And now, she was living the same life her mom had at this age. Only with one very big difference—her mom had had a devoted boyfriend by her side, whereas Chloe felt very much alone.

NINETEEN

MONICA

On Sunday morning, Monica woke to a text from Rachel. Her heart did a quick leap.

Starbucks?

She pressed her temples. Only a coffee invite.

Monica swayed. She didn't love the idea of being around Rachel while carrying Chloe's information. It felt deceptive and dishonest. She'd even skipped girls' night, feeling there'd be no way she could look her friend in the eye and pretend everything was normal. Then again, Rachel's call the other day had left a bitter taste in Monica's mouth. In the last two days, she'd had time to process what she couldn't in that moment. The accusation—intended or not—that, somehow, she wasn't a good-enough mother. That her boys were sad and neglected, all because Monica was trying to work hard to support them. She worried seeing Rachel would bring out that resentment. Even thinking about it made her teeth clench. Rachel had once cancelled coming to an award dinner honoring Monica because Jacob's T-ball game got rescheduled. Monica had been stunned

—T-ball? Really? But Rachel had come back with something like, "They're only young once." Monica had wanted to scream, *But do they have to take every single piece of you?*

Monica cracked her knuckles. Would Rachel be suspicious if she made an excuse not to meet? Monica was a horrible liar. Her parents always knew, between the hives and the darting eyes. The time she'd tried marijuana in tenth grade only to be confronted at the door when she returned home and tried to convince them she'd hit a skunk. She could never play poker. Even at that moment behind a phone, Monica felt herself getting blotchy.

But...

She loved their Sunday coffee runs. And avoiding Rachel would only make things worse. Reinforce she was doing something wrong. She'd go. She'd go, put on her best act, and pray Rachel didn't bring up Chloe's name.

After throwing on a J.Crew henley and jeans, Monica called out to the boys. "Anybody want strawberry lemonade and a muffin?"

Lucas and Logan came running in their matching striped pajamas, hair all mussed from a good night's sleep.

See, Monica thought, *they're perfectly happy kids.* And she was a good mom, taking them to Starbucks when she could have gone alone.

She replied to Rachel.

Be there in twenty.

When they pulled in, Rachel was already there with Jacob and Savannah. The kids gathered around a single tablet, taking turns playing the hot new elementary school game. The women greeted each other with one-arm hugs. Monica tucked her blonde waves behind her ears. *Act cool. It's just a normal day.* She wished their husbands were there as buffers, but that was wishful thinking at best—lately, Roman's absence from their daily activities went without saying.

The barista called out their orders, and Rachel hopped up to grab them. Monica took the momentary interlude to heave a giant breath. The secret hung on the tip of her tongue, and everything in her wanted to blurt it out. Seeing Rachel in person took the pressure to a whole new level. She wasn't sure she could truly look her in the eye.

But then she remembered her promise to Chloe. She clamped her jaw shut. At least for now.

Rachel cupped both hands around the drink and took a sip. "If only I could get a permanent caffeine drip." Her hair was tossed in a ponytail, but it didn't lie flat, and there were bumps sticking out like she'd done it without looking in the mirror. It didn't matter. Somehow, she managed to look naturally beautiful without a stitch of makeup and in yesterday's clothes.

"Talked to Chloe last night," Rachel said.

Fuck.

Monica choked on her own saliva. "Oh yeah? About what?" The response came too quick. Too perky. And with her terrible poker face.

"If she was coming home for Jacob's birthday. You guys are still coming over, right? Please say yes—I got half a sheet cake."

"Of course." The truth was she'd forgotten. Monica made a mental note to double-check her calendar to make sure she didn't have any late-afternoon appointments. "Did she say yes?"

"She was weird. Sort of dodgy and in a *mood.* I asked if she was PMSing, and she got huffy. It was almost like she didn't want to come home, even though she never misses birthdays."

Monica gave a nervous laugh. "Well, she's in college now, so..."

"Maybe. I don't know. She's seemed off ever since Preston broke up with her. I think it messed her up pretty bad."

"Mmm."

"I just hope she would tell me if something was wrong, you know? Like if it's more than just the breakup? You hear all those horror stories about depression, and God knows social media doesn't help..." Then, in the same breath, "Savannah, give Lucas a turn."

Monica felt the walls closing tighter. "I'm sure she would. It's probably just school stuff." Her mouth tasted sour.

"Is there something wrong with your drink?" Rachel asked, pointing to Monica's untouched cup.

"Oh, whoops." Monica picked up her latte and took a sip. The hazelnut flavor blend she usually found delicious was like drinking venom. Each swallow only fueled the uneasy stirring in her stomach. The lie was growing. Breeding and compounding, as though it would burst from under her skin like a hideous wart.

"Can you believe that..." Rachel proceeded on a tangent about some new piece of gossip from town or the school or somewhere online—Monica couldn't focus. She nodded along, and inserted the occasional agreement, but her mind was elsewhere. Specifically, with a newly pregnant girl in a dorm room forty minutes away. Her feet sweated in her slip-on sneakers. It wasn't fair of Chloe to ask her to keep this secret. Watching Rachel go about her morning like there wasn't a bombshell waiting to explode felt like one of the worst things Monica had ever done. She couldn't take it much longer.

"Earth to Monica. Are you listening?"

Monica snapped to. Rachel's eyebrow was raised in a look of confusion.

"Sorry," Monica said. "Guess I really do need this caffeine." She forced a sip down her throat.

"I was talking about Vienna Scott. Did you see her post about their girls' trip to Sonoma?"

"Vienna? She's the blonde, right? Has a kid in the boys' class?"

"Yes. You know her—she's like the queen bee, everyone always flocking around her. Anyway, can you imagine flying across the country just for a friend getaway?" Rachel rolled her head as she took in a breath. "Must be nice."

Monica would pay double to fly to California at the moment, if it meant getting out of this conversation. She wished she hadn't agreed to come. She'd miscalculated her ability for improvisation.

In the end, it was the shortest coffee date they'd ever had. After Monica forced half the latte down her throat, she announced she had to get home to do laundry—even though they had a housekeeper who helped with that. Rachel looked mildly offended but hid it well. There would be plenty more coffee Sundays in their future. Mornings where Monica didn't feel like she was navigating grenades with each sentence.

She shooed the boys out, gave Rachel a quick side-hug, and left her cup on the table. In the car, she held the wheel with both hands, feeling her pulse in all ten fingertips. She thought again about how dangerous secrets were. And now she was certain of something else: Promises were even worse.

TWENTY

CHLOE

IT WASN'T CONFIDENCE BUT UNCERTAINTY THAT DREW HER to the health center. And when Chloe walked through the double doors of the sizable Nordenberg Hall, which housed Student Health Services on the ground floor, her armpits were damp with sweat.

"Can I help you?" the woman at the registration desk asked. Her thin, dark hair rested on her shoulders, and even from a seated position, Chloe could tell the woman was tall. Long, slender fingers gave her away.

"Um," Chloe fumbled, feeling unprepared and stupid, as though she didn't expect to have to actually speak. The truth was she didn't have an appointment. She'd come spontaneously, seeking... seeking what? "Sorry, I'm— I mean, I don't—" Her eyes darted around the small lobby, landing on a wall of brochures lined in neat rows. "I just wanted some information." She pointed to the wall with a nod, as if to indicate her purpose. The woman replied with a smile and returned to the papers on her desk.

Chloe stepped aside, letting a boy with a red nose take her

place at the window. She wished she were only here for a sinus infection. She'd take bronchitis even.

At the display of brochures, Chloe scanned the headings, past the one with the image of a Band-Aid over a brain and the words "Depression & Anxiety," the one for Covid boosters, and one with interlinked male and female symbols and the heading "All About Safe Sex" (too late for that). She was looking for something specific. Pink, maybe. Or with a woman on the front. Perhaps even... a baby.

Then she spotted the blue Planned Parenthood pamphlet, and she quietly pulled it out, holding it close to her body. "Abortion Care," the front read.

Chloe flipped it open, skimming the material as though it would answer her burning questions. She read through the section about what to expect, and another about financial assistance. None of it was new—she'd googled these things not long after discovering the pregnancy. And still, she craved more information. Something she wasn't finding online or in tri-fold brochures. Nowhere did it say, "Get an abortion." Nowhere did it tell her, "Have the baby." Those decisions didn't come from a piece of glossy paper; they came from within.

"Did you find what you were looking for?"

The voice behind her made Chloe jump. She spun to find the receptionist, hands clasped in front of her, a gentle smile on her face. Her nametag said Joy, and Chloe considered the contradiction of a woman with such a name working with ill people all day.

Joy eyed the brochure in Chloe's hands. Chloe, in turn, sputtered, "Oh, whoops. Wrong one." She hastily shoved it back into its holder and grabbed the one next to it. "Achieving a Balanced Diet," it read, along with a picture of the food pyramid. "Yep, this is it. Hard to stay healthy with that cafeteria food." She gave a nervous laugh and felt her face burn.

An uncomfortable pause hung between them for a beat, until Joy spoke. "Why don't you come sit? I'll get you a glass of water. And there are cookies on the counter. Help yourself." She pressed a hand to Chloe's back, leading her across the room. It was more of a request than an offer, and Chloe mumbled something unintelligible in protest, but Joy simply pulled her along. "Come, come."

Chloe sat in the corner on an oversized chair whose cushions swallowed her in, and for a second, she considered the comfort of it may never let her back up. Within moments, Joy was there, placing a small glass of water and a cookie onto the small table between them. She took the seat opposite and crossed her ankles.

"What year are you?" Joy asked.

"Freshman," Chloe replied. The cookie looked so good—was it raisin or chocolate chip?—and she picked it up and took a nibble, all the while wondering why she didn't just stand and leave.

"Have you been to the health center before?"

Chloe shook her head.

"We have all sorts of services, both physical and mental. And even if there are things we can't do here, we can certainly make referrals or point students in the right direction for additional information."

Chloe lowered her eyes, as though Joy could see right through to her brain and the twisted web of thoughts that had been haunting her. She should take her cookie and leave. She didn't want to discuss her predicament with a total stranger.

Joy leaned closer. "Would you like me to make you an appointment with our on-staff doctor? Or perhaps a counselor? We have females if that might make you more comfortable. I know we're booked today, but I can probably get you in tomorr—"

"Thanks," Chloe said, "but no. I'm okay. Like I said, just picking up some healthy eating info." She flashed the pamphlet but darted her eyes. Joy stared, and Chloe prayed the woman wouldn't push.

"All right. Well, you know where we are if you change your mind. Our students' health is our top priority." She gave Chloe's knee a light tap.

Chloe couldn't get up fast enough. The woman was nice and all, but this had been a mistake. Now someone else knew—or thought she knew—what was going on. Chloe had a momentary panic that Joy would somehow be able to look her up in the university system, flag her account: *Pregnant! Pregnant!* Search her parents' names and make a call that would ruin everything.

All of it was impossible of course. But that didn't stop Chloe's mind from spinning. When she exited the health center, she sucked in a mouthful of air and speed walked away, slowing down only once she'd crossed over into the next block.

The blue pamphlet with the double Ps resurfaced in her head. The details about the procedure, the sinking feeling in her gut when she thought about it. But was there an alternative? Could she move forward knowing what she knew?

Somewhere forty minutes north, her parents went on with their days, unaware of the life growing inside her. A grandchild they may or may not ever see. Chloe struggled with keeping something from them—she was raised to be honest; had always thought she and her mom would be the best friend type. Confidantes. But that was childish logic. Rachel barely knew what classes Chloe was taking. She probably couldn't even name Chloe's favorite band, or how Chloe liked her steak cooked.

So why, Chloe reasoned, should she care now how her mom would feel? With each step, she tossed her options from side to side. She leaned one way, then the other. Decisions that gnawed at her brain. One minute she imagined herself with a newborn in her arms, and the next she wanted to call to book the next available appointment at a clinic. She wondered how other girls in her situation had felt. Were they just as scared? Did they feel just as isolated? She bet they had boyfriends by their side, someone to hold their hand and tell them it was going to be okay. But she didn't have that. Not anymore. And no matter what her decision, she knew she'd be doing it alone.

Chloe took her time returning to the dorm. It was between classes, and students flooded the pathways between buildings. In a school of thirty-four thousand, there were days she'd walk around and not recognize a soul. But like a cruel twist of irony, life taunting her, she glanced ahead and saw Preston among a group of girls. His gorgeous smile showed off his white teeth, and even from a distance, she could tell he'd recently trimmed his hair. One girl laughed and pressed a hand to the pec muscle she knew was underneath his coat. That was *her* pec muscle.

Chloe set her mouth into a stiff line, shoved her hands further into her pockets, and took a detour back to the dorm. So much had happened in the last few months, it felt like another life. Weren't she and Preston just walking campus hand in hand? What happened to the fairy tale she'd dreamed of? Now, she was solo and he surrounded by adoring eyes. How could he move on so quickly? A surge of jealousy made her burn. *I can get other guys too*, she thought. But the declaration did nothing to ease the pain. It only added to it. Who would want to date a girl with a baby?

TWENTY-ONE

MONICA

March

Ross Park Mall was Monica's destination of choice, not only because it was a short twenty-minute drive away, but because it had a little bit of everything for every shopper. Rachel always liked to hit up Claire's on the way out to get fun goodies for Savannah, and that's when Monica usually nipped into Gucci, a store she'd have felt bad dragging Rachel to. One look at the price tags and Rachel would faint.

But before she could consider a new bag or pair of sunglasses with the twin Gs, Monica had to find some more practical pieces. Nordstrom was just the spot.

"I can't believe wide-leg pants are back," she said, flipping through a rack of high-waisted trousers. She pulled out a pair; held it up to her body.

Rachel cocked her head. "I would drown in those."

She really would. Monica added the pants to her try-on pile.

"Chloe says skinny pants are out," Rachel said. "Who

knows? How am I supposed to keep up with trends when I only shop once a year—if that?" She laughed, running her hand down a striped shirtdress.

At the mention of Chloe's name, Monica stiffened. That was how it had been lately—Monica dreading any reference to the girl. Because bringing up Chloe meant remembering the secret. And remembering the secret came with a heavy serving of guilt.

Maybe, Monica thought, if she didn't acknowledge it, Chloe's name would be a fleeting moment. She'd talk about anything—anything—but Chloe.

No such luck.

"Speaking of Chloe," Rachel said, putting a hand on her hip. Monica's palms broke out in sweat. "She's still acting so weird."

"Hmm." Monica busied herself with a stack of sweaters, digging to find a medium somewhere in the middle. She'd avoid eye contact at all costs.

"Yeah. She's never been so quiet. I don't know. But I'm really starting to worry it might be..."

Oh God. Don't say it.

"... depression."

Monica released a giant breath. "Really?"

"You know, these teens are on their phones twenty-four-seven. Social media around the clock. They're not engaging with peers the way we used to. It's like their lives are all stuck in this little box. And don't even get me started on the pressure social media puts on girls. It's terrible. Be thankful you have boys."

Monica would have argued this fact. Boys were susceptible to mental health crises too. But for the moment, she was simply glad Rachel was on the wrong diagnosis train.

"It's scary," Monica said. "But Chloe's a smart girl. She's got a good head on her shoulders." As the words left her mouth, she cringed at the hypocrisy. Was a good-headed kid one that kept big secrets from her parents? Monica would say anything to appease Rachel. She tried diversion. "What about this?" She held up a silky blouse with barrel cuffs.

Rachel scrunched her nose; shook her head. "Not your color." She held up an emerald one instead. "You need jewel tones. That pink will wash you right out."

Monica took the blouse and put it in her pile despite knowing she wouldn't buy it. She was more of a neutral girl.

"I'm just not sure," Rachel said.

"About the blouse? What about black?"

"No. About Chloe."

Good lord. Not this again.

Rachel gave a sigh. "I feel like something's wrong. I just wish she'd talk to me." Then she jerked upright, eyes wide. "You don't think it could be—"

"I'm going to go try these on," Monica quickly interjected. "It's almost eleven. We still want to go to Banana Republic before lunch, right?" She didn't wait for Rachel's response before darting into the fitting room. Inside, she heaped the clothes onto the bench then bent over, hands on her knees. How much longer would she be able to keep Chloe's secret?

Monica pressed her fingers to her temples. When she stood back up, she took in her reflection in the mirror. The woman staring back at her looked like a fraud. Deceit written all over her face. She looked away, ashamed.

Monica sat there long enough for Rachel to think she was trying on the selection.

"Come out and show me," Rachel called, but Monica couldn't budge. Shopping had lost its thrill.

A good few minutes later, Monica emerged, clothes draped over her arm like castoffs. She shrugged.

"Nothing?" Rachel said. "I didn't even get to give my opinion. What about the emerald? It's perfect for you."

"Didn't fit right. And you know, I think I'm more of a straight-leg fan." She hung the trousers and everything else on the return rack.

"Bummer. Don't worry—we'll find something at Banana."

In reality, Monica was done shopping. She didn't want to stroll through any more stores, suffer through any more small talk. She wished they'd driven separately so she could make up an excuse to leave right then.

As they made their way to the exit that opened into the mall, they passed the shoe department, followed by the children's section. Monica's heart rate picked up just seeing the layette of pastel colors up ahead. It was as though the racks of infant sleepers and tiny crocheted jumpers were tormenting her.

Liar, liar, liar.

"I'm dying for a pretzel," Monica blurted, picking up the pace. But it did no good.

"Oh my God, Mon, look at this." Rachel stopped and snatched a smocked baby romper from a faced-out rack. Attached was a stretchy headband and the littlest pair of ruffled socks. "Can you even remember when our kids were this small?"

Monica gave a nervous laugh and fidgeted with her purse.

"Feels like yesterday, right? And also forever ago. Look at this one." She moved further into the rack, reaching for some other piece of incredibly adorable clothing, and Monica felt the situation slipping out of her grasp. "I miss buying these things," Rachel continued before quickly adding, "Not that I'd want to go back to the baby stage."

That was it. Monica fumbled her phone from her purse. "I have to take this," she said and walked in the opposite direction, heart in her throat. Just before turning away, she caught Rachel's perplexed expression.

The phone shook against her ear, and even though there was no one on the other end, Monica mouthed a fake conversation, the whole time hating what she'd agreed to.

TWENTY-TWO

RACHEL

If Rachel knew anything about Monica, it was when her friend was hiding something. Monica was a terrible liar. It showed all over her face. Just like the time Rachel knew Monica was pregnant without Monica even confirming. The discreetly declining drinks, the terrible excuses to skip sushi night. Rachel had a nose for out-of-character behavior, which was why she knew Monica wasn't really talking to anyone on the phone. It hadn't even rung, for goodness' sake.

She pretended to look thought the rack of baby clothes, the whole time watching Monica from the corner of her eye. Monica couldn't even fake talk well. What the hell was going on? Why was she being so weird?

Then it hit her. There must be something going on with Chris at work. She thought back to the call last month, when Monica had questioned Chris's work ethic. Something must have happened. Maybe Roman thought he'd made a mistake hiring him. Maybe Chris was about to be fired. Or wait! Perhaps this was about those embezzlement rumors. What if Monica knew—what if she was *in on it?* Rachel's muscles tensed, as scenarios flashed through her mind, one more disastrous than the next. Completely lost in thought, she didn't hear Monica return.

"Ready?"

Rachel about jumped out of her skin. "Jeez, you scared me." She brought a hand to her chest. "Yes."

They made toward the exit, falling in stride beside each other. Once her runaway pulse slowed, Rachel's curiosity got the better of her. "Everything okay? Your phone call I mean."

"Oh! Yeah, just work stuff."

On a Sunday? And why did Monica seem flustered over such a seemingly explainable response? If she wasn't wearing a turtleneck, Rachel suspected she'd find red blotches on Monica's neck. But she didn't push. She needed to talk to Chris first. If things were going to blow up with his job, she wanted to see it coming—or even warn him.

"Something fishy's going on," Rachel said to Chris that night after the kids had gone to bed.

"With what?"

"Monica was acting super sketchy today. Dodgy. Even pretended to be on the phone when I knew she wasn't. It was like she was avoiding talking about something."

"Maybe it's work related. You know how seriously she takes patient confidentiality."

Rachel shook her head. "No, this was something else. I think it was about you."

"Me?"

"I have a bad feeling. Remember what she said a while ago? How she basically confronted me about you leaving early? How she said the job is supposed to be your main focus."

"I don't think she really used those words."

"That's not the point. It was implied. Anyway, today was definitely giving me those same vibes."

"Well, I wouldn't be surprised if Roman said something to her."

"What's that supposed to mean?"

"It means it's a little hard to be eager about a job when you aren't happy."

Rachel groaned. "I know you're not exactly loving it, but I can't imagine they could credit you with poor performance. I mean, you're doing everything Roman asks, right?"

"And then some."

Rachel's eyes narrowed. "Chris." She drew out his name with a tone of caution.

"Nothing like that," he said.

"Promise?"

"I'm not a crook, Rachel. Whatever Roman's got going on is his own ethical dilemma."

"If it's even true." She added this to make herself feel better. Because if they really believed the accusations and weren't doing anything about it, didn't that make them complicit?

Her thoughts returned to Monica's odd behavior earlier. "I just don't want any of this campaign stuff to come between Monica and me. The way she acted today, it was so uncomfortable. If she knows something she's not telling me, I don't think I'll ever be able to forgive her. She knows what this job means to our family. I really hope we don't have a blindside coming our way."

"I think you're overthinking," Chris said. "And besides, if Roman doesn't approve of me, then he'll say something. Hell, maybe I should just quit and beat him to it."

Rachel's eyes turned to saucers. "Don't you dare."

Chris smirked.

"Stop—this isn't funny. I'm telling you something's going on."

"Which is why I should jump ship before it capsizes."

"Not until we know anything for sure. How would that

make us look as friends if we just assumed? Innocent until proven guilty, right?"

But Chris just lay back in bed and pulled the covers up. He clearly thought she was making something out of nothing. His level-headedness was usually a source of calm for Rachel. But this time she couldn't shake the paranoia. She thought she knew her friend more than anyone on the planet. So why then was she left staring at the ceiling long into the night?

TWENTY-THREE

MONICA

Monica called Chloe on the very short lunch break she usually didn't take. They hadn't spoken since Chloe's visit to the office over a week prior, and Monica was dying to get an update. "How are you?"

"Okay. The same," Chloe said. "Although I peed four times last night."

Monica laughed despite herself. "Your body's doing unbelievable things. Just wait until the last trimester."

"If I get there," Chloe all but whispered.

Monica's gut twisted. "That's why I'm calling. Obviously to check on you, but also... we really should try to make a decision." She'd planned to say *we* instead of *you*, hoping it would be less threatening. Open Chloe up. If her calculations were right, Chloe was about nine weeks along. And if she wanted an abortion, she was running out of time.

"You want me to have this baby, don't you," Chloe said.

Monica flinched at the bluntness. She stumbled over her words. "Well, I mean... No, I'm—"

"No, you don't want me to have the baby?"

"No, I..." Monica stopped. The words were getting twisted.

She cleared her throat. "What I was trying to say was no, I'm neutral. Truly. I will support you either way."

But she wasn't neutral, not really. She couldn't be. Not in her line of work. Her whole career was about bringing life into the world. Helping people get pregnant, not un-pregnant. It didn't mean she was against abortion. Abortion had its place, and Monica considered herself a moderate when it came to social issues. Women absolutely had the right to choose, which was why she had to keep reminding herself that Chloe wasn't her patient. Chloe hadn't come to her begging to be pregnant. She came already pregnant—and unsure whether that's what she wanted. It was miles from the mindset Monica encountered in her practice. The women she worked with would do anything to have a baby. She needed to keep the two scenarios in their own lanes. They weren't the same.

"What I'm more concerned with," Monica said, evoking her parental tone, "is letting your parents in on it. I was with your mom yesterday and—"

"You didn't tell her, did you?"

"No. But it was... difficult. I think you should tell them." It was selfish, sure. Monica wanted Chloe to tell Rachel for the girl's benefit as much as her own. She didn't think she could face Rachel in person again without the truth being out in the open.

"No way," Chloe said. "They'll freak."

"Maybe at first. But think about it—they love you. They'll support you."

"How do you know?"

"Because I went through this with your mom two decades ago. She experienced the same emotions you are now, and she was equally terrified to tell your grandparents. But do you know what happened? They came around. They accepted her decision."

"And that's why you think I should keep the baby."

There she was, back to that. "That's not what I'm saying. I think your mom and dad would accept whatever you choose. As would I. Even if you decide not to have the baby, don't you think it's fair to tell them? They would want to be there for you. You'll need support no matter what you choose."

The idea of an abortion had been fleeting for Rachel. An option she'd toyed with for approximately ten seconds before dismissing. She'd told Monica as much over the phone. She knew her life would change, but she and Chris had decided together: They were about to become parents.

But that was two decades ago. It didn't mean she wanted the same for her own daughter. And in fact, there had been moments over the years—maybe under the influence of a drink or two—when Rachel had made comments about never letting her kids follow in her footsteps.

But... *let?* Could she really control a nineteen-year-old?

There was a long stretch of silence. "Are you okay?" Monica asked.

Chloe's voice wavered. "I don't know."

"Have you thought about afterwards? I mean, how you would feel in both scenarios after the fact. If you went through with an abortion, how do you think you would feel?"

"Guilty, relieved. Who knows? Probably both?"

"And if you had the baby?"

"Regretful, maybe happy. Again, I see both."

Monica frowned. This was harder than she thought. She'd hoped Chloe would be more certain. That having support would make the decision easier. But Chloe sounded torn.

"Listen," Monica said, "I'll support whatever decision you make, and I believe your parents will too. At the end of the day, you need to do what you want to do, not what you think others expect you to do."

Chloe was silent.

Something tugged on Monica's conscience. Like words were

going unspoken. "Chlo," she said. "Deep down, do you know what you want to do? If no one or nothing else mattered. Is your gut telling you one thing over another?"

The tiniest voice replied, "Yes."

Monica nodded as if they were sitting face to face. "Okay then. I think that's your answer. Do you want to tell me?" She was dying to know.

"Not yet."

"That's fair. Sit with it for a bit. I'll call you on my way home, okay?"

"Okay."

When they hung up, Monica let her head fall back. A decision was made. But which one? And was Chloe going to inform her parents? Whichever choice it was, the next time they talked, Monica would reiterate the urgency to tell Rachel. It had to be done. The secret was no longer skin-deep. It festered in Monica's bones, like a cancer. Pretty soon it would hit her bloodstream and then it would be with her forever.

Like most things that resolve on their own when given the proper time and space, Chloe's decision didn't stay hidden for long. Monica didn't get a chance to make that call that evening. Not because she forgot, and not because she was too busy. But because as she pulled from her assigned parking space in the underground lot, a text from Chloe came in. It contained one simple sentence:

I'm keeping the baby.

TWENTY-FOUR

RACHEL

Birthdays were a big deal for Rachel. Especially when it came to her youngest. Eight whole years with Jacob. Rachel didn't quite know how to feel about it. On the one hand, she'd been raising kids forever and there was a certain satisfaction in them getting further from the needy stage. The constant affection. The inability to do anything for themselves. But this birthday also felt like a turning point. Eight was a sweet spot, where he still wanted to be around her and Chris but didn't require such exhaustive attention. Sometimes she watched Monica with Logan and thought how someone couldn't pay her enough to go backwards.

Rachel stood at the counter, prepping a fruit tray for the party. She stabbed a massive watermelon with a carving knife and used all her body weight to slice through. When that didn't work, she stood on a stool for extra leverage.

"Whoa, Mom," Savannah said, coming into the kitchen. "Does Dad know you're doing that?"

"I don't need Dad's help to cut a watermelon, thank you very much," she said through gritted teeth. She gave another lurch on the knife, and it split the orb in half, sending juice onto the counter. "See?" Perhaps an odd choice for March, but the watermelon was cheap and would feed a lot of people, including Monica's family, who were supposed to be there within the hour.

Savannah raised her brows and walked on, unimpressed. Rachel snorted. *Thanks for the help!* The kids had no clue how much it took to put on a party. Hell, they had no clue what it took to run a household; how much she did for them day in and day out. Her daughter simply saw a mom carving a watermelon —what she didn't see was Rachel getting up early to make the rest of the food, to hang *Avengers* decorations around the house, to pick up the cake from Walmart. It was ten forty-seven a.m. and Rachel was already zapped.

She thought of Chloe still asleep upstairs. What was the point of coming home on weekends if you were just going to sleep the whole time? Chloe had shown up yesterday morning and Rachel had barely seen her in the subsequent twenty-four hours. Jacob's double-header soccer games didn't help, but still, she'd have thought her eldest would want to be a little more involved.

Rachel looked around the kitchen, tallying what still needed to be done before their friends arrived. Inflate balloons. Fill the ice bucket. Run the vacuum. She felt a tension headache coming on. She put her hands on her hips. That's it. Chloe had slept long enough. The girl could help.

Rachel scurried upstairs and tapped on Chloe's door with her knuckles.

"Come in," mumbled a groggy-sounding voice.

"Are you really still sleeping?" Rachel asked, stepping into the room.

Chloe lay in bed. She lifted her eye mask up over one eye and squinted. There were clothes piled on the floor in small mounds. A travel makeup bag overflowed onto the dresser. It was the room of both a kid and a young woman—a juxtaposition that would have stirred Rachel, had she not been annoyed.

"What's wrong with you? Do you have mono or something? You're sleeping all day."

Chloe scooched up to sitting, back against her pillows. Her tawny hair parted in the middle like her mother's and hung limp. She tucked both sides behind her ears. "Actually," she said, casting her eyes down to the floral bedspread, "I haven't been feeling well."

"You haven't?"

Chloe shook her head. "Uh-uh."

"What, like a virus? Is there something going around campus?" Rachel knew how easily germs spread when so many people were in close contact. Working at a preschool meant she was constantly surrounded by kids with snotty noses and dry coughs.

"No. I think it's something else."

"Think?" Rachel's chin jutted forward. *Spit it out*, she wanted to say. She didn't have time for this—there was so much still to do. She'd come up to ask for help, and now Chloe was stringing her along.

Chloe huffed out a giant breath. She folded her hands in her lap; lifted her head. "Mom, I have to tell you something."

Rachel stiffened. Her blood froze. Nothing good came from an announcement like that. She remembered the fleeting thought she'd had that day at Nordstrom, before Monica had bolted into the dressing room, preventing her from voicing it aloud. She'd all but forgotten since then. Until now.

Chloe put her hand up like a stop sign. "Wait, I should tell Dad too."

"He's cleaning up the garage." Rachel's voice was monotone, her eyes fixed without blinking. "What is it? Just tell me."

"No really. I don't want to have to say it twice." Chloe swung her legs off the side of the bed and stood. She smoothed the tank top that had twisted on her torso from sleeping. Rachel eyed her. Was Chloe wearing a push-up bra?

Chloe passed Rachel to leave the room, and as though her lips wouldn't move, Rachel stood mute. This "something" could be anything, but that didn't explain why a full-body chill swooped over her. She tried to talk herself off the ledge. Maybe Chloe got busted for drinking. Maybe she failed a big exam. Oh, please let it be a failed exam!

Rachel turned to follow her daughter, who'd already made it downstairs. Her brain went haywire. They were only a little way into the semester. They probably hadn't even had an exam yet. The realization made her hiccup. What else could it be?

A tiny earthquake traveled her body. Not that. It couldn't be that.

Chloe was going for the door when Rachel stopped her. "I'll get him." She needed to speak to Chris first. Needed to gauge his reaction and let it calm her. She was letting herself get hysterical over what could be nothing.

Chloe hung back, letting Rachel go.

In the garage, Chris lifted a plastic storage tub onto a high shelf. He was wearing a T-shirt and worn-in jeans—the ensemble she'd known for so long but which had become less familiar in his new role that required a certain finesse. Sweat dripped from his forehead, and he wiped it away with his forearm. He bent for another.

"Chris," Rachel said. She could hear the panic in her voice.

When he met her gaze, he stopped and set the tub on the ground. He knew this look. The same look as any of the other times tragedy had struck: Jacob's broken arm, Savannah being bullied by another girl at school. All of those times felt the same —something was wrong with one of her kids. She could feel it before there was even confirmation. Almost like a sixth sense. And when Chloe had looked her in the eye and said she had to tell them something, Rachel had felt it then too. They were about to be handed another blow. Why else would Chloe be so serious? Why else would she have insisted on telling them together?

"What is it?" Chris asked, and just by his tone, Rachel knew he instinctively recognized the same. A parent's intuition.

"Chloe wants to talk to us."

"About what?" he said slowly.

"I don't know. All she said was she had something to tell us." Rachel bit her bottom lip. Chris looked from her to the door and back again. "I'm scared. What if she says she's—"

"Don't." He spread his fingers, pressing the air down. "Don't go there."

"I can't help it. You know that's where my mind goes first."

Chris lifted the last tub onto the shelf then gave his hands a clap to clear the dust. "Come on," he said, like a man resigned to his fate.

How could he be so calm? Shouldn't they prepare themselves?

He led the way back to the house and into the living room where Chloe was now cross-legged on the couch, pillow hugged in her lap. Rachel and Chris pulled in the large, square ottoman and sat so their hips touched. Rachel's back was straight as a board. A pupil at attention.

"Where are Savannah and Jacob?" Chloe asked, which made Rachel shake even more. Not only did Chloe want to tell them something serious, but she didn't want her little brother and sister around to hear? This couldn't be a speeding ticket.

"Outside," Rachel managed. "Playing at the neighbor's."

Chloe swallowed. Rachel tried to do the same, but her mouth was a cotton ball.

"I've been keeping something from you guys," Chloe began, a deep breath after each sentence. "There's really no easy way to say it. And I know you're going to be upset, but just hear me out, okay?"

Rachel's eyes bounced around to every inch of her daughter, from her balayage hair to her painted toenails. What was this secret? Could she see it written somewhere on her body? If she stared hard enough, would she figure it out?

"I'm pregnant." Chloe's voice cracked when she said it, and her chin trembled. But she didn't hang her head; didn't cry. Only gripped the pillow tighter.

Rachel folded forward, dropping her head into her hands. A sudden sob escaped her. "I knew it." She felt Chris's heavy hand on her back. "I knew that's what you were going to say." Rachel felt like she'd had the wind knocked out of her. Everything felt tight, and she struggled to take a deep breath.

"Jesus, Chlo," Chris said, leaning down, elbows on his knees.

"I'm sorry," Chloe said.

When Chris sat back up, his face was red. "I'm going to kill Preston."

"It's not his fault," Chloe sputtered. "I mean, I'm equally to blame here."

Rachel put a hand on her husband's thigh. "Yes, Chris, you were Preston once too, remember? There are two parties involved." Now wasn't the time for homicide.

She returned her attention to Chloe. "What about your pill? This is exactly why I put you on it in the first place, so something like this wouldn't happen." It was a rhetorical question; one Rachel didn't expect an answer to. Obviously, Chloe wasn't taking the pill properly.

Rachel had a brief flash of feeding her children *Flintstones* vitamins when they were little, and a stabbing feeling at wishing she could oversee their care forever. Pop onto campus every evening to watch Chloe press the little white tablet from the foil. In her mouth, down to her belly. There. Safe and secure.

But that wasn't reality. Chloe was an adult now. She had to be responsible for her own actions.

Rachel pressed her palms into her eye sockets as though enough pressure could reverse the dilemma. "Oh, Chloe, Chloe, Chloe. This isn't what I wanted for you. Your life is now changed forever." The lump in her throat dissolved into tears, all the memories of her own unplanned pregnancy rising to the surface. She'd been so afraid. Felt so alone. Telling her parents was one of the hardest conversations of her life, and she'd never forget the disappointment on their faces. Is that how her face looked now? Chloe now sat in Rachel's position, and the agony of that tore through Rachel like a hot blade.

"I'm sorry," Chloe kept saying. "I didn't mean for it to happen."

"Of course you didn't," Chris said. "No one plans to get pregnant at nineteen. That's why we always lectured you about being safe. We trusted you."

That's when Chloe broke. She collapsed into the pillow, shoulders shaking. Despite Rachel's own pain, her heart splintered watching her daughter's reaction. Anger and empathy and remorse swirled together into a venomous cocktail in her veins. She wanted to punch a wall. Run out the door and down the street. Curl up in a ball and shut out everyone.

But she also wanted to hug her daughter. And so, despite it all, warmth won. Rachel slid in next to Chloe and wrapped an arm around her. Even Chris's face softened. Neither of them could stand seeing their children hurting.

"Don't hate me," Chloe cried.

"Oh, honey. We could never hate you. That's impossible. It's just..." Rachel sighed. "You're following in my footsteps, and it's the one thing I hoped wouldn't happen."

Chloe lifted her head. "Was I really such a tragedy in your life?" Her face flushed. "The way you talk about it, it makes it seem like I literally ruined your lives. I mean, think about how that makes me feel." She breathed fast, her chest rising and falling in quick succession.

"That's not what she meant," Chris inserted at the same time Rachel said, "Don't twist my words. Of course you're not a tragedy. You're one of our greatest blessings."

"That's not how it sounds." Chloe pulled away from her mother, folding her arms across her chest. "I thought you guys would be more supportive since you've been through it."

Now it was Rachel's turn to get defensive. "I don't think you understand how hard it is to have a baby."

"Well," Chris said, "that's assuming she's not going to—"

"Chris."

Chloe set her jaw. "I'm not having an abortion. I thought about it, but no. I'm keeping the baby."

An acid river churned in Rachel's gut even though she hadn't yet eaten anything more than a nibble of the fruit she'd diced earlier. She felt hot. So hot. And yet so cold. Numb. Time slowed. She couldn't believe what she was hearing.

"I really think you should consider all the options. Abortion isn't the only thing. There's adoption, and..."

Chloe shook her head. "I've already talked to—" She cut off her own sentence. "I've already thought about everything. I talked to Ava."

Rachel blew steam through her teeth. Chloe was having a baby. And her decision was firm. Even if Rachel wanted to convince her of another option, Chloe wouldn't budge. That stubbornness, the strong will Rachel loved in her, presented in pressed lips and tight fists. The choice had been made.

"Chloe..." Rachel said, sucking air through her teeth in skepticism. It felt rushed. Too sudden. Shouldn't they talk it through?

Chloe flew up from the couch. "You're never on my side. All you care about is Jacob and Savannah, so why does it matter what I do? It's not like you know anything about my life. Why shouldn't I have this baby?"

She didn't wait for an answer before storming off, back to

the dungeon of her bedroom. Rachel and Chris watched her go, unable to form any words quick enough. When all that remained was the dust of her sudden departure, the two looked at each other. Rachel experienced disorientation she could only compare to fiction. Spinning. A swarm of bees in her ears. Not quite in her own body.

There was nothing to say, so she and Chris leaned into each other. It could have been a moment to pull them apart—a chance to place blame—but perhaps that would come later. Instead, Rachel buried her face into her husband's collarbone and let the tears flow freely.

TWENTY-FIVE
MONICA

I told them.

THE TEXT CAME THROUGH JUST AS MONICA, ROMAN, AND the boys pulled out of their driveway to head to the Morelands'. Monica took a sharp intake of breath. She'd been anxious all morning, worried about how she'd act around Rachel at the birthday party, feeling guilty every hour that passed knowing something her friend didn't. It had been two weeks of hell since Chloe had confided in her. The lie was eating her from the inside out. But with Chloe's text, and the wave of relief that accompanied it, everything changed. "Oh, thank God."

"What?" Roman, who was driving, gave her a sideways glance.

"Nothing." A million pounds lifted from her shoulders. She wouldn't have to pretend anymore. Wouldn't have to bear what felt very much like a serious break in friend code.

She replied to Chloe: **Oh, good!**

But as she relaxed into the leather passenger seat, another thought crept in. If Rachel knew Chloe was pregnant, Monica would be encountering quite a different scene than she'd originally planned for. This wouldn't be their typically festive birthday party. Was Rachel going to be a mess of tears when Monica arrived? A hot ball of fury? Monica would have to be in support mode. She readjusted her expectations. And then another jolt hit her like a dart: Not only would she have to comfort her friend, but she'd have to play dumb. It was one thing to not harbor Chloe's secret any longer, but there was another aspect Monica would have to withhold—the fact that she knew first. She wanted to cry. Would the charade never end?

She shot off another quick text to Chloe: **Did you say anything about me?**

A few seconds passed before the little reply dots appeared: **No.**

Another dodged bullet. Monica laid her phone upside down on her lap.

"I hope they didn't get those cheap-ass buns again," Roman said. He drove with one hand on the wheel, the other casually on the gear stick, his chambray shirt sleeves rolled to his elbows.

"It's just a hamburger bun."

"Yeah, the flimsy, generic kind. They fall apart and soak up ketchup like a sponge."

Monica bit her cheek. Her husband was a bit of a snob when it came to cuisine, even the picnic variety. Bread had levels of integrity. It might have been why their grocery bills were so high. "Be nice," she said.

"I'm always nice." He gave her the smooth grin that used to make her chest flutter.

"Yeah, Mom," Logan said from the back seat. "Daddy's always nice."

She coughed, and Roman gave her a look.

"Sorry," Monica said. "Dry throat."

. . .

Before the car turned off, Lucas and Logan were already out the door, dashing across the driveway. They wouldn't knock. They wouldn't ring the doorbell. They'd just go in—comfortable with the rhythm of a family not their own.

As Monica exited the car, she gave herself a firm reminder: *Act surprised.* If there was ever a time to improve her poker face, this was it. Rachel would undoubtedly share Chloe's news, and Monica could *not* let on that she already knew. Her throat burned, so she popped a Tums from her purse. This would only be a small lie, she told herself. Trivial in the grand scheme of things. Rachel didn't need to know this tiny detail—it would only make things worse. Best to keep her in the dark.

Monica found her friend in the dining room, tossing a plastic superhero covering over the table. Rachel wore a frown to go with her mom jeans.

Shit.

"Hey, girl," Monica said, trying for optimism. "I brought your favorite." She held out the box of Prantl's cookies. Rachel's eyes glistened, but it wasn't joy over shortbread—it was grief.

"I'm so glad you're here." Rachel dropped the tablecloth and came toward Monica with outstretched arms, like a child going to its parent after a scary dream.

Monica put the cookies down just in time to wrap her friend in a hug. "What is it?" Her stomach sank, and she was glad Rachel couldn't see her eyes; afraid they'd give her away. Rachel tried to let go, but Monica held her, scared to meet her friend face-to-face. After another few seconds though, the embrace felt overdone, and Monica dropped her arms.

"You're not going to believe it," Rachel said, voice shaking.

"Wha-What is it?"

"Guess." Why was she torturing her like this? "Oh, you'll never guess. It's Chloe. Turns out it wasn't depression. She's pregnant."

"Oh, Rach. Are you serious?" Monica put on her best look of horror, praying it was convincing.

"She just told me half an hour ago. I'm still processing."

"Fuck."

Rachel folded her arms across her middle. "I can't believe it. I mean, I can—I know how easily it happens. But after all our preaching. All the precautions."

"You can't blame yourself."

"Then she yelled a bunch of stuff about me not caring about her and never giving her attention. Talk about adding salt to the wound. Apparently, I'm a terrible mother."

"You're not." Monica rubbed Rachel's arm. "Don't say that. Chloe's obviously upset."

"She should be. This is going to permanently alter her life. And she just wants us to act like it's no big deal?"

Monica didn't have a response. She couldn't understand the first-hand experience of an unplanned pregnancy. Couldn't tap into the sudden assault of emotions. But she'd been there by Rachel's side when it was her. And that she could speak to.

"She's lucky to have you and Chris as parents."

Rachel's eyes narrowed. "You don't seem surprised."

"Oh, I am!" Monica brought a hand to her chest. Damn her acting abilities. The truth was she'd had weeks to process Chloe's news, while Rachel had just learned of it moments ago. "I just mean, imagine the young girls who don't have support."

Rachel's reaction—an exasperated laugh—indicated it wasn't the response she'd been looking for.

"Like I have time to help raise another baby?" she said. "I can barely juggle all the balls I already have. Chloe made that perfectly clear."

"You know what I mean. You're a great mom, Rachel."

Rachel looked away, her face crumbling. "I had so many plans," she whispered just loud enough for Monica to hear.

. . .

The buns were indeed soggy, but Monica ate nonetheless. She made eyes at Roman with a silent, *Don't you say a word.*

The news was out. After Rachel had told Monica, Monica had told Roman. Her husband had blanched, a sputtering, "She's what?" coming from his lips.

"I know, it's shocking," Monica had said. "It's like déjà vu. Two college kids pregnant all over again. Rachel and Chris have only met Preston like twice."

It had taken Roman a minute to process it. Monica understood—they all still thought of Chloe as the little kid with Kool-Aid stains around her mouth. Adjusting to the thought of her being pregnant—being a *mom*—was a lot to digest.

"Is she coming down?" Monica said quietly to Rachel. They sat around the table, while the little kids set up a makeshift picnic in the other room. Rachel picked at her pasta salad but didn't eat. Even Chris, with his abundant appetite, barely touched his plate. The mood had taken a somber turn. Monica was torn between wanting to be there for her friend and wanting to escape the tension.

"I tried," Rachel said. "She's been burrowed up there all weekend. I'll try again." She clicked away on her phone, shooting off a text message to her daughter one floor above.

It wasn't like Chloe not to be at least cordial. Usually, she was the first one to sweep Monica's boys up into a hug. The get-together felt off without her. Then again, this wasn't a normal gathering—not with the news that had turned life on its head. Monica understood Chloe's isolation, and part of her was relieved not to have to throw another actor into this grand façade.

Rachel's phone beeped. She read the response then flashed the phone to Monica.

I don't feel like socializing.

"Don't force her on our account," Roman said. He was on his third beer already, eyes getting that glazed look. "I'm sure she's got a lot on her mind. The last thing she wants to do is eat a hotdog. Can you even eat hotdogs when you're pregnant?"

Like the thunderbolt it was, Chloe's pregnancy dominated their conversation. Retrospective what ifs, imminent logistics. The four adults bounced questions off each other, intermixed with Rachel's occasional moments of quiet tears.

"She could, as they say, take care of it," Roman said, making air quotes around the last part. "I mean, that's probably for the best, right? It's much more acceptable today, what with women's rights and all that stuff. If it were my daughter, I'd—"

"But it's not your daughter," Chris said, and that very much ended the discussion.

"Let's change the subject," Monica suggested. She'd managed to eat the cheeseburger, but with all this talk, it wasn't sitting well. She wanted to get as far away from the topic of Chloe and the pregnancy as possible.

"Eight months until election day," Roman offered. He addressed Chris. "Things are really going to ramp up. Lots of push in this final stretch."

Chris nodded somberly. Monica wondered how he could possibly think about work in the face of such personal news. Wondered if Chris was still reeling from their dinner-gone-wrong.

"We can't let anything derail our progress," Roman continued as though speaking in unnecessary code.

"Right," Chris said slowly, and something told Monica it was only for her benefit. Like Chris was shielding her from his true feelings about her husband. The money rumors had ceased —thank God—but they'd left behind a layer of dust that hadn't quite settled.

The two men stared hard at each other. Pressure blanketed the table, and Monica wished they'd just stayed home. Made an excuse not to come to the party. She could have talked with Rachel over the phone. Everything felt too heavy for a day that was supposed to be light and breezy.

"You guys are doing great," she said to break through the stress. "I'm sure we'll all be celebrating on November seventh. Right, Rach?"

But Rachel was lost in a past conversation, her eyes clouded over. Monica reached out to squeeze her hand, bringing Rachel back to the present.

"What? Sorry."

"I said, we're bound to be celebrating on election night. I know it doesn't feel like a happy time, but remember you have us, okay? We'll always support you guys. And Chloe. She's like our own."

Roman pushed back from the table. "I've got to run."

"What?" Monica's face twisted into a question mark. "Why? We haven't even had cake. We drove here together."

"Politics never sleeps, babe. You know that. Can you and the boys get a ride home later?" He raised his brows at Rachel.

"Um... I guess?" Monica fumbled over a thick tongue at the same time Rachel piped in with, "Sure. I can drop you guys later if you want to stick around."

Disappointment crashed into Monica. This was supposed to be a no-work day. It was a Sunday, and Jacob's birthday party for goodness' sake. But Rachel's face screamed for her to stay, and Monica couldn't abandon her friend as much as she wished she could leave too.

"Are you okay to drive?" she asked Roman.

"Totally fine. Sorry to eat and dash. Chris, my man, I'll see you first thing in the morning. Rach, thanks for the meal. Everything was... delicious."

Roman went to leave but stopped abruptly just as he was about to turn the corner out of the room. Someone blocked his path.

"Chloe," he said brightly. "I was just leaving. Sorry to miss you."

Chloe passed by him and took the chair he'd left open at the table.

"Hi, hon," Monica said. Her eyes instinctively went to Chloe's midsection.

Chloe cracked a pithy smile and wrapped her arms around her knees. She looked like she had the weight of the world on her mind. Too much for someone so young.

Monica turned to tell her husband to drive safely, but he was gone. So much for a proper goodbye. She resolved herself to enjoy the remaining time, if possible.

"Glad you decided to join us," Rachel addressed her daughter. "Are you hungry?"

"No."

"I brought Prantl's," Monica said, sliding the box Chloe's way.

Chloe studied the box for longer than a beat; walked her fingers across the table. "Maybe just one then." She picked a snickerdoodle and nibbled the edge.

Later, everyone watched as Jacob opened presents. They oohed and ahhed, directing their attention to the boy of the hour. It might have appeared like any typical birthday celebration, but there were so many words left unsaid, so many unknowns hanging in the air, that to Monica, sitting there was more a chore than any sort of merriment. The only peace of mind came from the fact that Rachel hadn't and would never discover Monica's deception. She'd never know Monica had withheld such sensitive knowledge. Monica was in the clear. And that alone allowed her to sip her vodka-spiked lemonade, the alcohol dulling everything else.

TWENTY-SIX

CHLOE

THE PREGNANCY TRACKER APP SAID SHE WAS TWELVE weeks along, and the baby was the size of a plum. Chloe held up a hand in the shape of a circle then moved it to her abdomen, picturing a purple blob curled up inside. The photos looked like an alien—oversized head, tiny limbs, webbed appendages. Nothing cute about it. Rachel had accompanied Chloe to the first appointment, where the blood test had confirmed her due date: September twenty-ninth. She wondered if it was a girl or boy. There were tests to find out early, but Chloe chose to wait.

Back on campus and trying to assimilate into college-student life, that date seemed a lifetime away. The idea of actually delivering the baby was a distant thought. After all, it wasn't even April yet. Tulip buds popped through the mulch around campus. Easter weekend approached, and Chloe wondered if her mom would still give her a basket, or if getting pregnant meant she'd outgrown visits from the Easter Bunny. Now, all the magic of youth would be passed on to her own child. She'd be the one stuffing plastic eggs with colorful jelly-beans instead of the one finding them. A piece of her mourned this slingshot into adulthood.

Chloe took in her reflection in the full-length mirror she and Ava shared. Her silhouette was the same—slender and toned—and no one would ever have suspected there was a baby beneath her abs. It wasn't until she stripped off her clothes that the tiniest bump protruded below her belly button—just enough to make her pants feel ever so snug. Almost like she'd overeaten at Thanksgiving dinner, only this bloating didn't subside with digestion.

"You look totally normal," Ava said.

Chloe pulled her shoulder blades together. "My boobs are massive."

"Each individual woman's body demands to be accepted on its own terms."

Chloe gave an amused hoot. Honestly, Ava and her quotes. "I hope I don't gain a ton of weight." She remembered her mom being pregnant with her siblings. Rachel had looked like she'd smuggled a basketball under her shirt and that's it. All belly. And then gone the minute the kids came out. Chloe thought maybe she'd be lucky like that too.

"Are you going to tell him soon?" Ava pushed her blue-light glasses up her nose. A press badge hung around her neck, credentials to cover a campus speaker on behalf of the newspaper staff.

Him was Preston, and Chloe had been procrastinating, still stuck on the idea of doing motherhood alone. But no one else seemed to agree, and so she resigned to give in. "I was thinking I would today."

"Wait, today?"

"My parents are pressuring me. They said he has a right to know." Chloe hadn't spoken to Preston since she'd discovered the pregnancy. They'd spotted each other in social circles, but she'd largely tried to avoid him—and instances of drinking—by sticking close to the dorm, or even going home.

"Shit. Are you nervous?"

"Hard to tell with the daily nausea." Chloe slipped on white sneakers and grabbed her school bag. "I just want this semester to be over."

"Well, I'm glad you stayed. They would have paired me with some rando."

The decision to finish the semester had been a collective one. Her parents agreed that as long as she felt okay, Chloe should complete her freshman year. Get as many credits under her belt, so when she went back—and she *would* go back, Rachel said—she'd be that much closer to graduation. But it hadn't been easy. Chloe struggled with continued exhaustion and morning sickness, along with a new aversion to any type of egg. Scrambled, fried, even the thought of those yellow puffs, it didn't matter. The smell of breakfast coming from the cafeteria was enough to make her choke on her own breath.

"I know you feel like shit, but won't you hang for the weekend?" Ava asked, to which Chloe gave a rueful look. "Tomorrow is the Take Back the Night walk."

She gulped involuntarily. "I'm not exactly in the walking frame of mind."

No, it would be back to Wexford for the weekend. The next few weeks would revolve around keeping her head down, getting through her classes, and not much else. She tried not to let herself think about packing everything up after finals. When she stepped off campus that spring, would it be forever?

Ava twirled a piece of hair that hung over her shoulder. "Text me as soon as you talk to Preston. He better not be a dick either. Remember what Gloria says: Women are—"

"I got it, Av. Thanks."

"Good luck."

Chloe nodded and dragged herself to class.

. . .

Not long ago, she'd had Preston's schedule memorized. But this semester was a whole different story. A hollowness opened in Chloe's chest. She used to know everything about him—at least she'd thought she had. Now, the only thing she could be sure about was his dorm, Holland Scott. If she had a chance of catching him, it would be near there. So that's what she did.

After class, Chloe walked up Fifth Avenue and situated herself on a bench outside the ten-story building. It was as good a place as any to get work done while she waited. The mild spring air felt nice, a refreshing change of pace from her own stuffy dorm. She pulled out a textbook, intermittently looking up from the pages when co-eds passed.

Sure enough, Preston strolled her way within two hours. Chloe slammed the book shut and hopped off the bench. When he saw her, his gait lapsed for a step then continued. It's not like they were enemies—he'd been the one to suggest they remain friends. Still, Chloe's gut cramped. She took a few steps toward him.

"Hey," she said.

"Hey." He scratched his head; looked over his shoulder.

"Do you have a minute?"

"I, uh... Yeah, sure. What's up?"

Chloe led him to the bench. She couldn't bear going up to his room. Too many reminders.

"This is hard to say." She breathed slowly and deliberately, trying to stave off the vomit that threatened to rise. Preston went rigid. Once again, the words were about to spill out. Two simple words that would change everything. She wished there was a softer way to say it, but there wasn't. "I'm pregnant."

Preston's face paled. His fingertips gripped his phone tighter, turning white. "For real?"

"For real."

"And you think it's mine?"

Chloe flinched. "What, like I'm sleeping with different guys every night? Do the math, Preston."

"We haven't had sex for months. Not since..."

The memory of the ski lodge weekend popped into her mind uninvited and she reflexively pressed her knees together. "I'm twelve weeks along. Almost done with the first trimester."

Preston heaved giant breaths, swiveling on the bench as though waiting for someone to jump out of the bushes and yell *Gotcha!* He raked a hand through his hair. "You've got to be kidding me. Fuck."

Chloe sat silently, letting him process the news. It was a lot. She remembered how she'd felt when that little pink cross had shown up on the test. Like the life had been sucked from her. Preston needed a minute to catch up. Instinct compelled her to apologize like she had to her parents, but if there was any fault to be had, he was equally guilty. This was *their* doing, not hers. If she'd had her way, she wouldn't have told him at all. The sting of the breakup was still very much present, and after the hurt had subsided, it had been replaced with a bitterness that told Chloe she could raise this baby alone. She didn't need his help. But her parents had insisted she tell him, and so there they were, on a metal lattice bench with a colossal blow between them.

"I'm not asking for anything," she said. "But I thought you should know."

His eyes welled, which broke Chloe's heart even further. She stuffed her hands under her thighs to keep from reaching out and stroking his face. She could see his life flashing before him, and she understood the shock of it all.

"My parents are going to kill me," he finally said.

"You don't have to be involved if you don't want. I'm prepared to do it on my own." Her voice dropped. "I mean, it's not like we're together or anything."

Preston's shoulders slumped. "Chloe, I'm not an asshole. I

care about you as a person. It's just... Holy shit." He lowered his head into his hands.

"I'm finishing out the semester and then will obviously be taking time off."

"When's it... I mean, when are you...?"

"September twenty-ninth."

Preston blinked at the ground.

"Listen," she said, "I'm just as scared as you. This wasn't exactly in my plans. Will you just keep it to yourself though? I'd rather not become the talk of campus."

He nodded. There wasn't much more to say. When he sat back up, their eyes met and stayed locked for a long minute. Then, without words, they hugged.

"Can I do anything for you?" he asked, and her bones turned to mush. She bit the inside of her cheek. This wasn't a reconciliation, she reminded herself.

Chloe stood. "We'll talk, okay?" The details were so up in the air. In just a few weeks, they'd be dispersing campus back to their hometowns—Chloe forty minutes north, Preston several states away. Did she think he'd tag along to doctor's appointments? Did she want him to? Too much uncertainty and pain lingered in the air for her to stay any longer on that cracked sidewalk. Instead, she mustered a vague smile, turned, and walked away.

Being around her parents since the announcement came as a hot barb. A catch-22—wanting to escape campus and dreading showing her face to the two people she looked up to most. Still, it wasn't enough for Chloe to stick around Pitt for the weekend. Not even Ava's puppy-dog eyes and pleas to lay low together were enough. She felt bad for missing Ava's Take Back the Night event, but being in company with her counterparts only reminded Chloe how different she now was—even if she alone knew why.

On Saturday morning at home, Chloe woke to a knock on her bedroom door.

"You up?" her mom asked. Chloe peeked at the alarm clock on her nightstand. Ten forty-three a.m. She felt like she could sleep another dozen hours.

Rachel stepped in holding a cardboard package. "This was by the door. Must have come when I was taking Sav to dance."

Chloe sat up and took the box. An orange Etsy label was on the outside. She didn't remember ordering anything.

Chloe used her nail to pierce the tape, then opened the top flaps and pulled out a basket filled with goodies laid upon shredded paper strips. She held up a lavender candle that said "Mama" across the label and a zip-top packet with the words "Tea 4 Two."

Chloe eyed her mom, who shrugged and said, "Not me," then returned to the items filling the basket. Essential oils, a face mask, a little baggy of ginger mints. Tucked in the back was a card, which she pulled out and read. The front featured an illustration of a woman slung on a couch, drool coming from her mouth, and the heading, "Tired as a mother—" Chloe read the inside message aloud.

Chickadee—

Just a little care package. Hope you're feeling better soon.

XO

Monica

"That was nice of her," Chloe said, bringing the candle to her nose. "Ginger's supposed to help with upset stomachs, right?" When she looked back up, she saw her mom's face had fallen flat, mouth in a thin line.

"Yep," Rachel croaked.

Chloe unwrapped a candy and popped it into her mouth. "How cute is this?" She held up a bath bomb shaped like a pacifier.

"Adorable."

"What's wrong? Are you mad or something?"

Rachel crossed her arms. "Why would I be mad?"

"I'm pretty sure I can tell when you're pissed about something. Is it this?" She gestured to the basket on her lap.

"Don't be silly, Chloe. It was a very thoughtful gift."

Chloe thought for a moment. Hadn't she heard those very words from her mom recently? Then it came to her—the Stanley cup. The same look. The same response. Was her mom... jealous?

"It's just a little pick-me-up," Chloe said reassuringly. "Don't overanalyze it."

Rachel collected the empty packaging. "I don't need you telling me what to analyze, *thankyouverymuch*." Then she was gone, leaving Chloe with a ginger mint tucked into the pocket of her cheek and a look of confusion on her face. Too tired to follow, she fell back onto the bed and sent a thank-you text to Monica. At least she knew someone cared about her.

TWENTY-SEVEN

RACHEL

"She's my goddamned daughter, not yours," Rachel muttered to herself as she descended the stairs heavy-footed. What did Monica think she was doing? This news wasn't something they were celebrating with pregnancy announcements and mommy massages. It wasn't exactly something she and Chris were *happy* about. So why did Monica feel the need to act like a chipper grandma-to-be? And wasn't it crossing some sort of line by sending gifts without checking with her first?

Rachel's internal temperature rose. Her heartbeat pounded in her ears like a bass drum, and her mouth pulled into a scowl.

"Whoa," Chris said in mock terror. "Who pissed in your Cheerios?"

"It's nothing," she grumbled.

"Doesn't seem like nothing."

"It's just... It's Monica." And then it was like someone turned on the faucet that was her mouth. "She sent Chloe this pregnancy care package full of a bunch of prenatal stuff." Chris stared wide-eyed, clearly not grasping the seriousness. Rachel huffed. "Forget it. You won't understand." She stormed off, but Chris followed.

"Wait a minute. Sending a gift is a bad thing?"

"It's not just about the gift. It's that she's treating this pregnancy like some sort of joyous occasion. Pampering Chloe feels like rewarding her for getting herself in this situation in the first place. If I wanted to celebrate, don't you think I'd be the first one spoiling my daughter? Those gift baskets are expensive."

Chris cocked his head. "So, is this about Chloe or is this about Monica?"

"You know what?" she said, feeling her mood turn vinegary, "I'd appreciate if you were behind me on this. Am I the only one who isn't thrilled about my daughter having a baby before she's even old enough to buy a beer? Are you seriously ready to be a *grandpa*?" Her voice choked up. There was so much more she wanted to say, but she held back.

"Of course I'm not thrilled, Rach. But I'm trying to wrap my head around it. Chloe's made her choice, and there's nothing we can do about it but move forward."

She wanted to tell him then—tell him how it was more than the fact that Chloe's life was about to quadruple in complexity. It was about her too. But it felt selfish, and the last thing she wanted was another reason to feel subordinate to everyone else. Instead, she wiped her eyes before the tears had a chance to fall, then grabbed a light jacket and headed for the door. Air would help. She needed a minute alone to collect her bounding thoughts.

Their street connected to two others to form a half-mile loop, and it was the perfect distance for unpacking a distressed mind. Rachel pumped her arms as she walked. How could she say what she really wanted to—that this baby wasn't just altering Chloe's life but hers as well. Going back to school would be out of the question. If she could barely make it work now, it would be near impossible with a newborn in the picture —one Rachel would undoubtedly have to help raise. She thought of the college application she'd submitted in February, the thrill she'd felt at the possibility of being accepted. Now, she was back to square one. Stuck with her job at the preschool, an unfinished college degree hanging over her head.

Everyone seemed to have accepted their new reality. Monica was damn near giddy. Didn't she understand what a blow this was? But then, if the roles were reversed, Monica could afford all the help she needed. Hire a night nurse. Pay for the best day care. The thoughts were ridiculous—the boys weren't even double digits yet, another thing that separated the two women. The one who did things right, and the other who fucked up.

Rachel loved that Monica and Chloe were close—but not this close. Not when it stepped on her toes. Monica should be a friend to Rachel first, not the other way around. It felt like a slippery line had been crossed. Normally in these situations, Monica would be the first person Rachel would turn to. A phone call, any hour of the day. The two knew everything about each other. Now, she felt utterly alone.

As she walked, a bitterness sprouted. She built walls around the mental image of her family. She needed to protect not only herself but her daughter too. She was a damn good mother. Hell, she'd given up everything for her kids—her life revolved around them. The one time she'd considered putting herself first had backfired. Rachel steeled herself. It served her right. She'd made her choices all those years ago, and now she had to live with them. Her feet dragged. She could suck it up. She'd have to. If only it didn't feel as though a part of her had died.

Later that week, after days without communication with Monica, Rachel's stomach clenched when the text she was anticipating finally came through.

Are we still on for Friday?

They said it to each other every week as though it were a question instead of a ritual for years.

Rachel's finger didn't even hover before quickly swiping out of the text without replying. It would take her another full day to respond, a curt: **Can't, sorry.**

She didn't think about how Monica would interpret it, didn't care how it landed. Her world was coming undone, and she needed space, even from the one person she was usually attached to like a boat to its anchor.

TWENTY-EIGHT

MONICA

Can't, sorry.

No explanation, no lighthearted, *Let's reschedule*. Just two words in the way someone would talk to a stranger. A drifter on the street. Monica got a quick shock of heat through her body. It was so abrupt. So... detached. Maybe Rachel had found out? Maybe she was furious at Monica? Still, part of her was soothed by the cancelled plans. She wouldn't have to dodge any awkward conversation.

But not calling or texting, not seeing each other weekly was something that would be easier said than done for two people who relayed nearly every recap of their days, from starting periods to new dinner recipes. The thought alone of putting distance between them robbed too much light from her life. Yet it felt like her only option.

Monica was nearly asleep when Roman creaked open the bedroom door.

"I didn't expect you so late," she mumbled, craning her neck.

"Dinner was slow, and we got to talking. You know how it goes." He slipped into the master bathroom and shut the door.

Got to talking. About what exactly? Monica didn't know where or whom he'd been with exactly, only that it was campaign business. Asking him didn't really matter anyway because he usually just replied with, "Oh just some donor."

All the dinners, all the events, blurred together. She barely had enough mental capacity to hold her own work issues let alone adding a husband who was running for office. Add in two kids plus public scrutiny and it was mental overload. Maybe she didn't care what he was doing, as long as she didn't know. But then that thought scared her. Because if she didn't care whether he was an ethical person, what did that say about her own values?

When Roman returned from the bathroom, he pulled back the covers and got into bed. He cradled his hands behind his head, staring at the ceiling. "Supposed to be ninety tomorrow—talk about perfect timing. Are you still able to bring the boys?"

Monica heard him talking, but she was lost in her own thoughts. His voice drowned out.

"Monica? Did you hear me?"

"Hmm?"

"I said are you still bringing the boys tomorrow?"

Monica flipped through her mental calendar. "Where?"

Roman groaned. "The ice cream truck. My fundraiser. Remember? Free cones for the first hundred people?"

"Oh, right." She spoke as though in a dream. "I think Rachel's planning to take them."

"Are you okay? You're like not even here right now."

Monica bit the inside of her cheek. Admitting the truth meant opening a potential can of worms—her distraction was largely a result of his behavior. Instead, she offered something else.

"I'm just thinking of Chloe." It wasn't untrue, and even though it might not have been top of her mind, not the fiasco taking top bill, it still held a permanent place in her catalog of mental stressors.

"Ah," he exhaled. "I'm still surprised she's going through with it. The baby, I mean."

"She made up her mind."

"But don't you think she should get an abortion?"

Monica propped herself on her elbow. "Not if she doesn't want one. What's it matter to you?"

Roman huffed. "Jeez, don't attack me. I'm just thinking about our friends' daughter, that's all. She's literally nineteen. It's not like we're living in the fifties. People get abortions every day."

"Of course they do. But it's clearly her decision. And it's up to the rest of us to support her." She studied Roman's profile. His jawline looked tight. "Besides, she's getting further along now. Most people don't get abortions this late."

"Yeah, but it's still possible."

Again, Monica's pulse spiked. She was the baby doctor. *Stay in your lane, buddy. Stick to politics.*

Roman turned to face her. "Anyway, it's not a good look."

"Good look?"

"For me. For the campaign."

A frown crossed Monica's brow as she tried to put two seemingly separate things together in her mind. The jigsaw pieces didn't fit. "Don't you think you have enough other things to focus on? You know, like your reputation."

"Ouch, Mon."

"Well, those rumors certainly weren't positive, and you didn't seem too concerned."

Roman groaned. "I'm so tired of defending myself. I'm running on a platform of values. It doesn't exactly look great for my right-hand man to have a pregnant teenage daughter."

Monica blinked. It took her a second to form her words. "Wait, you're concerned about Chris?"

"I'm concerned about all of us. Chris is a face of the campaign now, and what, all of a sudden we're supposed to just announce, 'Oh, by the way, my daughter got knocked up out of wedlock?'"

"Are you serious right now?"

"Yes," he said, wide-eyed. "You mean to tell me you don't think it could have a negative effect on voters?"

Monica sputtered and scooted to the edge of the bed, putting distance between them. An image of Sarah Palin and her teenage daughter briefly flew through her mind. "No, actually. Your campaign wasn't the first thing that came to mind when thinking about a girl—who's like my own child—suddenly finding herself pregnant." She gave a laugh of disbelief. "I can't believe you're making this about you."

"I'm trying to look out for Chris too." His voice rose to meet hers.

"Right."

"Listen." An edge of defensiveness crept in. "I haven't worked this hard for it all to collapse because of Chloe forgetting to use her birth control."

Monica's mouth fell open. *Who is this man?*

"All I'm saying is that there are options other than having the baby, and that it would probably be in everyone's best interest. My success is Chris's success. Don't you all get that?"

She couldn't speak, her brain jumping into immediate moral judgment zone. The Morelands were their friends. Chloe was a surrogate daughter. How could Roman be so selfish?

The air was not only thick but polluted. Monica turned to her other side, facing away from him. She couldn't get any closer to the edge if she tried. Roman groaned, then the bed shifted with his weight. Monica heard him fluffing his pillow before finally everything settled. The room was soundless. But the adrenaline pumping through her veins was loud enough to keep her awake for hours.

TWENTY-NINE

CHLOE

July

The last time Chloe had gone to a Pirates game, she'd spent an hour giving herself Dutch braids and bedazzling the back of a McCutchen jersey with rhinestones. Today, she hiked maternity shorts over her swollen belly, the elastic band nearly reaching her bra. The underbelly style never seemed to stay put, so Chloe had opted for the ones with an extra foot of fabric at the top. They were ugly as hell, but she couldn't deny the comfort and sense of support the compression provided. Never did she imagine wearing such things—at least not at her age. Especially not while hanging out with a bunch of girls in midriffs and cutoffs.

They were pregaming at a friend's house in Mount Washington. From the upstairs window, Chloe could see an incredible view of downtown Pittsburgh, where the Ohio River met the Monongahela. Yellow bridges connected the banks like a grid of metal. She nestled into the couch cushions, switching hips when one side got sore. The baby kicked, and she laid a hand reflexively on her belly.

"Kamikazes!" someone shouted. "How many?"

Ava bounced a finger in the air, counting heads of everyone in the room. "Seven!" she called back to the voice in the kitchen, before quickly realizing her error. "Oh, whoops. Actually, six!" She gave Chloe a look and brought a palm to her forehead. "Sorry. I keep forgetting, even though…"

"Even though I can almost balance a cup on my stomach? Look, it's my new party trick." Chloe placed her red Solo cup on the ledge created by her pregnant belly then released her hands. "Ta-da!"

The girls laughed. It was easier to break the awkwardness with humor than let the real thoughts sour the fun. Chloe suspected they'd only invited her out of pity. That and to take advantage of her sober status—nothing beats a pregnant lady when you're looking for a designated driver.

Still, Chloe had been excited to get out of the house for a chance. Her shifts at the mall were getting more difficult—extended time standing meant her feet swelled and her ankles all but disappeared by the time she got home. Even now, she was dreading the walk from wherever they'd find a parking spot into PNC Park.

"Seven shots," a girl named Maggie said, carrying a tray of shot glasses and placing it on the coffee table in front of the couch. Everyone reached to grab one. Maggie extended a glass to Chloe.

"Oh," Chloe said, a bit startled. Did Maggie really think she was going to take a shot of vodka? "No, I—"

"Relax. It's just water." Maggie gave a laugh that indicated she was clearly already buzzed. "Just didn't want to leave you out."

She stepped back, completing the circle of friends. Sunburned hair spilled down her back, the glint of a belly-button ring sparkling just above the waistband of her shorts. Chloe missed her own belly button.

"Hail to Pitt on three!"

Everyone clinked glasses.

Chloe appreciated the gesture—Maggie and Ava, they all meant well—but the act only made her feel more out of place. Flinging back a shot of water felt silly. She did it anyway.

Her friends would all be returning to campus within the next month to start their sophomore year. By the time mid-term exams rolled around, Chloe could be in labor. The contrast made her head spin, almost as if she were partaking in the drinks right along with the rest of the group. Instead, she snuck off to the bathroom to pee for the third time in an hour and popped a Tums from the travel container she kept with her at all times. Her newest accessory—heartburn relief.

When she returned to the living room, a couple of people were gathered near a bowl of salsa, and Chloe swore she heard someone say "Preston," but the sentence dropped off the second she entered the room. She got it—teenage pregnancy was still taboo in many of her friend circles. She was the topic *du jour*. When girls wanted to spill some tea, it was Chloe and her pregnancy that satisfied the gossip seekers. It made Chloe feel even more divided—one part of her craving normalcy with friends, the other never wanting to leave the safety of home.

As though his ears were burning, a text from Preston came through just at that moment.

Test results?

He was referring to the glucose test Chloe had had earlier in the week, the one where she'd had to chug a neon-orange drink and get bloodwork to see if she had gestational diabetes. For as much as she wanted to navigate the pregnancy solo, Chloe had been keeping Preston up to date on her appointments. Still, she got a twinge every time he reached out. Sadness. Regret maybe.

Not yet. They said by Tuesday.

K.

She stared at the phone, trying to process how this person with whom she now shared such clipped communication was once the same person who knew about the mole below her bikini line.

Her phone buzzed again with another message.

I emailed my professors about the baby so they know in case I have to split mid-class. They're cool with it.

You don't have to do that.

You don't want me there?

Chloe bit her cheek. Did she? Having just her mom would be easier. Potentially less... dramatic.

I don't know.

I'd like to be there when my baby is born.

The water churned in her gut.

K.

"Ready to go?" a guy named Nick said to the room.

Chloe slid her phone into her crossbody purse.

"Who's driving?" someone else asked, followed quickly with a snicker and an elbow to Chloe's bicep. "Just kidding, Chlo. You know we still love ya."

She let them jostle her around, happy to still be included but already predicting her annoyance level would peak before the third inning. Being the only sober one in a group of college kids, on a sunny evening in July, at a major league baseball game no less? About as fun as it sounded, which was to say not in the least.

"Sure you don't want me to drive?" said one of the guys in a backwards baseball cap. "We don't want to take the wrong bridge."

"Women need men like fish need a bicycle," Ava snapped and gave his hat a slap, making it topple to the ground.

They made their way outside and piled into two cars. Chloe shimmied behind the wheel of Ava's Honda.

"Are you totally bored?" Ava whispered, sliding into the front seat.

"What? No, I'm fine."

"This can't be much fun."

"I don't have to drink to have fun, loser," Chloe chided.

But the truth was more than just alcohol. Chloe had felt herself fading from her friend group over the last seven months. As though the tiny human inside her ushered in a new set of priorities. A laundry list of responsibilities. And a flipped perspective on everything big and small. None of the things she used to think about seemed important anymore, none of her previous concerns relevant. Sometimes she didn't feel nineteen at all.

Throngs of fans were already flooding the stadium by the time they parked a few blocks away. While they waited for the light to change at a crosswalk, Chloe watched a line of people cross on the other side. Among them was a young family—husband, wife, and a little girl with pigtails held back with yellow-and-black ribbons. The mother had a shuffle Chloe instantly recognized, and when Chloe looked closer, she saw that, sure enough, the woman was pregnant.

"See?" Ava said, noticing the same thing and pointing. "You're not the only one."

And while Chloe nodded with a smile, the comparison missed the mark. That family was nothing like her. They had each other, and she had no one.

She absentmindedly ran a thumb across the heart tattoo on her inner wrist, a remnant of another life. Would Ava disappear once the baby came like so many of her mom's friends had? Chloe pictured a day when her child would ask about the little heart shape, and Chloe's response would be, *Oh, just something I did with a friend I used to have*. Could this pregnancy really alter her life to such a degree?

It could. And it made her sad for something she was already in the process of losing.

THIRTY

RACHEL

August

Rachel had to remind herself to slow her pace when walking next to Chloe. At nearly eight months along, Chloe had a noticeable waddle now. The two crossed the parking lot to the car after leaving Chloe's latest checkup.

"I swear this baby's going to be an acrobat," Chloe said. "Or a gymnast or something. I don't know how there's even any room left in there for it to move around."

Rachel chuckled. "You'd be surprised."

"Look at me," Chloe said, stopping mid-stride and opening her arms. "I'm massive."

"You're not."

"I am."

"You're all belly. You've only gained, what, fourteen pounds? That's nothing. Even the doctor said so. And besides, you've got youth on your side. You'll bounce right back."

Rachel remembered those days, the ones near the end of pregnancy where she couldn't get close enough to the table and regularly dropped food on her belly. There are hardly any words of comfort for someone who feels so out of control in their own body, so utterly done with being pregnant. But to her, Chloe looked beautiful. And despite the shock of the pregnancy, she'd come to love laying a hand on her daughter's growing bump and feeling her grandchild move inside.

Chloe collapsed into the passenger seat and pulled the seat belt all the way across to buckle. "It's like the baby's tap dancing on my bladder."

"Hang in there. Only six weeks to go. You're doing great."

The doctor had measured Chloe's belly, taken her blood pressure, and felt for the baby's position—head down today, to which the OB had given a satisfied thumbs up.

"I saw a TikTok this morning where a woman literally swelled like a balloon. I'm not joking—her ankles were the size of her thighs. Shit's fucked up."

"Chloe."

"Sorry, but it is. Pregnancy is no joke."

"It's one of the greatest miracles in life."

"Okay, Oprah."

Rachel gave her a look. "What I'm saying is that you're right, some women have it way worse, but we keep doing it because it's worth it."

"Guess I shouldn't complain."

Rachel thought back to one day not long before Savannah was born, when she'd burst into tears at her inability to tie her own shoes. "A little complaining is okay." She gave Chloe a wink.

Next to her, Chloe tapped away on her phone.

"Don't forget to text Preston," Rachel said.

"Okay."

"Tell him the baby's measuring six pounds already."

"Okay."

"And that your doctor wants to do another ultrasound, and—"

"Mom, I got it. I can handle my own conversation."

Rachel clamped her mouth shut. She was just trying to help. The long distance between Chloe and Preston wasn't exactly making the pregnancy easier, and she often wished her daughter had the same level of partner support Chris had given her.

When they pulled into the driveway, Chloe waddled into the house, Rachel following behind. Chloe dropped onto the couch with a groan. "How can one trip to the doctor make me feel like such a sloth?" She propped her feet on the ottoman and leaned back against the cushions.

Must be nice, Rachel thought but quickly erased the judgment before yelling up the stairs. "Jacob! We're leaving in ten minutes!" Their house was a revolving door—people in, people out, going from one thing to the next. Rachel couldn't recall the last time she'd napped on the couch in the middle of the day.

"Jacob!"

Chloe winced at the volume and pitch. She brought a hand to her ear. "Mom, seriously?"

"Sorry. You know how he has selective hearing. I have to remind him every other minute. Jacob!"

"Mom." This time her face screwed up, and she sucked in air with an audible *oooooh*.

"What is it?" Rachel asked.

"My stomach just got super tight."

"Probably Braxton Hicks. Not painful, just uncomfortable, right? Like cramps?"

Chloe nodded; took a sip from her Stanley.

"Yep, that's them. Trust me, you'll know real labor when it comes." There was no denying the real thing—having done it three times, Rachel could attest.

"Which of the eighty-five activities are you off to today?" Chloe asked.

Rachel put her hands on her hips. "Very funny. Jacob has a checkup, then straight to basketball."

"You don't have to go to every game, you know. You can drop them off. They'll survive if you're not there."

Rachel paused to consider a brief interpretation. Was this Chloe's way of asking her to stay? To hang out? Watching a show or scrolling their phones sounded nice, but Rachel had no time for that. Didn't Chloe get it? Well, she would soon enough. Give her another handful of years.

"I don't like to miss games," Rachel said because it was the truth. "And besides, it's not good to sit around all day." But then another idea came to mind. If Chloe wanted to spend time with her, she could join. "Why don't you come?"

"Too tired."

"You could practically walk. The school can't be much more than a mile. Maybe it would be good to get some fresh air and move a little."

Chloe blew out a laugh. "Yeah right. I haven't walked that far since I visited Monica's office, when I first found out I was pregnant."

Rachel's eyes pinged to Chloe like she was a bullseye, and Chloe's expression quickly went from carefree to panicked. Rachel's gaze narrowed. "You went to Monica's office?"

Chloe gaped. "What?" A curtain of red crawled up her neck.

"You said you visited Monica's office when you first found out you were pregnant."

"Oh, I... Wait, no... I'm getting mixed up." She gave a light-hearted laugh, but Rachel saw right through it. It was one of her motherhood superpowers, to sniff out dishonesty. Suddenly the room took on a foulness.

Rachel squared her shoulders. "Don't lie to me. I can tell when you're lying."

Chloe released a breath. "Fine. Yes, I went to talk to Monica."

"When?"

"When I was at school. Do you need an exact date? What I was wearing? I don't know—it was sometime in February."

Rachel was quiet for a moment. She felt the corners of her mouth pulling down, weighed, like the rest of her, by hurt realization. It came with a jab to the jugular. "You told Monica you were pregnant before you told us?"

Chloe shifted. "I was scared, okay? I didn't know what to do. She's always a good person to talk to."

"And I'm not?"

"You're not exactly as available as she is. Plus, I had a feeling you wouldn't react well."

Rachel faltered a step at that, like Chloe had plunged a knife into her lung. She took a gulp of air.

"Look, Mom," Chloe continued, "it's not a big deal. It was only like three weeks before I told you guys."

"Three weeks?" Rachel's eyes watered involuntarily, and like an automatic response, so did Chloe's. They were two emotional messes in a tension-filled standoff. And it was in that moment when Rachel understood that emotional pain hurt far worse than physical pain. "I can't believe you didn't come to me first." Her voice was small.

"Why are you always making things about you? I'm the one who's pregnant here. I'm the one who's about to have a baby and who can barely breathe and who gets random jolts of lightning crotch at odd hours of the day."

"And you don't think I know exactly how that feels?" Her volume rose. "That's exactly why I thought you'd have confided in me. I'm not some horrible mom, okay? We're a team. Or at least I thought we were."

Now it was Chloe's turn to recoil. "It doesn't have to be

some sort of competition between you and Monica, you know. Just because she knew first doesn't mean anything."

"But it does. You're not a mom yet. You don't get it." So many things Chloe couldn't possibly understand. How standing there in the living room, Rachel felt like she'd just been picked last for the team. Where had she gone wrong? Somewhere along the way, Chloe had let go of her grip, and when she'd needed a hand again, it was no longer Rachel's. She'd been replaced. And Chloe was blaming it on her.

Just then, Jacob came bounding down the stairs in his basketball shorts and jersey. "Ready!" he said, unknowing smile on his face. Neither of the women moved. He did a double take between his mom and sister. "Um, hello?"

"I'll meet you in the car," Rachel said more firmly than intended, and Jacob cowered from the room.

Rachel stared at her eldest daughter as though looking at a stranger. Who was this person she thought she knew so well? No longer a child, she now kept secrets from the one person who would give her life for Chloe's happiness?

Chloe returned the stare, and Rachel wondered what was going through her mind. The strain between the women was a coiled spring, ready to pop. And that's when the hurt began to morph into something else—resentment.

"Look," Chloe said, "I'm sorry if—"

"I have to go," Rachel cut her off. She took two steps toward the door, then paused and looked back over her shoulder at Chloe. "And here I thought I've been living my life for you guys all this time."

"Mom, I—"

But Rachel left before Chloe could finish.

Perhaps it was harsh. Perhaps it was unfair to say to someone already experiencing a roller coaster of emotion. Chloe was just a kid. But sometimes kids needed to hear the truth.

THIRTY-ONE

RACHEL

Rachel was still stewing the following day, and not even a Saturday morning with an extra cup of coffee could perk her up. It might have been the weekend—which meant no rushing off to work—but there were no days in which Rachel could afford to sit around doing nothing. Something always needed to be cleaned; someone always needed a ride.

She rinsed the breakfast dishes in the sink so absentmindedly, she didn't realize she'd grabbed the knife until the sharp sting of soap and water made her wince. A trickle of blood snaked down the drain. Rachel cursed under her breath, grabbed a paper towel, and pressed it to the cut. When she peeled it back to take a peek, she saw it was no bigger than a deep paper cut, but she still kicked herself for being distracted.

It was all Monica's fault.

Rachel struggled to process what she'd learned the day before. Chloe had gone to Monica first. Her daughter had sought advice, comfort, from another source—a source that wasn't her. And to add insult to injury, Monica had kept it from her. For three whole weeks. It might as well have been a year.

Rachel couldn't wrap her head around it. How could Monica have thought that was okay?

Despite all her attempts not to *go there*, the scene bullied its way into Rachel's head. Chloe crying in Monica's arms, Monica stroking her hair, a request for secrecy, and then a promise. She imagined the words coming out of Monica's mouth: *I won't tell your mom*. Did she feel guilty? Any guilt at all? Or was Monica not the friend Rachel had always thought she was?

"I'm running to the store. I'm out of one-inch nails," Chris called from the other room. "Need anything?"

"No," she hollered back. Their house was always in some state of remodel, some DIY project—the garage, the basement, the foyer bathroom—getting a facelift.

She heard the door shut and Chris's truck start. Jacob and Savannah had barely finished breakfast before bounding outside to meet their neighbor friends, and with Chloe at work at the mall until two, Rachel found herself in a rare position— alone. The quiet enveloped her like a plush blanket.

If only she could quiet her mind.

Rachel looked around. Crumbs littered the kitchen floor under the base cabinets, and somewhere upstairs, she knew there was an overflowing laundry basket that could use her attention. But the couch called to her, and so she reheated the remains of her coffee mug, and eased down onto the cushion with an exhale. Just a minute—she'd give herself just a minute to relax.

The doorbell made her jump mid-sip, and she nearly spilled coffee down her shirt. She got up, curious. Who would be ringing the doorbell on a Saturday morning?

As Rachel approached the entryway, she caught a glimpse of someone through the narrow windows flanking the door. A red-and-green strap of a handbag, slung over a shoulder. Gucci. She'd know that purse anywhere—it was Monica.

And instead of opening the door with a smile—or instead of

Monica coming in without even knocking, as she'd done for years—Rachel did something completely out of character. She hid.

Rachel darted from view, tucking herself around the corner. Her heart thumped in her chest. She held her breath, as though Monica could hear it through layers of drywall and insulation and siding. At the same time, a sense of panic washed over her, and Rachel questioned her own sanity. Why was she hiding from her best friend? She would have laughed at how ridiculous she looked, the absurdity of the situation, had she not been crippled with confusion.

Monica rang the bell again. Rachel imagined her cupping her hands and peering through the window, but didn't dare peek. She thanked God no one else was home, for surely one of the kids would have answered the door. There would have been no excuse for hiding with a house full of people who were none the wiser.

Monica knocked. Why wasn't she going away?

After another brutal few seconds, curiosity got the best of Rachel. She ever so slowly leaned her head out, just enough so that a single eyeball could see. Monica had stepped back from the door, perhaps resigned that no one was home. Her face wore a frown of disappointment, which gave Rachel a sense of vindication. *Good. You don't deserve to talk to me after what you did.*

But then Rachel's eyes were drawn to a bag in Monica's hand. A small gift bag, white with some sort of small, pink lettering. Her body burned. Another gift for Chloe. How dare Monica overstep *again*?

If Rachel had had any hesitation about not answering the door, it completely dissolved once she saw the present meant for her daughter. She whipped herself back around the corner, seething. Jealousy pecked at her insides, but Rachel wouldn't let herself accept it at face value. Jealousy was for people who were insecure. *She* was the one in the right here. Monica had been in the wrong.

Finally, after what felt like an hour, Rachel peeped at the door again. The stoop was empty, Monica gone.

Rachel approached the window to confirm, her feet feeling heavy, her limbs drained of energy. She wouldn't let herself feel guilty. And at the same time, she knew her toxic thoughts would destroy her if she didn't let them out. She needed her sounding board; she needed to talk to Chris when he got home.

In the meantime, Rachel plopped her mug into the microwave for the third time, then climbed the stairs to her bedroom and rage-folded a pile of laundry on her bed.

THIRTY-TWO

MONICA

When Monica returned home, she took the slice of carrot cake from the little white bag and put it in the fridge. It had been meant as a pick-me-up for Rachel. A token of comfort. It was no secret the pregnancy news had sent Rachel reeling, and Monica hadn't exactly been the best of friends lately. A little sugar high and reconnection was just what they needed. So, she'd been disappointed when she'd showed up ready to reclaim the closeness they'd somehow misplaced only to discover no one home. She'd considered hanging the bag on the doorknob but decided not to. That would be too easy.

She'd try again another day.

It had been months since they'd seen each other—not since before Rachel's curt **Can't, sorry** text message. Monica had sensed something then, and she'd given her friend time to cool off. But nothing had ever come between them before, and so she had no reason to think that this would end up being anything but a tiny blip in their timeline.

The truth was, Monica didn't feel quite like herself without the balance of Rachel. It was like the scale was off, too heavy on one side, too light on the other. Too... *something*. She was desperate to see Rachel, to put an end to this weirdness.

Only, the weekend whizzed by, and before she knew it, another work week was underway. Monica barely had time to come up for air let alone make an unscheduled visit to Rachel's house with a slice of cake. Instead, on Wednesday night, after putting the kids to bed, Monica opened the fridge door, stared at the container for a beat, then grabbed a fork and ate the cake, savoring the rich cream cheese frosting. Let something sit long enough and it's bound to get moldy.

THIRTY-THREE

RACHEL

THE TIMESTAMP ON HER EMAIL SAID SEVEN TWENTY-THREE a.m., but Rachel didn't see it until three in the afternoon when she finally opened her laptop. Chloe was always jagging her for not setting email up on her phone, but Rachel had enough frenzy in her life—she didn't need a string of little red notifications piling up on her phone too.

A tingling radiated from her chest when she saw the sender: Community College of Allegheny County. And then the subject line: *Congratulations!* It had been so long she'd assumed it was a rejection. Elation quickly morphed into something sharp. This wasn't the circumstances under which she'd expected to hear from the school. Chloe's pregnancy had all but thwarted her plans. A few months ago, this was all she'd ever wanted, but now it came with a bittersweet swirl in her belly. Still, her fingers couldn't click it open fast enough. The university logo centered against the red-and-white header.

Congratulations! It is with great pleasure that we write to inform you of your acceptance to the continuing education program.

Rachel's eyes glossed over. She fanned herself with an electric bill next to her laptop and tipped her head skyward to keep the tears at bay. If only...

She finished reading the personalized email, which detailed the program, graduation requirements, and remaining credits she'd need to complete the degree. None of this was new—she'd done thorough research and knew exactly the steps she'd need to take. But that was before a baby was in the picture—a baby that would be coming in a matter of weeks. There was no denying it now. Long gone were the weeks when Chloe's stomach looked like a washboard. Now, she carried a defined bump. Rachel remembered that stage, when she'd felt pretty and feminine. Before the beached whale phase kicked in. Pregnancy suited Chloe. She glowed in all senses of the word, despite her complaining.

Rachel blew out a long breath. Chris was somewhere in the house, and she needed another minute to process before she saw him. The email should go straight to the trash folder. That's what it was, after all. Garbage. A lost dream. Wishful thinking. But despite that clarity, she just couldn't hit delete. Maybe she'd keep it as a form of self-torture. Perhaps when Chloe's baby went to school, Rachel could too. Grandmother and granddaughter. But that would make Rachel—she counted in her head—fifty-nine at least. She swallowed a cry.

Chris's footsteps startled her, and Rachel moved to block his view of the computer.

"I've been meaning to ask," he said. "Has Chloe decided about Preston?" It was a topic they'd been tiptoeing around with their daughter—whether or not she wanted Preston in the delivery room. Chloe remained adamant about doing everything herself, much to Rachel's puzzlement. But with the due date approaching, Rachel had said she'd broach the subject again. It was meant to be part of their conversation the previous day—before things turned ugly.

"We didn't get that far."

"What's that supposed to mean?"

"We got in a bit of an argument."

"About Preston?"

"No, about Monica."

"Monica?"

Rachel exhaled, ready to tell the story. "Monica knew about the pregnancy before Chloe told us. Chloe went to her first. I guess she wasn't sure what she wanted to do initially and thought Monica was the only person she could talk to."

"Makes sense. I'm sure she was nervous as hell to tell us."

Rachel gawked. "No, it doesn't make sense. We're her parents."

"She told us eventually, didn't she? What's it matter?"

She coughed her disbelief; folded her arms across her chest. "Great. First Chloe and now you. I thought *someone* would be on my side."

"What's that?" Chris pointed at the laptop Rachel evidently was doing a poor job of shielding from view. She went to shut it quickly, but he reached out first and held the lid open.

"Hey!" she said.

But he was already reading with a perplexed expression. "What's this?"

"Haven't you ever heard of privacy?" She tried to put herself between him and the computer. It only made the situation appear more suspicious. The jig was up.

She moved aside, and Chris leaned in. It didn't take long for his eyes to grow. They didn't need to verbalize things to communicate with each other—she knew his silent language as much as he knew hers. And this reaction wasn't exactly one of positive enthusiasm. "You applied?"

Rachel's heart beat out of her chest. This wasn't how she'd wanted it to go. She'd imagined an acceptance letter followed by Chris spinning her in the air and later a champagne toast. It was fantastical perhaps, but she couldn't help her brain going to idealized places. Even if he didn't give her a twirl, he'd at least come around. But now? It was impossible. And in turn, his reaction was bound to match.

"Back in February," she admitted. "I was going to tell you."

"Were you?" His tone bordered on accusatory. "A little like the pot calling the kettle black, don't you think?"

"What's that supposed to mean?"

"You got all bent out of shape when you found out Monica had kept a secret from you. Meanwhile you were doing the same thing to me."

"I..." She didn't have a comeback, at least nothing that wasn't hypocritical.

Chris's lips pressed into a grimace. "We never keep secrets."

"Yes, I was. But then... Chloe."

He coughed an exhale. "I didn't realize you were serious about all this."

"Why wouldn't I be serious? I've been talking about it for years. It's like a piece of me is left unfinished. Plus, I could get a better job and—"

"Here we go. It's always about a better job."

"I'm talking about me, not you."

Chris shook his head. "Why do you always want more? Can't you just be happy with our life?"

Rachel's face burned. "I am happy with our life."

"Then why this?" He pointed to the screen like it disgusted him.

"Because it's something for *me*. Why can't you understand that? Everything I do around here is for other people. You, the kids. For once it would be nice to do something I want to do."

"Oh, forgive me for being so needy." He lifted his hands in defeat, then went to the sink and poured a glass of water.

Rachel waited for him to finish, using the seconds to collect her thoughts. What else could she say to make him see it from her perspective? It didn't matter. At the end of the day, it was a pointless conversation. They were arguing about something that was no longer possible.

"Before you go and get any pissier, you should know that it's not going to happen anyway."

He met her gaze. "What's that supposed to mean?"

"I can't go back to school now with the baby coming. Chloe will need me." Another person for her to take care of. Her soul sank a little. She dropped her eyes to the floor; hugged her arms across her body. "I'm stretched too fucking thin."

Chris rolled his head and rubbed the back of his neck. "I'm sorry. I don't want you to feel like that. You know I'm here to help."

"It's not the same."

"Listen. I get it, okay? It's just..."

"I really don't want to talk about it anymore."

"Well fine then." He stood straight, indignant, then turned and busied himself at the refrigerator.

Great.

They were arguing in circles, so far off in the fog they didn't know where it had even begun.

The conversation died there, with neither of their positions having any more to say. It was all out on the table but very much scattered like crumbs left behind.

Later, as the crickets conducted an orchestra outside her bedroom window, Rachel slid under the covers, unable to shake the chill from her bones despite the summer evening air trickling through a crack in the window frame that was never quite plumb.

Chris faced away from her, his breathing deep and regular. He hadn't even said goodnight. Bitterness swirled in her belly. How dare *he* be the one to hold a grudge? She was the one who'd been betrayed by her closest friend. She was the one whose dreams had popped like a balloon in a matter of seconds.

Rachel stared at the ceiling. Deep down, she questioned herself, put herself in the hot seat. Was her reaction justified? Maybe she was overreacting. Maybe she needed to take a step back and see things objectively.

But she simply couldn't.

The same feeling of being ganged up on threatened to choke the breath from her lungs. Chloe and Chris were taking Monica's side and it wasn't fair. Rachel felt utterly alone.

THIRTY-FOUR

MONICA

When the phone rang in her office, Monica had just returned from an egg retrieval, her last appointment of the day. The patient, in her mid-thirties but still unable to conceive after nearly eight years of trying, had had tears rolling down her face as she'd lain on the table. Her husband had stood by her head, their hands locked together. "You're doing great, baby," he'd repeated softly. The way he'd looked at his wife, a mix of awe, respect, and with a love that filled up the room, had made Monica's skin warm. After working with them for the good part of two years, she'd come to see the two as the quintessential couple. The definition of devotion. It was both beautiful and heart-wrenching to see, because no matter how hard she fought it, a grain of jealousy planted in the depths of her. In truth, the couple reminded her of Rachel and Chris.

The caller ID was blocked, which should have been her first clue not to answer. So many robocalls. If it was important, they'd leave a message. She didn't have time to get sucked into a scam, and she wasn't good at cutting people off mid-sentence let alone hanging up. So it was curious why she ended up answering, but on the third ring, she did just that.

"Hello?"

"Is this Dr. Cross?"

"Speaking." If people were looking to book appointments, they always called the office. Very few who had her cell number would address her as anything but "Monica," or sometimes even "Mrs. Nash," which made her lips pinch.

"This is John Garrison from the *Pittsburgh Post Gazette*. I'm calling to get a statement on the recent allegations brought against your husband."

Monica gaped. Hadn't they debunked the financial stuff? At least that's what Roman had told her. "I'm afraid I don't know what you're talking about."

"There have been accusations of inappropriate sexual behavior from a staff member on your husband's campaign."

"How did you get this number?"

"The woman reported unwanted text messages and sexual advances."

A pause. "That's impossible," she sputtered, but at the same time, her chest burst open into flames. The room was suddenly a hundred degrees.

"I'm afraid the allegations are real, ma'am."

Monica wanted to tell him not to call her ma'am. Ma'ams were women over sixty.

"We're working on a piece that will go live tomorrow. Do you have a comment?"

"Who is this *accuser?*" Monica asked, putting emphasis on the label. Dirty. Not to be believed. Just like Haverty.

"Unidentified. All we know is she's thirty-one."

Monica's ribs squeezed. A whole decade younger than her. "This is bullshit," Monica said. "My husband is an upstanding man and a good husband. He would never cross the line." She heard typing in the background.

"Okay, now what about—"

But she didn't let him finish before she hung up. She

shouldn't have said anything; should have kept her mouth shut. Her hands shook, and she clasped them together to lessen the trembling. It couldn't be true. Roman wouldn't do that to her. They might not have the strongest marriage on the planet, but he'd never violate such morals. Such workplace ethics.

Would he?

Monica slowed her breathing. She looked down to where her clutched hands sat in her lap. Her fingers intertwined just like the couple during the IVF procedure. Only, instead of her partner, a support system to bear the weight of such an onslaught, she was alone.

"Do you have something you want to tell me?" Monica had sat there for close to an hour, letting herself process the bombshell. Among the first things to do was call Roman. She'd actually been surprised he'd picked up at all.

"About what?" he asked, voice still cool and calm. Could he really be that naive? Surely he'd heard the news about to drop? Or did he just think he could smooth-talk his way out of this one too?

"I just got a call from a reporter asking me about allegations against you. A staffer is saying you sexually harassed her?" After she'd hung up with the reporter, she'd dived into Google, searching her husband's name. Nothing came up—not yet.

Roman sighed. "I'd hoped they wouldn't drag you into this. It's all false, Mon. Just like the money stuff. You know I wouldn't do those things."

"Wouldn't you?" An edge of emotion rose in her voice, one she didn't like.

"Of course not. Politics are nasty. People will say anything to bring someone down. Haverty is a bully."

She analyzed his voice for any sign of defense, but he never balked. "Who is this woman?"

"It must be Katy Fischer. She's the only one who fits the description."

Her heart plummeted. A name? So easily? "So there really is a thirty-one-year-old on your campaign?"

"Well, yes. Like I said. But she left weeks ago. Decided politics weren't her thing. I think she said she was going to work for a non-profit."

How could he be so calm when she felt like she had a lit fuse inching toward detonation? Monica tried to picture the woman—she gave her perfect highlighted hair and perky boobs—and imagine why someone would willingly attempt to destroy someone else's life. What was in it for her? Why make accusations if they weren't true?

Snapshots of the past year and a half flashed through Monica's mind like a film reel. The late-night dinners, the sudden disappearances, the questionable excuses. Constantly on his phone. But then there were also the spontaneous foot massages on a lazy Wednesday, the movie dates with the boys, a bouquet of flowers on their anniversary. Could Roman really do the things this woman claimed?

"Mon? You still there?"

She snapped back to the present. Her hand left a damp print on her desk. "So it's not true?" she said quietly.

"Not true."

He said the two words with such conviction, Monica felt she had no choice but to believe him.

When she didn't immediately reply, he added a coyness to his words. "Hey, c'mon. You're the most unshakable woman I know. Don't let these fools get to you."

She could only get out one word. "Okay."

"Alright. Well, I'm gonna get back to it, okay? I'd like to get home in time to tuck the boys in to bed. We can talk more tonight. Why don't I pick up dinner from that pasta place you like so much. Does that sound good?"

"Sure."

"Perfect." Then, just before saying goodbye, "Oh—what did you end up saying? I mean, to the reporter."

"I told him there was no way. That you're a... a good man."

"That's my girl. Okay, gotta go. Talk later." And he hung up.

Monica laid her phone down on the desk in slow motion. Everything rattled around her head, none of it coming together to make any sense. For ten long minutes she sat there, going through possibilities. Maybe this, maybe that. While her heart said one thing, her head said another. She'd dismissed the money rumors, but could she turn a blind eye to two accusations? It was enough to make the room spin.

Something hard caught in her throat. In a matter of hours—minutes?—an article would appear online. An article that would destroy her husband's reputation—maybe hers along with it. She felt dizzy. It was one thing to deal with marital issues privately, but it was another to have dirty laundry out in the open.

THIRTY-FIVE

RACHEL

To say things had been tense in the Moreland home would be an understatement. Everyone could feel it. The clipped dialogue, the coolness. Rachel tried to get over the resentment, but it was as though the emotion followed her like a hungry monster. A dark shadow she wished she could wave away. And despite feeling so alone, she wanted nothing more than to *be* alone. If no one was going to understand her position, then why torment herself in their company?

But then the next night, Jacob begged to watch a movie after dinner—with both Mommy *and* Daddy—and she'd had no choice but to be in the same room with the man who apparently harbored resentment about her dreams.

"Shit." Chris looked at his phone and sat up. It didn't sound like an I-forgot-to-record-the-Penguins-game shit, or an it's-going-to-rain-for-seven-days-straight shit. This one was grisly. Multi-layered, panic mushrooming on top of fear. Rachel knew her husband's inflection. She could detect something grave without having to see his face. But she did see his face, and even in the dark of the living room, she could tell it had drained of color.

"What is it?" she asked, immediately thinking of Chloe.

"Fuck," Chris said, and that's when Rachel knew it must be really bad. They didn't casually drop F-bombs in front of the kids.

"What?" she asked with more force.

He gave her a quick look and jerked his head, signaling for them to speak in the other room. Rachel followed him.

"What? What?" she said when they were out of earshot. She felt like a broken record. *Just tell me!*

Chris held out his phone, the screen aglow with an email. Rachel took it and read aloud.

"Wanted to give you the courtesy of seeing this before it goes live," she read. She scanned back to the top. The email had been sent to Roman, and Chris was cc'd. It was from an editor at the *Pittsburgh Post Gazette*. Below the intro was a news article, including a headline in bold. Rachel's mouth dropped open.

BREAKING: WEXFORD MAYORAL CANDIDATE ROMAN NASH ACCUSED OF INAPPROPRIATE RELATIONSHIP WITH STAFFER

"Oh shit," she said.

"Yeah," Chris said, nodding.

"On top of all that financial stuff? It can't be true. Not both, right? Haverty's really taking things too far. Right?" She looked at him like she was waiting for him to agree. Like Roman didn't already have strikes against him, even small, trivial ones, the hypothetical-but-feels-real kind.

Chris set his jaw. "Read it."

She returned to the screen with a knot in her stomach.

A 31-year-old female staffer for Roman Nash's mayoral campaign alleged Tuesday that the popular conservative candidate conducted multiple instances of sexual harassment

over the course of the last year. The staffer, who wishes to remain anonymous, said she was the victim of unwanted and unsolicited sexual contact, including inappropriate touching and text messaging. According to the affidavit obtained by the Wexford Police Department, Nash, 46, sent the woman messages on more than one occasion asking for nude pictures. In one such message, Nash is quoted as saying, given the chance, he would "make her feel things she'd never felt."

This latest accusation comes on the heels of other complaints about the former political science professor. Several sources claim Nash has misused campaign funds, even going as far as to allege embezzlement, all of which Nash vehemently denies. As of print time, no formal charges have been made, but authorities say they're investigating the claims.

Nash's political aspirations began over a year ago when he announced his candidacy for the mayor of Wexford, a city of 21,000 about a half hour north of Pittsburgh. He is the husband of Dr. Monica Cross, a prominent fertility specialist. They share two young sons.

Now, with less than three months until the election, the fate of Nash's campaign hangs in the balance. Despite the lack of formal charges, sources close to the complainant allege a civil suit could arise. Nash's campaign team has issued a statement saying they are taking the allegations seriously and are conducting an internal investigation. Nash himself has yet to comment publicly on the matter. The Wexford Police Department has confirmed they are investigating the complaint and are urging anyone with information related to the case to come forward. City officials and other political figures have called for Nash to drop out of the race in light of the accusations.

Rachel suddenly found it hard to breathe. Not only was this Chris's boss but her best friend's husband. The man who was supposed to be Monica's happily ever after. Rachel's heart shattered as if the article were talking about her own husband. It couldn't be true.

Or it could and she just didn't want to let herself accept that level of deceit.

"Oh my God," she said.

"I know. What the hell was he thinking?"

"Did you know about this?" Rachel asked, wide-eyed, an accusatory tone in her voice. "Mishandling funds is one thing, but sexual harassment...?"

"What? No! Don't you think I would have said something? C'mon, Rach, what do you take me for? Monica's my friend too, you know."

"So you never saw anything?"

"Nothing that was ever beyond the lines of how Roman always acts."

"What's that supposed to mean?"

"You know—Roman's suave. He's smooth." Chris slid a hand through the air like it was riding a wave. "But I never saw anything this glaring. I would have definitely told you."

Rachel studied his face, the way the surprise made a series of lines on his forehead, the same way they had at that dinner. He didn't know. They might have always suspected Roman of being a little... a little what? She couldn't quite put her finger on the right word. But there had never been any proof. Not until now.

"What the hell does this mean for me?" Chris muttered, and that's when Rachel's concern took on a whole new level. Chris's job depended on Roman's success. No campaign, no campaign manager position. "I was just securing a big donation from the Building and Trades Council. Fuck."

"Don't worry," she said even though she felt enough worry for the both of them. Instinct told her to swoop in with optimism. It's what they did—held each other up.

"Rach. Come on. Get serious. This is bad."

She winced. "It really is."

"But..." He made a pained face. "Are you really surprised?"

She gaped, but it was fake, and they both knew it. After a beat, she shrugged. "No."

Chris rubbed his brow. "Think Monica knows?"

Rachel couldn't form words. Her mouth had gone completely dry. She pictured Monica reading this same email, alone in her room after tucking the boys into bed. Roman was probably out somewhere like always. But no, the email hadn't been sent to Monica. Only Roman. Surely he wouldn't run to show her such a thing?

"I need to call her," Rachel said suddenly, the realization more urgent than anything in the world. Things had been under enormous strain, and the little monster wasn't far from her side, but this was too big. Everything else, all the feelings, had to pause. Rachel took a step toward the living room where she'd left her phone, but Chris stopped her.

"Wait, Rach. I don't know. What if they're fighting or something?"

He was right. Monica and Roman could be in the middle of a heated brawl. Maybe he had shown her to warn her. Then again, what if he'd stormed off and she was by herself needing someone to talk to. Rachel felt torn in half. "You don't think I should call?"

"Maybe give it a day. Would you want to discuss something so private the minute you found out?"

She considered this. Perhaps not. But then again, Monica was her go-to call for everything under the sun. How could she *not* call?

In the end, she took her husband's advice. She'd give it a day, keep an eye on the news to see if this was going to blow up or fade away. Then she'd call.

THIRTY-SIX

MONICA

THE ARTICLE HAD SIXTY-EIGHT COMMENTS AND NEARLY three dozen shares, and it was only six thirty in the morning. Monica read through fingers planted firmly over her eyes. When she got to the quote about the text messages, the crude things Roman had said, she lowered her hand to her mouth to keep anything from coming up.

It still felt so surreal. She couldn't imagine Roman doing these things. But then again, a darker part of her conscience could. And that alone made her ill.

Monica couldn't get herself to read the comments—they might very well undo her completely. All these people and their opinions. Readers were brazen behind a screen. She could never imagine they'd be so brutally honest in real life. There was no way public reaction would be anything but vicious. Monica wondered if she'd be sucked into it too. What did these allegations say about her as a wife?

Before she could get too far, the phone rang, all but sending her heart through her throat. Oh God, not another reporter. She couldn't handle it.

Rachel's name flashed across the screen, and Monica blinked in surprise.

When she answered, a spring of emotion caught in her throat. Their relationship had been off kilter for months, and even though she'd done her best to brush the reality away, hearing her friend's voice now brought everything into focus. She needed Rachel.

"Hi," they both said, like they were experimenting with the most basic of greetings.

"I'm guessing you just saw the news," Monica said. "I don't know what to believe."

"I know, right? It's like who is this guy? I didn't want to believe it either."

Monica stiffened. "Didn't? Wait, you aren't just seeing this?" The heat was building back again, and she fanned herself with a stack of papers from her desk. If it wasn't so hot outside, she'd open a window and stick her head out to catch a breeze.

"Oh. Well— I mean—not long. Just last night."

"How did you see this last night?"

"The reporter sent an email to Roman and Chris."

Monica's chest flared. Only one of their husbands had shown his wife, and it wasn't hers. "And you didn't call me?"

"I thought you might need a minute."

"I can't believe you heard about all this and didn't immediately call me. You could have given me a heads-up, then I wouldn't have been caught so off guard." It wasn't true exactly. The reporter had called first, told her the article's publication was imminent. But that was beside the point. Rachel didn't need to know this tiny detail.

"I'm sorry. I just thought—"

"Thanks a lot," Monica huffed.

"Mon, don't be angry with me. I'm calling to check on you. How... how are you?"

"How am I?"

"Well, yeah. This kind of news isn't exactly easy to digest."

She felt a sudden defensiveness rise. Like she wanted to protect something, herself perhaps. *This type of news*. What was Rachel implying? Monica straightened her back. "Maybe not if you think it's true. Why wouldn't I just disregard it? Being upset would indicate I believed it." Even she didn't buy what she was saying.

"Okay..." Rachel drawled.

Monica could tell her friend was treading lightly. She didn't care if she was snapping. Rachel deserved to be on the defense here.

"Anyways, I better go," Monica said. "I have a lot to think about."

"Okay, well if you want to talk, I'm here."

They'd usually work it out together. Hour-long phone calls or immediate drop bys were a no-brainer. Crises were always easier to bear with each other's support.

Not this time.

"I'm good. See ya." Monica disconnected and laid her head down on the pillow, where a little puddle of tears collected. What was happening? Why was her world falling apart? She replayed the conversation with Rachel, and each time her heart rate spiked. Her very best friend hadn't called her with incriminating information about Roman. Was it really because she was giving Monica space? Or was it something darker—did Rachel think the allegations were true all along?

THIRTY-SEVEN

RACHEL

At the game, Rachel could barely focus. Her hands delayed in clapping for baskets. Once she realized Jacob was on the court only when she heard another mom cheer his name. She was mentally back in the living room with Chloe the week before, hearing her daughter say the words, *I love Monica more than you*. Well, that's not exactly what Chloe had said, but that's how it felt. She imagined Chloe walking from campus to Monica's office months ago, scared and alone, seeking comfort and answers. She could have been the one to provide Chloe with that. She *should* have been the one to provide Chloe with that. The fact she wasn't both pained and enraged her. Once again—at least in the eyes of her daughter—Monica had come out on top. For Rachel, who'd given her life to the role of mom, there was no greater sorrow. She'd failed.

And then there was Monica. The friend she loved so much and yet had never felt more estranged from. The two things compounded, pressing her down. Their phone conversation earlier that day still lingered like a scab that pinches with every movement. The gymnasium felt like a sensory overload.

When Chris arrived after picking up Savannah from an

after-school function, Rachel watched as parents across the court leaned together, silent words slipping from corners of mouths. Eyes watching as Chris strode across the floor to meet her in the bleachers. He, it seemed, was guilty by association. Everyone touched by Roman Nash bore a dark mark, a scarlet letter, regardless if they had any fault of their own.

"How's he doing?" Chris asked, sitting and giving Rachel a quick peck on the cheek.

"What? Oh, Jacob. He's, uh, he's playing great."

"Nice." Chris removed his jacket. He wore his shirt and tie from work, something Rachel was still adjusting to.

"I'm afraid to ask about your workday," Rachel said.

Chris gave his head a quick tilt. "How do you think?"

"Yeah. I imagined so."

In less than twenty-four hours, Roman's campaign had entered a state of deterioration. A few of his bigger donors had pulled out, all but taking with them most of the public trust. For all Chris and Rachel knew, there was a strong chance he wouldn't even make the ballot. The stress showed on Chris's face—Rachel was sure some of the gray flecks in his stubbly beard hadn't been there a month ago.

"Do you guys have some sort of fallout plan?" she asked, leaving out the direst part of her question. The truth under the surface. Would Chris still have a job?

"I mean, we're doing all the positive PR we can. Roman hired a crisis management consultant, but I don't know, Rach. These rumors, they're not good, and they're not going away. I don't know what's worse in the public eye—the financial stuff or being unfaithful to your wife."

"Well, how is he at work? Like, does he *seem* guilty?"

"You know Roman. He's as confident as ever. I haven't seen one bead of sweat."

It made Rachel waver once again. She couldn't help going back and forth—guilty, not guilty. She'd talk to one person and her opinion would go this way. Then another person, and it would go that way. When Chris mentioned Roman's steadfastness, she concluded there was no way the allegations could be true. After all, how could someone carry all those secrets without breaking? But then she'd be slammed with doubt, all certainty flying out the window.

The idea that she might not really know someone who had been so much a part of their recent lives made her head—and heart—hurt.

"I would really love to *not* talk about it," Chris said, loosening the tie at his neck. Rachel patted his thigh, and a pang of guilt hit her like a barb. They wouldn't be involved in any of this if she hadn't pushed Chris to take the job. After the blowup at dinner all those months back, she'd thought Chris would quit on the spot. But he'd held on, she knew for one reason—her.

The buzzer sounded at the end of the quarter, and they clapped. The boys took the bench for a brief respite. Chris sighed and shook his head. The game resumed.

As if on cue, not seconds later, a steady murmur wafted. Right and left, people gave each other eyes, whispered and looked. Rachel followed their gazes. In walked Monica. She'd removed her white lab coat but still wore the smart pencil skirt and tucked-in blouse. Her blonde hair tousled to her shoulders. For the briefest moment, their eyes locked. Discomfort passed between them. The seat next to Rachel—Monica's usual seat, when she actually made it of course—remained open. But instead, Monica took a seat a few rows down.

"I can't believe she's standing by him," Rachel heard come from a woman to her left.

And then another voice: "She's so pretty, but there must be something wrong with her."

Rachel's insides lit up like a furnace. She wanted to tell these people to fuck off. Why was Monica the focus and not Roman? Monica hadn't done anything wrong, and she certainly didn't deserve to be treated like a pariah. Where were the rally cries, the women ready to swoop in and lift her up? Despite all her grievances, Rachel still felt a strong sense of loyalty for her inner circle.

Staring at the back of Monica's head, Rachel wanted nothing more than to vault the five rows that separated them and wrap her best friend in an embrace. Her feet danced, itching to move, but she remained seated. Something held her there, and she knew exactly what it was: Chloe's admission. Bitterness and jealousy kept her rooted in her seat. Those emotions, stronger and more powerful than any feelings of love and sympathy, prevented Rachel from doing what she knew was right. And so, she stayed put. Gagged. Defiant, yet tortured.

Chris looked back and forth between the women. "Why is she...? Aren't you...?" He pointed toward Monica.

"No," Rachel said. She pretended to watch the game, but it was hard to see through glassy eyes.

"I swear," Chris said, "women are so—"

"Drop it," she hissed. "I don't expect a *man* to understand." It was a comment that came with more quip than venom.

But she did. She did expect him to understand. He'd known Monica just as long, had been a third wheel to their friendship before any romance bloomed. It was far too complicated to dissect in the middle of a basketball game.

He tapped her knee, a silent, *I get it, but I don't get it and we can talk later if you want.* And in the moment, that's all she wanted from him.

THIRTY-EIGHT

MONICA

Monica hugged her stomach. Nothing she told herself eased the unrest. The minute she'd called Roman yesterday after getting the call from the reporter, he'd denied everything. And yet, judgment told her otherwise. Monica was a smart woman, so why did she feel so foolish? First the financial allegations and now this? Instinct told her there was a fire raging somewhere she didn't know about. If only she hadn't been asleep when he got home. Now, a whole day later, they still hadn't talked in person.

A bead of sweat rolled down her cleavage. Too many questions, too many scenarios. All of which were catastrophic from her position there on a hard wooden bleacher. She didn't have answers, only thought after darker thought. Everything pointed to the big unknown: Was Roman really a wolf in sheep's clothing?

Monica watched the game in a daze. She clapped when others clapped, not registering which team the applause was for. Coming here had been two-fold, a mix of mom-guilt and defiance. She'd never let anyone think she was broken.

It wasn't just the allegations on her mind but the fact that the seats to her immediate right and left remained open. She was isolated in a gymnasium full of people. Rachel sat five rows back. Mere feet separated them, yet it felt like an ocean. An ocean Rachel had formed when she hadn't called Monica before Roman's news broke, and one Monica had solidified when she'd chosen a seat so far from her best friend. She couldn't shake the feeling of being trapped, stuck in her own thoughts and fears. Her mind was a whirlwind of emotions, and she didn't know how to calm it down.

A hug would help. A shoulder to cry on. Rachel's shoulder.

A woman in a "basketball mom" T-shirt walked past and gave Monica a snide side-eye. Later, another, only the second look also contained pity. Monica didn't know which was worse. She was *that woman*—the woman she never thought she'd become.

At halftime, she texted Roman.

We need to talk again.

Yesterday's phone confrontation hadn't been enough. She had questions, and she wanted answers. Wanted to confront him face to face, read his body language. The article had been out for twelve hours, and she didn't even want to think how many comments there were now.

I'll be home around 9, he replied.

Three hours. That's how much time she had to prepare her interrogation.

THIRTY-NINE

RACHEL

Someone was calling her name, but Rachel was in such a daze it took her several seconds to realize.

"Rachel!" a woman's voice cried.

Rachel spun on her heels. Parents sprinkled the school parking lot, dispersing from the basketball game. Then a hand rose, a wave. It was Vienna Scott, mom to a little boy on the team and alpha woman in the parent circles. Her golden hair shimmered in the sun.

Rachel put on a smile and returned the wave. She was friendly enough with the other parents at school. PTO, youth sports, volunteer field trips. They were the kind for whom Rachel only knew the bare minimum—names, kid's ages, maybe where the spouse worked. She wouldn't have considered them great friends—more cordial acquaintances. Making adult friends required another level of dedication Rachel didn't possess, despite efforts to the contrary. Still, she'd be lying if she said she hadn't wanted to join their group outings to the water park, or so-and-so's themed birthday party. The girls' trip to Sonoma. For the longest time it had been just she and Monica, and that had sufficed. Until it hadn't. Until things got weird and Rachel felt companionless.

Rachel fell back from her family as Chris led the way to the car. Soon, Vienna was beside her.

Vienna lowered her voice. "We were just talking about Monica and the whole scandal. Do you think it's true? You guys are besties, right? You probably know everything that's going on."

Rachel flinched at the forwardness but also the use of Monica's name instead of Roman. Shouldn't he be the one linked to the word "scandal"?

"We're very close, yes."

"It must be awful."

Rachel nodded. Better sense told her to cut the conversation short right then and there. Not feed into the gossip mill any further. But Vienna looked at her with wide eyes, hungry for any morsel of information, and it gave Rachel a twisted feeling of power—she was the one Vienna wanted to talk to. She knew more than her, and Vienna was pawing at her to share. Rachel grew an inch taller. "It's been a bit of a shock for sure. But Monica doesn't believe any of it."

"Does that mean you do?" Vienna asked, a sly sneer on her face.

Rachel's heart leaped. Why had she said "Monica" instead of "I"? Rachel didn't believe the rumors either—did she?

"Well," Vienna said, "I mean, let's be honest, men don't cheat for no reason. Don't get me wrong—I'm not blaming Monica. It's just, you know... her job really pulls her away from her family, right? I've seen you take her boys to games and stuff. It must be hard on them with her working all the time."

Rachel followed along dumbly, still processing it all, but also in a state of partial agreement. She *did* take the boys to their sports often. And Lucas *had* expressed sadness to her about his mom not being there.

"Anyhoo," Vienna said, giving Rachel's arm a light tap, "nice bumping into you!"

Opposing sensations gripped her—one that made her feel low, the other high. It was Monica at the center of town chatter, and that gave Rachel a sharp taste in her mouth. Then again, Vienna had drawn her into her orbit in those brief minutes—a place she would have usually balked at, but with the absence of her best friend as of late had made her feel included.

As she made her way to the car, Rachel realized she'd been missing something for months now—the thrill and satisfaction of friendship. If Monica was falling away from her, where would she find a replacement?

FORTY

MONICA

Logan needed extra cuddles, so Monica was lying on the dinosaur-covered twin bed when Roman finally got home. She tried to sneak from the room, but each time, Logan's eyes flew open and he pulled her back down next to him. After another ten minutes, when his breathing deepened and the clasp of his fingers finally loosened around her arm, Monica slid out and tiptoed away. She found Roman in the den with a short glass of clear liquid in hand. Something told her it wasn't water.

"Is that vodka?" she asked, unable to help her accusatory tone.

"It's been a day, okay?"

"I guess so. But not even a mixer?" As though a splash of Sprite would make it all better. But it wasn't time for that discussion. One thing at a time. Adultery took precedence.

Roman sipped and sucked air through his teeth. His Adam's apple bobbed as he swallowed. Monica put a hand on her hip, waiting for him to talk. Surely he must know how she felt, whether the accusations were true or not? Why wasn't he in immediate defense mode? Why wasn't he assuring her everything was fine? *Don't believe it. We're solid. I love you and only you.*

But he said not a word, simply crossed his legs and leaned back into the leather armchair.

Unable to wait any longer, Monica squared her shoulders and planted her feet. "Don't you have anything to say to me?"

"About what?"

"Don't play dumb, Roman. It's been all over the news today."

He rolled his head. "Monica, I told you it's all propaganda. The staffer... They're trying to frame me for something I didn't do."

"So you're telling me it's not true, just like before?"

"That's exactly what I'm telling you."

Her pulse pounded. She shifted in place. "You have to understand how it sounds to me. It hasn't been just one allegation but several."

"What are you saying—you don't believe me? Have I ever given you reason not to trust me?"

The late nights, the wandering eyes. The smooth-as-butter way about him she'd once found irresistible. Everything came flooding back. But could he lie right to her face? Could he sit here and play her as a fool? She started to doubt herself again. Maybe it was all in her head. Maybe she was going crazy.

Monica took a step forward. "I'm saying it's hard to drown out the noise. Everyone's looking at me differently. People are whispering."

He put on a phony frown. "Oh, I'm so sorry you had to deal with grown-ups whispering at a kid's basketball game. How about me, huh? Think it's been easy for me?"

"Well maybe you should be more careful with things you say and do." Her voice climbed, and she hoped they wouldn't wake the boys.

Roman stood and closed the space between them, his face inches from hers. She could smell the alcohol on his breath.

"I don't have anything to hide. And trust me, if I wanted to sleep with someone else, I could." He walked away, taking the vodka with him.

Monica's mouth dropped open as she watched him leave. Something inside her cracked then, as though the very foundations she'd placed her life on were no longer solid but instead made of quicksand. This family she'd built, this marriage—was it all a sham?

An imaginary red flag waved for her attention. *Hello? Don't you see me?* But she kept falling back on what she wanted to believe, what she wanted to be real. She'd pressed Roman, and he hadn't budged—and she didn't know how to interpret that. It hadn't given her much reassurance. And with such a resolve, Monica wondered if she'd ever know the truth.

FORTY-ONE

RACHEL

"Let's talk."

There it was. Chris put a hand on the edge of the bed where he sat. Rachel joined him, collapsing as though her body-weight had doubled. Seeing Monica in person for the first time and not even speaking to her—felt like a lead ball tied to her foot, pulling her down to the seabed. She wasn't good at hiding her emotions, and for that reason, Chris could see them written all over her face.

"Whatever's going on with you and Monica needs fixing," he said.

Rachel sighed. "It's complicated."

"You guys have been best friends for twenty years. I mean, hello, you're Rachel and Monica. You're a duo. Your reruns are still on TV every day."

She smiled a little at that, but it wasn't enough to lift her drowning spirits.

"Female friendships aren't like guys'. There's so many layers. So many..."

"Big feelings."

"Big feelings."

"But it has to be something you two can work out, right?"

Rachel considered it. She couldn't imagine their connection severing over a water bottle and a care package. It was Chloe's trust that had pierced her deeper—that her daughter had turned elsewhere in her darkest time, and that Monica hadn't told her. Her eyeballs hurt. She pressed stiff fingers against them.

"I've been thinking," Chris continued.

Rachel pressed harder. "Oh dear."

"About something else."

"Good."

"About you going back to school. I think you should do it."

Rachel dropped her hands. Her head flew up. "You what?"

Chris gave a soft smile. He grabbed both her hands. "I was a dick earlier. It was selfish. You deserve to do things for yourself too. I know how much you want this."

"But the baby."

"We'll make it work."

She shrugged. "I don't know. It seems too impossible now."

"Well, it's not like you'd be going back full-time or anything. A class here and there will be okay, right?"

Rachel looked away, considering. Was it feasible? She'd reluctantly tucked that dream back in the drawer. And given what Chloe had said—about Rachel always making things about her—the decision to finish school certainly fell into the selfish category.

"I can't," she said. "There's just too much going on at home. And Chloe will need a lot of help with the baby."

Chris put his hands on her face, forcing her to make eye contact. "Rachel. You can be a good mom and still put yourself first sometimes. The kids will be fine."

She turned it over in her mind once more. The pros and cons pulled like a yo-yo. "I'll have to think about it."

"Good enough for me," he said, pulling her in for a kiss. She let him linger at her lips before he slipped a hand up the back of her shirt and unclasped her bra.

"The kids…" she said.

"Are watching a movie." He trailed his mouth down her neck.

With so much on her mind, a brief escape would be heaven. So she fell back onto the bed and didn't think about anything else.

FORTY-TWO

RACHEL

September

The up and down was making Rachel feel unbalanced even though both her feet were on level pavement.

"Curb walking encourages the baby to move lower," Chloe said, one foot stepping up, the other on the road. Up, down, up, down. "I saw it on TikTok."

"What happened to good old-fashioned castor oil?"

"Ew, Mom, no. That's so not a thing."

Since when? Rachel thought. Had so much changed in the nine years since Jacob's birth? Chloe got the majority of her birthing information from social media. Lamaze classes via the world wide web.

"Maybe those tacos will help," Chris said, hovering close enough to catch Chloe should she trip. "I'm pretty sure you used an entire bottle of hot sauce."

"Trust me, my esophagus knows. But I want this baby out."

"You technically still have another week," Rachel offered, even though she knew the feeling—anything after thirty-five weeks might as well have been fifty.

They circled the block, Chloe bumping along on the curb, until they made it back to the house. The little kids begged to watch the new live-action Disney remake, and for once, they had no activities preventing them from settling in for a nice family night.

Chloe curled against the arm of the couch. The opening song filled the room. Moments later, she brought a hand to her belly. "Ooooh. That one felt different."

Her father pounced. "Different how?"

"Stronger."

Though Chris would never have admitted it, Rachel could tell he'd been a nervous wreck the last few weeks, scrutinizing Chloe's movements, peppering her with anxious questions. It was as though their daughter had reverted to a toddler, one he was in charge of keeping safe.

"Probably more Braxton Hicks," Rachel said from the other end of the couch.

Chloe shook her head. "Uh-uh. It didn't feel like that."

Rachel and Chris met eyes; exchanged a silent look: *Is this it?*

They waited.

Less than five minutes later, Chloe gripped the throw blanket. "There's another one."

Rachel glanced at her phone, feeling a small uptick in her own heart rate. "That was quick. The Braxton Hicks were never that close together, were they?"

"No. And they definitely weren't this strong. Ow!" Chloe winced, and Chris was at her side, a tentative hand to her back.

"Let's time them for a bit," Rachel said, trying to stay calm. "We don't need to rush in. First babies take a while. And you don't want to get sent home for false labor—I did that twice with your sister."

They agreed to stay put and monitor the contractions through the rest of the movie, but before the two hours were up,

Rachel was already calling the neighbor to come watch Savannah and Jacob, and Chris was racing upstairs to grab Chloe's hospital bag.

There was no doubt about it—these were real contractions. The curb walking had worked. It was go-time.

Rachel tossed on a jacket, while Chloe perched on the edge of a bench near the door typing something on her phone.

"Did you text Preston?" Rachel asked, yanking her own phone charger from the wall and tossing it in her purse. What else did she need? How long would they be there? A mild frenzy whipped up in her, and she took a deep inhale to settle it down.

"He's on his way."

"It's late to be starting such a long drive."

"Mom, he'll survive," Chloe said. "Don't forget, I'm the one having a baby."

Rachel pictured Preston rushing out the door to get there from Ann Arbor in time. The image filled her with nervous energy. She couldn't imagine not having Chris at her side when each of their children were born. The fact that Preston was coming at all was something only recently solidified.

Chloe hunched forward, holding on to the banister by the front door. "Are you coming?"

"Sorry! Coming!" Why was she fluffing pillows at a time like this? Rachel helped Chloe up by the arm, and just as they opened the door, the neighbor was hurrying up the walkway.

"Baby time!" Rachel said. "Thank you so much."

And then they were gone, Chris driving fifteen over the speed limit all the way to the hospital.

"Breathe, honey," Rachel coached next to Chloe in the back seat. They held hands, something they hadn't done for years but felt as familiar as yesterday. There in the car, Chloe was a kid again, looking to Rachel for reassurance. And Rachel returned it with gentle strokes of the arm. *It's okay. I won't let anything bad happen to you.*

When they arrived, Chris dropped the women off at the revolving door. They didn't have to say a word to the desk attendant before he quickly took Chloe's name and ushered her into triage.

There, a kind nurse checked Chloe's dilation. "You're at three centimeters."

"That's it?" Chloe cried.

It's what Rachel had been worried about. The slowness. "Three's great. You're doing great," Rachel assured her.

The nurse clicked away on her computer. "Let's get you admitted and up to delivery."

Watching her daughter labor was an out-of-body experience. Rachel felt as though the pain were transmitting from Chloe's body to her own. She'd do anything to take it away. Only she couldn't. This was birth. This was what had to happen. More than once, Rachel prayed something—someone—would snap their fingers and it would all be over. *Bring a healthy baby into the world, but please, please relieve my daughter's anguish.*

"I can't do it," Chloe moaned. It was midnight, and Rachel didn't need to hear the words to know her daughter was exhausted.

Rachel gripped Chloe's hand so their sweaty palms suction-cupped together. "Yes, you can. You're doing it."

The arrangement was for Rachel and Preston to be Chloe's two support people in the delivery room. But Preston was still over an hour out, so for now, Rachel alone offered words of encouragement.

Chloe writhed. "Where is the epidural? What's taking so long?"

"The anesthesiologist is with another patient," the nurse said. "He'll be here any minute."

Tears rolled down Chloe's cheeks. "Please make it stop," she cried.

Yes, please. Please.

But Rachel didn't want to let her own fear show. She had to be the calm one. And so she laid a cool washcloth on Chloe's head. "Keep breathing."

After minutes that were days, the anesthesiologist arrived and carefully placed the catheter in Chloe's back. Relief came almost immediately, Chloe's forehead relaxing. Rachel, in turn, did the same. For the first time since they'd arrived, she felt like she could take a full breath.

"Can you feel anything?" the anesthesiologist asked, checking the monitor.

"Just pressure. Nothing sharp."

"Good."

"Now it's time to rest," Rachel said, brushing the hair from Chloe's forehead. "Let your body do the work."

Chloe's body shook, the effect of skyrocketing hormones and the medicine pumping around her spine. Rachel draped another blanket over her, then sat back in a chair and watched as Chloe's eyelids fell. Her mind traveled back to the first time she'd lain in a hospital bed about to give birth. The swirl of emotions. The support waiting down the hall.

Monica.

The thought of her friend brought a stiffness to Rachel's jaw. She'd always thought she'd experience this with Monica by her side. Now she didn't even feel the urge to text Monica to let her know the baby was on its way. That alone sent a pang deep in her core.

Sometime later, the doctor returned, and with a gentle tap to Chloe's leg, said, "Going to check you again."

Chloe opened her eyes, groggy. "How long was I asleep?"

"Over an hour. I'm glad." As much as Rachel would have loved to catch some sleep too, she'd been unable. Too much adrenaline. If she closed her eyes, she might miss something, and what if Chloe needed her all of a sudden? Now, Rachel's eyes stung from being open far too long.

The doctor plunged her fingers under the blanket where Chloe had tented her legs. Chloe sucked in a sharp breath.

"I know, sorry," the doctor said. Then, "Yep, you're about nine. Almost fully effaced. Things are moving along pretty fast. Good for you!" She withdrew her hand, snapped off her glove, and strode away with a nod to the nurse. "I'll be back."

Rachel gave a little clap, but Chloe shuddered. "I'm scared."

"We're going to turn down the epidural a bit so you can start feeling things," the nurse said.

Chloe's head rattled. "But I don't want to feel anything."

"You have to feel a little or else you won't know when to push. Trust me, this will help get baby out. Try to stay relaxed. You've got one centimeter to go, but I think it will be quick."

"She's right," Rachel added. "You're so close, Chlo."

The door opened. But it wasn't the doctor who entered. Instead, Preston tentatively crossed the room like a nervous fish out of water—probably because that's exactly what he was. His bloodshot eyes looked like he'd been straining to focus on the road in the dark. A backwards baseball cap covered his dirty blonde hair.

"Hi," he said to the room as a whole. He shifted nervously a few feet from the bed, and Rachel couldn't help but feel a little bad for how overwhelmed he must be.

"You made it just in time," she said. "Here." She moved out of the way so Preston could take her spot next to Chloe. When she stepped back, she took in the two of them, both so young, but about to experience the greatest blessing of their lives.

Chloe went to speak but was seized by a contraction and

clamped her eyes shut. She pushed out a long breath through her teeth.

"You feel that one?" the nurse said, while Rachel continued in her soothing voice, "That's it. Breathe it away."

When it tapered, Chloe opened her eyes.

"Hi," Preston said again.

"Hey."

"How are you?"

Oh, Preston. It was maybe the dumbest question ever, but Rachel couldn't fault him. This whole experience wasn't only unpredicted but alien—Rachel could attest first-hand.

"I, uh... brought you some flowers." He held a pink-and-yellow bouquet. Before Chloe could thank him, a contraction surged again. Watching the monitor, they were almost back-to-back now, never really receding fully.

"I'll put them over here," Rachel said, taking the bouquet and appreciating the sweet gesture for her girl.

"Okay," Preston said. He looked around anxiously then placed a clumsy hand on Chloe's shoulder. Her eyes closed again.

Then just as suddenly, as if the lights went on, her eyes snapped open. "Something's different," she said, alarm in her voice. "I feel like... like..."

"Hang on," the nurse said, coming again to the foot of the bed. "Let me see." She checked Chloe once more, and then, with a smile: "Yep. You're ten. Let me call the doctor."

Chloe's head fell back, and two tears slid down her temples. She moaned.

Rachel felt like she was about to jump out of her skin. This was really happening. Now. Her grandchild would be born imminently. "You're doing so great, sweetheart," she said.

Preston, still big-eyed and with a slightly ill complexion, quietly echoed, "Yeah, you're doing great."

The doctor flew in, slipped her arms into a sterile gown, and pulled a rolling stool to the base of the bed. "Alright, Chloe. I'm going to have you scoot down a little, okay? Good. Feet right in here. Perfect. Now when you feel like you want to push, you're going to take a deep breath, hold it, and bear down while we count to ten."

"I don't want to poop on the table," she said to Rachel.

"Trust me," the nurse interjected, "it happens more than you think. Don't worry."

Chloe bared her teeth and pushed.

"Great," the doctor said. "Keep going. That's it. Nine and ten. Good."

Rachel held her breath through the whole contraction. It rose and fell. Everyone paused. Seconds later, the doctor, watching the monitor, gave Chloe a small dip of the head, a silent go ahead. With Rachel on one side and Preston on the other, Chloe sucked in a gulp of air and pushed again. The two held back her legs while the nurse counted a slow march to ten.

"Very good," the doctor said when Chloe released the air in a whoosh. "That was perfect, Chloe. Baby's already coming down. I'm not a betting woman, but if I had to, I'd say baby will be here within the next three pushes."

Rachel let out a little squeal and bit her lip, but Chloe was all focus.

"Okay, here we go," the doctor said when the next contraction hit. "Legs back, chin to chest, every ounce of you pushing. Nice, Chloe! Keep going, keep going, keep going. Excellent."

Rachel peeked down between Chloe's legs. She could see the top of the baby's head making its way down. Dark hair covered its head. A smile of amazement stretched across Rachel's face.

They released. Chloe panted. "It hurts," she cried.

"You're so close," everyone said in unison.

The doctor adjusted her mask. "Let's get baby out on the next push, what do you say?"

"Really?" Chloe's lip trembled.

"It's up to you. Give it everything you've got."

And then they started again. "One, two, three," the nurse counted. "Head's almost out, Chloe. Keep pushing!"

The tears flowed then, Rachel completely overtaken by amazement. She'd had three babies of her own, but this perspective—it took her breath away.

"Slow now," the doctor said, standing and reaching between Chloe's legs. "One shoulder, and two shoulders. And... here's your baby." She pulled the infant up and onto Chloe's chest, where the nurse promptly wiped away the goo and slime of birth. It happened at what felt like the speed of light, and Rachel gasped, hands shaking as she brought them to her mouth.

"Oh my God," Chloe said over and over. Her breath hitched. Rachel looked on through a screen of tears. She'd done it—Chloe had given birth.

"It's a girl," the nurse said. "She's beautiful."

"A girl," Chloe and Rachel cried simultaneously. The baby shrieked from the assault of birth, and Chloe gave her gentle shushing.

"Congratulations. Does she have a name?" the nurse asked.

Rachel turned to Chloe with bated breath. The anticipation had killed her for months, but Chloe had been adamant to keep the name a secret.

"Laina," Chloe said. "It means 'little rock.'"

Laina. What a perfect name for the person who would hold a solid, strong place in her daughter's life. Rachel wasn't the mushy type, but she couldn't deny the name felt symbolic.

Laina faced away from Rachel, but Rachel stroked her little head. "Look at all this hair!" she exclaimed. It took Rachel by surprise, her own children mostly bald at birth. "It's so dark!"

The color must have come from...

But no. Preston's was the color of a sandy beach, Chloe's

only a shade or two darker. Nothing like the raven hue before her.

There was still frenzy in the room. The doctor between Chloe's legs. The nurse sucking the baby's nose and mouth with a bulb syringe. Hands everywhere. Rachel blinked, high on dopamine and yet utterly spent. A crash of sensations.

Inches away, Chloe whimpered. She stared into the face of her newborn. Tears fell from her eyes, and Rachel reached out a hand to wipe them away. "Oh, honey," she said. "It's okay. She's here. You did it."

But Chloe didn't meet her with a smile of relief. The tears weren't tears of joy. Rachel quickly realized they were something else. A different emotion etched across Chloe's face.

"What is it, sweetheart?" Rachel asked, her stomach taking a sudden drop. Her gaze moved from Chloe to Laina. Rachel scanned the infant. Was there something wrong? Was the baby okay?

Two eyes. One button nose. Rosebud lips. A tiny chin. Everything exactly as it should be.

She looked closer. The hair, a surprise for sure. But then it clicked. Something just below the hairline. Ears, pink and covered with peach fuzz. But something unique too. Something Rachel instantly recognized because she'd seen it before. The way the lobes attached to the sides of the face. Slanted and narrow, not the fatty drops of skin like her own.

They were Logan's ears. Logan's and Roman's. And now this baby.

Rachel's pulse took off in a sprint. The hair might have been the first clue, but the ears reinforced it. And now those traits—two of many features that made one of the most adorable babies Rachel had ever laid eyes on—added up to a shocking possibility.

Rachel looked to Chloe then back to Laina like she was trying to put confusing pieces together. Trying to make them fit when they simply refused to snap together. Nothing made sense. It was like she was staring at baby Logan, the resemblance uncanny. But that was impossible.

Wasn't it?

Again, she returned her gaze to Chloe, whose face by then had all but crumpled. "Chloe?" she squeaked.

Preston looked between the women like a lost puppy, and finally, Chloe turned to him. With trembling lips and a minutes-old newborn in her arms, she spoke three words that made Rachel's world stop.

"She's not yours."

FORTY-THREE

CHLOE

Nine months ago

When her skin began to prickle and itch, she knew she'd had enough sun. After rotating—back to front, front to back—for the majority of the afternoon, Chloe sat up and pulled the earbuds from her ears.

"Well, hello, Sleeping Beauty," her dad said, which made Chloe roll her eyes. She was still half asleep, drowsy from both a long midday nap and the effects of the sun. Down at the water line, the younger kids played in the surf. Chloe glanced along the line of adults sitting in a row of beach chairs, drinks in hand. This family vacation might not have topped her list of things to do on winter break, but it had proved a decent distraction from Preston. Her parents had even let her have a drink or two. Each time the alcohol had hit her bloodstream, it was like a mini escape from reality. Time healed all wounds. Well, so did liquor.

"I'm fried," Chloe said, pressing the skin on her arms, watching a white spot appear and disappear. She longed for a cool shower and air conditioning. "I'm heading back to the house. Want me to take anything?"

Rachel handed her a bag stuffed with sand toys and some wet towels, telling Chloe to hang them up to dry. "I'm sure we won't be too much longer."

Chloe pulled a loose shirt on over her bathing suit and ambled the quarter mile back to the house, switching arms to carry the towels that were heavy with soaked-up water. She replaced her earbuds, listening to the latest Taylor Swift album on repeat.

At the house, the cool inside air was a welcome reprieve from the heat. Chloe stripped off her bikini, got in the shower, and let the water run over her skin. When she emerged, the tan lines were more defined than she'd expected, and she scolded herself for too little sunscreen and shade. After donning a cami, light sweater, and cut-off jean shorts, Chloe was clean and ready to spend the rest of the evening in dry mode.

Just as she was getting ready to take a book to the seersucker couch, the door opened. *That was fast*, she thought, surprised the rest of the crew were back already.

But it wasn't the rest of the crew, only Roman. As he came through the door with a bag in hand and striped towel over his bare shoulder, he pushed his sunglasses onto his head.

"Hey," he said. "I had my dose of sun for the day."

Chloe made a sound of acknowledgment then turned back to her book.

Roman unloaded his things in the entryway, dropping a travel cooler on the counter and pulling any wet things from the bag. Chloe watched from the corner of her eye. When he bent over, she saw the muscles stacked up his back like a ladder. He was lean, not bulky, but still toned—more so than her own father, who had a softness to his build, an overall burly appearance. Roman's skin always looked so perfect, with his mysterious undertone and clean-shaven smoothness. His good looks had struck Chloe since she was old enough to notice men, and it had been something to be careful of, lest she let her girlhood thoughts run away from her and find herself blushing in front of him. Over the last year or so, she'd picked up on an increased flirtiness from Roman, something that felt both weird and gratifying. She couldn't put it into words really. And regardless of any thrill she got from it, she quickly remembered who the man was on the other end of the attention.

Roman crossed in front of her, stretched, and plopped onto the couch, inches from where she sat, legs curled up to the side. He reached a hand out and swatted at her hair. "Look at you, all fresh and clean."

She blushed.

Roman scooted close enough that Chloe drew her legs down, giving him room. She stared at her book, pretending not to notice—or care. Was she inviting this? A warmth overtook her, a beating deep in her lower half.

"I know you probably don't want to hear this," Roman said, "but there are a lot of fish in the sea."

"I know," she said, not wanting to appear still hung up on Preston. She was too mature for that. She was *so* over him.

"I just mean, you're so pretty, I'm sure the guys will be all over you."

"I don't know about that."

"Well, it's a good thing I'm not in college anymore."

Chloe's belly fluttered.

"You know," Roman said, "I've always thought you were most beautiful with no makeup on."

"Yeah right," Chloe said, feeling the heat in her face stretch down her neck.

"It's true. And that little mole of yours, right there. No, the other side." He turned her by the chin then tapped on a tiny mole under her eye.

Now their faces were aligned, and despite Chloe's every

effort to keep her eyes downcast, she couldn't fight the urge to meet his gaze. When their eyes locked, she held herself there for a second, then looked away. He brought her face back. What was he saying?

She knew exactly what he was saying. Roman had always been the flirty type, but it was harmless. This was *Roman*. Monica's husband. Monica, who was like a second mom, who'd been in the waiting room when Chloe was born, attended her preschool graduation, helped do her hair for junior prom. An aunt of sorts. And if Monica was an aunt, did that make Roman an uncle? A pulse throbbed between Chloe's legs, and she was at once mortified and intrigued.

"You don't have to be scared," he said.

Her heart beat out of her chest. She was scared. Scared of what was happening, scared of the thoughts spinning at dizzying speed. Scared that at any moment her parents could walk through the door. He fingered a piece of hair near her face. She could smell the salt water and sunscreen on his skin.

Chloe recoiled. "I should probably—"

"It's okay. Don't worry." He placed a hand on her thigh. "God, you're so pretty."

The flattery hit different than it did coming from Preston. This felt more intense. More dangerous. Like a shot of dopamine and the blur of one too many margaritas.

The flirting made her feel alive, his compliments a confidence boost. Here was a man who thought she was the full package. Who needed an immature college boy?

But the feeling also made her skin crawl. Left her with an excess of saliva and the desire to spit. The thoughts were wrong. She shouldn't find any pleasure in them.

Their noses were inches apart. She should scoot back—put more distance between them. They shouldn't be sitting so close.

But she didn't move. And perhaps it was that alone—the fact that she stayed—which gave Roman permission to cup her face and pull it to his. When their lips met, Chloe felt like she was in a dream. No way she could be kissing Roman. *Roman!*

His lips were soft, the pressure gentle. It lasted only a few seconds, then they were staring at each other again, faces flushed. Chloe's heart rested at the base of her throat.

"I've been wanting to do that," Roman said, quickly adding, "Recently, I mean. I feel like you get me. Like I can trust you."

She gave a polite smile; nervously frayed the hem of her shorts. Chloe could see he was breathing hard too and felt glad it wasn't just her.

"You know, that boyfriend of yours was an idiot. You deserve better." He leaned in, bringing their lips together again. Only this time with an urgency that made Chloe's eyes briefly fly open.

Roman pressed his body against hers. She felt his strong torso through her sweater. Before she knew it, he'd scooted her down flat on the couch, coming to rest on top of her.

"Is this okay?" he breathed through kisses, at the same time unbuttoning her shorts and slipping them down.

She didn't stop him, and she didn't know why. Because she wanted it? Because she missed the way Preston used to make her feel? At some point, Monica's face entered Chloe's consciousness, and she had to squeeze her eyes shut even harder.

Tell him to stop.

No, it's too late for that.

And oh, why does it also feel so good?

The whole time, Chloe was in a state of sustained amazement. She knew what was happening but also couldn't believe it. She was both turned off and on at the same time. All Roman kept repeating was, "You're amazing. You're amazing."

Chloe glowed as though a spotlight was shining down on her. Confidence surged through her body. She focused on the compliments instead of the person from whom they came.

The act was rushed and over in about the same amount of time as the build-up.

When he finished, Roman didn't lie next to her like Preston used to. Chloe remained on her back as he pressed himself up. She still wore her sweater, hiked up to her chin. She pulled her legs into herself, suddenly embarrassed to be exposed.

While Roman pulled on a pair of shorts, Chloe snuck to the bathroom. She used a wad of toilet paper to wipe herself then stared at her reflection in the mirror. Her pupils were pinpricks, heart rate still sky high. Her lungs constricted, making it difficult to catch a full breath. She couldn't formulate anything coherent. Only that she'd just had sex with Roman and part of her had liked it. Any deeper probing would have had her retch into the toilet a foot away. No, she couldn't go there.

When she returned, they stood awkwardly on either side of the room.

"Are you okay?" he asked.

"Yes."

"You're not going to—"

"No."

They were speaking in stilted code, neither one wanting to put words to what they'd done but both agreeing then and there that it would never leave this room. Chloe wouldn't dare tell a soul. This was her secret to bear. And in that moment, she somehow knew it would never happen again. This was a one-time thing.

A mountain of guilt rose in her core. She'd slept with Monica's husband, a betrayal worse than any other. It was twisted in so many ways, the layers of identity and family blurring together. Still, somehow, she knew it would remain hidden forever. Roman wouldn't be telling anyone, and neither would she. A forbidden deed never to see the light of day.

"I better get going," Roman said, tossing on a faded shirt and ball cap. "I'm supposed to be at the store getting dinner."

"Oh," Chloe said. "Right." Wetness continued to leak into her underwear.

Roman left without another word. Chloe returned to the couch, curled up her legs, and opened her book. When the rest of the family returned not half an hour later, they'd suspect she'd read multiple chapters, but only Chloe knew the truth: She'd stared at the same page the whole time, never reading a word.

The bright pink cross was really a dagger.

Pregnant. At nineteen. Almost the exact scenario her mother had found herself in. Chloe was continuing the tradition of careless behavior or bad luck or whatever it was.

When she'd gawked at the results on that little white stick, Chloe's mind had immediately gone to Roman. That night at the beach was, after all, the last time she'd had sex. Panic had filled her veins, turning her blood ice cold. She was pregnant with Roman's baby. And that's when she'd known abortion was her only option. She couldn't possibly have this child. All other options had gone swiftly out the window, regardless of how she might feel about them. Chloe wouldn't have considered herself staunchly pro-life, but she also didn't condone terminating pregnancies out of convenience.

It had weighed on her for days, and she'd lost six pounds from the mental stress. Every time she'd weighed out the options and talked herself into keeping the baby, reality had smacked her in the face. It was *Roman*. Her parents would kill her. Monica would be devastated. There simply was no way— no possible way—she could let this secret out. Done deal. She'd have to terminate.

But after a few days, a new thought shimmied its way to the surface, and Chloe kicked herself for not considering it from the beginning. Perhaps the baby wasn't Roman's after all. She'd been with Preston that one last time, just before their family vacation. What if, she pondered, she was already pregnant when she'd slept with Roman? In that case, the baby would be Preston's.

She was terrified either way.

Chloe flipped back through her calendar app, trying to remember exact dates, counting back then forward. When was her last period? When would she have been ovulating? Wasn't that how they calculated due dates? There was no clear way to be certain—the two encounters mere days apart meant little for determining which sperm deposit had hit the jackpot. It was fifty-fifty. The baby could be Roman's, or it could be Preston's.

You're so pretty.

I feel like you get me. Like I can trust you.

Good thing I'm not in college anymore.

Chloe had never felt more humiliated. She kicked herself for getting into this position. How stupid. How... gross.

The options before her took on a new light after that. Maybe she didn't need to have an abortion. The sole reason had been to conceal Roman's paternity. But if Preston was the father, did that change her choice?

Chloe took another day to think—to really think. On one hand, she knew having the baby and being a young mother meant setting forth on a new life course, one that wouldn't be easy. It would alter the lives of her family members too. She could opt to give the baby up for adoption—but no matter how hard she pictured it, she couldn't imagine having a child in the world, living with another family. Her mother would never go for it. Which brought her to the last option, and the one she'd originally thought was her only choice—abortion. Chloe read medical articles on her phone. Listened to a podcast in which women discussed their decision to go that route. It seemed like the thing that made the most sense. The only way to be sure no one ever found out about Roman.

That's it. Decision made.

Or so she thought.

After talking first with Monica and then Ava, doubt crept in. Would her parents be even angrier if they found out she'd had a secret abortion? Would the initial shock and disappointment of the pregnancy wear off to reveal supportive grandparents? Hypotheticals swirled like a hurricane, making Chloe feel as though she were going crazy. She needed to make a choice and stick to it.

It was a Monday evening, just over a week after her meeting at Monica's office, when Chloe reached her final decision. She couldn't pinpoint the precipice of change, but it came to her solid and strong. Despite the big unknown in the equation, she would keep the baby. She'd play it off during the pregnancy like the baby was Preston's—a safer, more acceptable option. How mad could her parents be at two college kids, when they'd once been in the same situation? Far less than if they knew she'd slept with Roman. It was a gamble she was willing to risk.

Nerves kept Chloe awake late into the night, and she woke the following day with a knot in her stomach. She'd have to tell Roman. He'd find out eventually, but she wanted him to hear it from her.

"Chloe," he said when she called the next day. "I'd hoped you'd call. I can't stop thinking about vacation." His voice was silky smooth, and it brought her back to that day.

"Actually," she said, "that's why I'm calling."

"Oh?" Maybe he thought she wanted to see him again. There was no way he was prepared for what she was about to say.

"I'm pregnant."

He coughed on the other end of the line, and it sounded like liquid—coffee, water, alcohol—spurting from his mouth. "Don't fuck with me like that."

"I'm not kidding. I took a test and it's positive."

"Well... uh... well..." he stumbled over her words. "Who's to say it's mine?"

"It might not be."

He let out a conniving laugh. "Naughty girl."

"But it very well could be."

"You're obviously going to take care of it, right? I mean, your parents will lose it if they find out you're pregnant."

"No, I've decided to keep the baby." Her body trembled. She flexed and clenched her fingers, back and forth.

Dead silence filled the line. Then, "You really think that's smart?"

Chloe paced the empty dorm room, keeping her voice low. "It's what I want to do. I guess we'll find out..."

It was at that point Roman's tone took a nasty turn. "Don't be stupid, Chloe. You want to go ahead with this, be my guest. But I'll deny everything. And don't forget, your dad works for me now. I can pretty easily make him jobless."

Chloe's jaw slackened. She stopped mid-stride. Was he threatening her? Her voice came out small. "Leave him out of this." Her father out of a job meant financial struggles for her family. She knew her mom didn't want him going back to manufacturing. They'd just been able to upgrade the living-room furniture like her mom had been wanting.

"Well, I guess it's mostly up to you. I know you think you're doing the right thing, but you should really consider the alternative. There are a lot of what ifs here. And everything could be avoided if you just—"

"I'm not getting an abortion." Something in his tone triggered her. This was her choice, not his.

"Fine," he snapped and hung up the phone.

The conversation rattled her. She'd known Roman wasn't going to be thrilled, but to blackmail her? It made Chloe think twice. Maybe she shouldn't have this baby. But the doubts were brief. Because every time they surfaced, she always circled back to the same thing: What if it wasn't Roman's?

Once she told her family about the pregnancy and decided to finish out the semester on campus, Chloe's world became a bubble. Partying was impossible, many of her friends had grown distant—as though they might catch pregnancy like pink eye— and she was terrified of running into Preston. Only Ava seemed to coax out Chloe's deepest thoughts as they talked late into the nights. And there, on a random evening when Chloe was feeling particularly hormonal and lonely, she spilled the truth to her friend. The secret she swore she'd never let leave her lips.

Ava stared at Chloe like she had two heads. "Roman? As in your mom's best friend's husband? As in the guy who's running for mayor of your town? What? How?"

Chloe nodded. She recalled the entire thing, giving Ava every detail. The things Roman had said.

"Jesus, Chloe." Ava pulled up a photo on her phone. "I mean, he is pretty hot for like an older guy. But still. Chloe!"

"I know. I still can't really believe it. It happened so fast, and I've been freaking out ever since. Sometimes it doesn't feel real. Like I made it up in my head or something."

Ava pointed to Chloe's stomach, which was still barely starting to show. "But you didn't."

"And now I'm fucked."

"You know," Ava said, pulling the pencil from behind her ear and tapping the phone, "it sounds like he took advantage of you. He was clearly in the position of power."

Chloe shook her head. "I didn't say no. I could have told him to stop." She didn't want to admit the way her body had responded to him, the reflexive pleasure she'd found on the flip side of the guilt.

"I'm not saying it was rape or anything. Just that he used his age and position to control the situation. You're obviously not someone he should have been sleeping with—no offense. It's just, you're nineteen and he's, what, fifty?"

"Late forties, I think."

"Yeah. That's not cool. What a creep. We talked about men like that in my news reporting class when we covered the Weinstein scandal. Predators."

Chloe cast her eyes downward. She wasn't owed any handouts here. She'd done what she'd done and now had to live with the weight of it. Roman wasn't a *predator*.

"I'm serious, Chlo. He shouldn't have done what he did."

"Neither should I."

"It's not the same. Power dynamics. He sweet-talked you."

Chloe hadn't thought of it like that before, but when Ava put it into context, a bit of smoke lifted, allowing her to see things differently. Maybe Roman had taken advantage of her naivete. Maybe he'd known exactly what he was doing and how he'd get away with it.

The thought made her sick. If she didn't already have enough guilt, now she had a double dose. Stupid. A lamb who couldn't even recognize a wolf right in front of its face. "Well, it's done," she said, wishing to change the subject. "I really think it's Preston's anyways. That's what my gut tells me." Gut or hope, one of the two.

Ava stared off into space like she did when she was lost in thought. "You should say something. Confront him."

"Roman?"

"Yes."

Chloe shook her head vehemently, remembering the threat from their phone conversation. She couldn't make matters worse than they already were. And besides, there was a fifty percent chance none of this would even matter. Deep in her bones, she knew this baby was Preston's and it had been conceived out of love—at least on her part.

"I'm not saying anything to anyone," Chloe said. "And you can't either, okay?"

"Duh."

They hugged. A pact.

It wouldn't hit Chloe until months later, when the allegations against Roman reached the media, that perhaps Ava had broken her promise. The reports said the subject was a woman in her thirties, but it was far too coincidental. The timing did little to convince Chloe that Ava wasn't behind it. And when she confronted her friend, Ava caved.

"I just couldn't let him get away with it," she said. "It was just so wrong. And let's be honest, it doesn't seem like the first time he's gotten into trouble."

"So you tipped the fucking media?"

"I didn't give them your name. I made up someone completely different from you."

"Ava," Chloe said bitterly, "you promised."

"I'm sorry! It's just... he doesn't deserve to win. He's not a good guy."

"Don't you see how this could tie back to me? It's not that hard to do a little research and discover there is no woman in her thirties. You're not some prize-winning journalist, Ava. You're a sophomore in college. You write for the school paper. This wasn't your business to spread."

Ava looked stunned and hurt, but Chloe's emotions took over, fueling her rage. Now there was yet another reason to keep everything under wraps.

She fled their room, slamming the door behind her. If she couldn't trust Ava, who could she trust? It was the lowest she'd felt since first discovering the pregnancy. The lie she'd worked hard to keep under wraps was slowly crumbling, everything tumbling into a pit with no bottom. How much longer until her parents or Monica put two and two together?

But they never did. Maybe they'd been too caught up in everything else. Or maybe, like they were wearing blinders, the adults only saw what they wanted to see.

That was, of course, until Laina made her debut and everything changed.

FORTY-FOUR

RACHEL

"SHE'S NOT YOURS."

When Preston backed away from the hospital bed with a look of such confusion, Rachel's breath skipped. He saw it too. The hair might have passed as a recessive trait, hidden deep in one of their ancestry lines, surprising but explainable. But combined with the ears, it gave Laina a distinct look—beautiful, but one that didn't match Chloe or Preston. One that Rachel remembered seeing when she'd visited Monica in the maternity ward after the birth of the boys.

"Chloe? I-I don't understand," she said, switching between looking at the dumbstruck boy and her daughter. Something was going on. Something huge. She'd been awake for twenty hours. Watched her daughter give birth. Her mind wasn't the sharpest. Maybe she was imagining things. Chloe couldn't have just said what Rachel thought she'd heard.

Rachel stared hard, trying to make sense of what she saw. Could it be that Laina was still scrunched and mangled from delivery? Newborns took a while to settle into their features, after coming out swollen and wrinkled. Maybe things needed time to settle? Maybe her ears were just pressed close and would gradually disconnect.

She was grasping. The evidence was plain as day.

If Rachel hadn't been there to witness the delivery herself, she would have almost guessed they'd given Chloe the wrong baby.

"I'm sorry," Chloe said, tears forming rivers down her face. Rachel raced to keep up. This was unimaginable.

"Is there something we should know?" the doctor asked, looking hesitantly at the triangle Chloe, Rachel, and Preston had formed.

Preston's chest rose and fell with heavy, fast breaths. "She's... she's not mine?"

Chloe shook her head. The staff in the room made uncomfortable glances at each other. But Rachel couldn't pay much attention to them. Of course Preston was the father. He'd been Chloe's boyfriend. They'd had sex, Chloe forgot to take her pill, she got pregnant. The family had operated with this storyline for months. Chloe and Preston were having a baby. She'd sent him sonogram pictures after each appointment. Anything contradictory to this didn't make sense.

"How could you?" Preston asked, and Rachel heard the hurt in his voice. His face had gone red, and his lips trembled as he spoke.

"I didn't know," Chloe said. "I thought there was a chance."

Rachel gaped. She looked to the nurse as if the woman could somehow fix this mess.

Instead, the nurse stepped between them and, in a quiet voice, said, "Sorry, but I have to get her weighed." She scooped up Laina, who let out a shrill screech, and laid her on a scale with a warming light above.

Preston took one last look at the child he'd thought was his, then pulled the neck of his shirt up over his mouth and fled from the room—but not quick enough to conceal the sound of his wounded cries.

Rachel turned back to her daughter. "Chloe, what is going on?" She didn't know whether to stay or follow the poor boy. "Is this true?"

"Obviously!" Chloe hurled. Tears flowed down her face.

Rachel braced her head in her hands. Her mind struggled to catch up. "He's devastated. Why didn't you— I mean, all this time—"

"Of course I feel horrible. But there was a possibility the baby *was* his. I wanted it to be his."

An elephant made its presence known in the room then. The thing neither of them wanted to say. The person whose name she couldn't manage to speak. It was impossible—and yet completely obvious. Still, Rachel grappled to understand how. Did she not know her own daughter at all? She felt like she might need to dash to the toilet and be sick.

Chloe looked away and bit her lip. The nurse returned with Laina swaddled in a pink-and-blue striped blanket, a newborn hat with a floppy bow covering the dark hair underneath. She laid her in Chloe's arms. "Six pounds, two ounces. A little peanut."

Rachel's mind whirred. An agonizing silence stretched between them. Finally, Chloe went to speak, but at the same time, the door opened and Rachel turned. Her body seized. Monica entered, wearing jeans, a lightweight sweater, and no makeup. What was she doing there? Did she *know?*

"Chris asked me to come," she said. "For support."

And in that moment, Rachel knew Monica was unaware of the calamity she'd walked into. Why would Chris send her? And at two in the morning? She knew exactly why—there's nothing like a new baby to act as a peace offering. How could she and Monica be fighting with a newborn in the picture? But they didn't know. Chris could never have predicted. This baby wouldn't be a means of connection but separation.

Rachel tripped over her words. "It's uh... it's not a good time." But Monica was already approaching the bed. Rachel panicked. What would Chloe say? How would Monica react? She looked back to Chloe, whose face had gone pale.

"Oh, chickadee, I'm so happy for—" Monica stopped. Her eyes bounced from Laina to Chloe and back again. Rachel watched the knowing come across her face like a dark cloud.

Chloe pressed a hand to her eyes. She looked down at the infant in her arms. Then, with a quivering chin, said, "I have something I need to tell you guys."

FORTY-FIVE

MONICA

Three hours earlier

Monica nearly fell out of bed when Chris called to say Chloe was in labor.

"Please come," he said. "I know it's late, but Rachel could use the support. Everyone's a little on edge."

"I really don't think she wants me there." Rachel hadn't said as much, but Monica could read between the lines. They hadn't reached this point in the timeline, planning out who'd do what —things had soured before Chloe even hit the halfway mark. Becoming grandparents hadn't been a common point of discussion before then. But now Rachel was about to be one, and Monica's lungs ached at the thought of not being part of it.

"Mon, you two need to figure out whatever it is that's going on between you. But right now, all that matters is that you're there for Rachel. She may not admit it, but she needs you."

Monica sucked in a breath. It was pushing eleven p.m. The boys were asleep. Next to her, Roman snored. Despite all that had happened—the allegations, her confrontation—she hadn't kicked him to the couch. Not yet. Logan might wake up from a bad dream, come to her room, and ask where Daddy was.

"Monica?" Chris said.

She hesitated, debating whether it was a good idea, even though she knew all along she'd go. Monica peeked at Roman. She'd leave him a note—she couldn't imagine being gone too long. "Okay, I'll come." Her mouth pulled into a smile. With everything going on in her life, Monica desperately needed something to celebrate. A baby—Chloe's baby—would be the perfect thing.

With a quick change, she was out the door. Her fingers drummed the steering wheel the whole way.

When she exited the elevator on the third floor of the hospital, Chris was waiting in the small lobby arranged with several chairs and an end table stacked with magazines. Though lit by overhead lights, only the dark of night came through the large windows. The space was deserted, and Monica felt like asking if there were indeed women having babies on the other side of the double doors.

"Is the baby here?" she asked.

"Hi." He stood and they gave each other a quick hug. "I haven't seen anyone yet."

"Who's in there with her?"

"Just Rachel. We got here a little after ten."

"Any updates?"

Chris checked his phone. "Rachel last texted forty minutes ago. Chloe was at five centimeters. She said she'd update again soon."

Monica let out a breath. "It'll probably be a while. Most first babies don't come quick."

Chris nodded, and they both sat. The air was charged, and not just because somewhere a few rooms away, Chloe was bringing a life into the world. Monica had barely spoken to the Morelands in months, and the few times she had, it hadn't exactly been a pleasant conversation with Rachel. Things had never felt so strained. She ached with longing for how things used to be.

"Thanks for coming," Chris said, in what sounded like an afterthought. He twirled his thumbs awkwardly. "I'm really sorry about the stuff with Roman."

"Oh!" Monica jerked a little, not expecting the topic change. Her mind had finally untethered itself from the news reports for a second. "It's okay. I mean, it's not okay, but thanks for acknowledging." She hadn't quite figured out the right response to people's concerns. Should she accept their apologies? What exactly were others apologizing for when they had nothing to do with it? Monica wished no one would bring it up ever again so she wouldn't have to formulate a reaction. She let out a tired laugh. "It's been a rough few weeks. I'm glad you called."

They waited in anxious anticipation for another hour. Monica kept an eye on the time, wondering if she should go ahead and cancel her morning appointments. If she was here all night, she'd need to go home and get some sleep. The note she'd left for Roman had told him where she was going. He'd get the boys ready for school if she wasn't back.

Beside her, Chris's head bobbed. The waiting room remained still with little activity at this hour. Only twice did the main door to the wing open, and when it did, they'd sat up alert, only to discover a staff member casually walking through. The waiting was excruciating.

Chris's phone beeped. He read the text aloud.

She's at nine! Almost ready to push!

"Ahhh!" Monica clapped. The message was just what they needed. A second wind.

"This is really happening," Chris said.

In the same breath, the elevator dinged, and Preston exited. Chris stood.

"Did I make it?" Preston asked.

"Just in time. She's getting ready to push. You better get in there."

Preston pressed the call button on the door, and within a minute, a nurse let him in. He slipped through the doors, leaving Chris and Monica behind. More waiting. Monica ached to be in there too.

"After the baby comes," Chris said, "Rachel and I will switch, so I can go back."

Monica nodded. That would give her and Rachel a good opportunity to talk face to face. So many things got lost over text messages. She wanted to look her best friend in the eye and mend all that had happened in recent months. Monica ran the reunion through her mind. They'd hug and apologize and set things right. Finally, things would be back to normal.

But first, they had a little more waiting.

A short time later, just before two in the morning, the door flew open again. Monica and Chris jolted from their chairs. Was it a nurse announcing the baby's arrival? Was it Rachel with tears of joy in her eyes?

It was neither.

Preston hurried out, head lowered, one hand to his eyes. The sound of his sobs reached Monica's ears. Instantly, panic washed over her. Something bad had happened. Something was wrong with the baby. Or Chloe. "Oh my God," she said, rushing Preston, who tried to push past her. "What's wrong?"

Chris joined her, and they each had a hold of Preston's arms, prohibiting him from leaving.

"What?" Chris bellowed. "What is it? Is Chloe alright?"

Preston wiped his nose on his shoulder and met their eyes. Monica had never seen such a mix of emotions—sadness and fury blended into something eerie.

"Ask her yourself," he said, then yanked his arms away and bolted through the exit door to the stairwell, in too much of a hurry to wait for the elevator.

Chris and Monica exchanged looks of concern and confusion, but before they could do anything more than stammer, a nurse toppled out the door.

"What's going on?" Chris demanded. "Is my daughter okay? What about the baby?"

"Mom and baby are fine," the nurse said, a bit flustered. "She's still getting cleaned up."

"She?" Monica said. "It's a girl?"

The nurse gave a nervous smile, hand to her forehead. "I was referring to Mom, but yes, baby is a girl."

Monica let out a soft cheer, but Chris couldn't focus. He pointed to the exit door. "Well, why was he crying?"

Chris's face was red with fear and exhaustion. Monica sensed that the whole setting—hospitals and childbirth and bodily fluids—wasn't entirely comfortable for him.

"I..." The nurse wobbled.

Chris turned to Monica. "Monica, can you—?" With Preston gone, it freed up a support position.

"I'll go. I'll check on them."

The nurse led Monica back to the delivery room. It smelled of salt and brine. Musty, earthy. An IV stand to the right, beeping monitor to the left. In the center, Chloe lay on the bed, disheveled hair in a top knot, flushed face the sign of great exertion. When Monica stepped through the threshold, Rachel turned and her expression went slack.

"Chris asked me to come," Monica said, suddenly feeling out of place. "For support." She prayed Rachel wouldn't kick her out. Being there felt so right, and she wanted nothing more than to reach out and hug them both. Instead, she approached gingerly. There, in Chloe's arms, was a little bundle. As Monica got closer, the baby came into view. "Oh, chickadee, I'm so happy for—"

And that's when Monica froze. She couldn't peel her eyes from the infant. Not because of awe and not because of delight, though until that second, those emotions filled her in entirety. But because the baby looked exactly like her Logan. The dark hair, the little ears he'd got from Roman—the ones she loved so much. If she'd put this baby alongside Logan's newborn pictures, they could have been—

The bottom fell out, draining all the blood from Monica's body. She felt as though she were on one of those amusement-park rides where the floor disappears, leaving riders in free fall. Where was the ground? Were her feet on it?

Chloe sniffed. "I have something I need to tell you guys."

Monica willed her heart to beat again. She reached for something to steady herself but felt only air. She tapped the toe of her shoe—yes, there was the ground. Somehow, she reached the edge of the bed and lowered to the bottom corner. Rachel remained standing, moved closer to Chloe in what Monica could only interpret as a power move. *My daughter.*

"The baby isn't Preston's," Chloe said, looking squarely at Monica.

Monica's wheels turned, but she wasn't dim. She quickly connected the dots: Preston leaving in tears. A baby that looked like a mirror image of her own son. Roman, who spent more time away at night than home with her. She thought of the sexual harassment allegations—the staffer—and now this? A baby?

Monica brought a hand to cover her mouth. If she moved it, the granola bar she'd eaten in the waiting room would come flying out. *Don't say it, Chloe. Don't say it.* She was vaguely aware of the nurse in the room but couldn't manage to ask her to leave.

"This can't be true," Rachel said, disbelief written all over her face.

Chloe looked between them, agony etched into her face. It was palpable, the torment Chloe emitted. Monica could feel it, and her heart broke for what she knew was about to be said. She didn't want Chloe to have to do it. And so, with as much grace as she could muster, Monica spoke. "It's Roman."

Rachel dropped her head, silent tears somehow deafening.

"Right?" Monica directed the question at Chloe. She remained impossibly calm, voice level, despite the siren going off in her head.

Chloe nodded. "Yes."

Rachel took a step back, hand to her heart as though checking for a beat. She shook her head, disbelieving.

"I'm sorry. I didn't mean to hurt you. It was just once, and I regret it, and—"

"Did he assault you?" Rachel hurled. "Did he— Did he force you?"

Monica's mouth went acidic. She knew the word Rachel wanted to say. The ugly "R" word. Rachel was thinking it, but would she say it aloud?

"No," Chloe said with a newfound fire. "It wasn't like that. I mean, it's my fault too. I should never have—"

"Chloe, stop." Monica stood and pumped her hands. "You don't have to explain." Then, to herself, as if everything suddenly made sense, "I should have seen this coming. I should have known."

"Monica." Rachel reached out, unease on her face, but Monica recoiled.

She stumbled to the door, half delirious, half stunned. "I have to go." Before the tears could hit her eyes, she made it to the waiting room, where Chris was pacing, arms folded across his chest.

"Are they okay?" he demanded. It had been all of eight

minutes since she'd left him, and in that wink of time, her life had turned upside down. His face paled. "Monica?"

"Yes. No. I don't know anything anymore." She choked on the last bit. "You better go in."

He hesitated for the briefest second then opened the door and disappeared, leaving Monica alone in the waiting room in the middle of the night with her heart in pieces. She pressed the elevator button with a trembling finger. When it opened, she moved on autopilot, stepping inside and preparing what she'd say to her sleeping husband.

FORTY-SIX

CHLOE

MONICA WAS THE LAST PERSON CHLOE HAD EXPECTED TO see walk through the delivery-room door. A sudden feeling of unpreparedness came over her. She'd only discovered the truth herself mere minutes before. There'd barely been time to process it: The baby was Roman's. And then Monica had shown up out of the blue, and Chloe had had zero time to plan how she'd break the news to the second-most important woman in her life. It felt very much like ripping off a Band-Aid. Sometimes faster is better, but the lead-up is torture. Chloe's body physically ached with guilt and remorse.

"I can't believe this," Rachel said after Monica had left. "Chloe, what happened?"

Her mother wanted details—all of them. Chloe gulped, thinking of coming clean about that afternoon at the beach. A family vacation, tainted. She hoped she could get away with retelling the bare minimum.

The door opening once more saved her. Chloe's father entered, pale-faced and stricken. The constant flow of people drained any last bits of energy Chloe had.

"What's going on?" Chris asked before noticing his

daughter and correcting himself. "Hi, sweetheart. Look at you." He kissed the top of Chloe's head. "I'm so proud of you."

The pain hit Chloe square in the chest. One more person to crush.

Even with the paternal glow radiating from him, his body language held a panicky edge. When he met eyes with Rachel, Chloe could tell he knew something was off. Nineteen years of reading her parents gave her this keen sense. She could only imagine what he'd already heard in the waiting room, first when Preston fled, and then Monica. Now Chloe would have to hash it out all over again. Disappoint another parent. Her head pounded. She craved sleep.

The nurse stepped forward. "You know," she said, "Chloe's just been through a lot, and this time is very important for mother–baby bonding. With all due respect, I'm going to suggest Grandma and Grandpa head back to the waiting room for a bit, okay? Maybe you can talk things over out there? Baby needs to try to nurse."

She guided them to the door as she spoke, giving a curt *mhmm* or *yep, okay* when either Rachel or Chris tried to protest. "I'll call for you both shortly. Let's give mama and baby some time."

Chloe's shoulders relaxed. Not a permanent distraction but a breather—however temporary—to let her mind process.

The nurse shut the door behind Chloe's parents, then turned back and crossed the room to the bed. "Well, this certainly has been interesting," she said. "But that's none of my business. What I'm concerned with is getting baby to eat. Are you planning to try breastfeeding?"

"Mhmm."

"Alright. Well, let's give it a go." She helped Chloe pull down her hospital gown and showed her how to position the baby. Laina rooted around then opened her mouth when she met Chloe's nipple.

"How does she know to do that?" Chloe asked.

"Instinct. Isn't it amazing?"

Chloe winced a little but mostly just watched in wonder. How had this tiny person been inside her less than an hour ago? It seemed wildly impossible. And yet, completely right. Laina pinched Chloe's breast with soft fingernails.

"You're both doing great," the nurse said, peeking at them and returning to her chart. "We'll get you settled into recovery soon. That's one floor up." She pointed to the ceiling.

Chloe closed her eyes, but behind her lids she saw Preston's face, and that made her choke up. She felt like a monster. A horrible, reckless person whose actions had impacted far more than herself. She imagined Preston speeding home through the early morning hours. Calling his parents. Word would spread on campus. They'd call her a slut.

But then another face flashed in her mind: Roman's. What would he say when he found out? Would he demand a paternity test? There'd be no way to deny it. Even looking at sweet Laina, it was clear who her father was. Regardless of what outsiders said, Chloe knew the truth: She'd been with two people. The answer was indisputable.

Her arms felt weak, almost like she couldn't bear to hold a six-pound baby. An ache stretched from her ribs to her knees, blood pumping in her pelvis. A new life was the gift at the end of her labor. This precious, innocent being who didn't ask to be born, didn't deserve to enter into a world of chaos. And yet the only thing Chloe could think of was that stretch of minutes where she hadn't done the right thing. When she hadn't spoken up. She'd been so stupid. She wished she could melt into the bed and disappear. The secret was out, and now she had to live with it.

Roman's child. Her child. Their child.

. . .

The room where they moved her was smaller. A chair that pulled out into a bed tucked into the corner. A TV mounted next to the white board where a nurse kept track of Chloe's meds and Laina's feedings.

Chloe pulled the blanket up to her neck. Her body went between chills and sweats like a yo-yo. Hormones adjusting, the nurse assured her. Laina slept peacefully, bundled like a burrito in the rolling bassinet next to the bed. It was the first time Chloe had been alone with her daughter after being attended by a steady stream of nurses. Chloe peeked at the little girl's face, angled toward her. She was perfect. Unplanned but perfect. A whopping three hours old.

She closed her eyes; drifted in and out of light consciousness. She was spinning on a playground, surrounded by younger versions of herself.

"What's it like to be older?" toddler Chloe asked.

She stared at her childhood self with wistful nostalgia then replied with a single word. "Hard."

A knock on the door and her eyes snapped open. Her parents entered with grim expressions and looking shrunken, as though the frenzy of the night had taken years off their lives. Outside, the sun remained below the horizon, the sky cast in soft shadows of alpenglow. They'd all officially been awake for twenty-hour hours, and it showed.

Chloe studied her parents' faces, determining what to expect. A lashing? A lecture? So much for the interlude of quiet. Chloe could barely keep her eyes open.

"How is she?" Rachel asked, coming alongside the bassinet.

"Good. She ate and has been asleep ever since." It struck her how normal the response came, talking about such adult things—breastfeeding, babies—from the perspective of the mother. She was a mother! Absurd! She felt more like an imposter, a child pretending to be an adult. Far too young to be discussing placentas and milk ducts and vaccine schedules.

"We need to talk about this," Chris said. His voice wavered.

Chloe tried but couldn't read his face. He looked at once like he might punch a hole through the wall as well as let loose a river of tears. His hair stood up messily.

He folded his arms. "When?"

"On vacation," Chloe said, not bothering to delay or spin a tale. It no longer made sense to lie.

"And that's it?"

"That was the only time. I regretted it immediately."

"He didn't force you?"

"No. I already told Mom. It wasn't— He didn't—"

Rachel sat on the edge of the bed. "So then why, Chloe? You're so much smarter than that."

"It was a dumb mistake. I was trying to get over Preston, and Roman was there and made me feel—"

"That's the problem," Chris interrupted, nostrils flaring. "He knows the things to say. He's a womanizer—I've known it from day one. I should never have let him around my daughter." His fist balled, and under his breath he muttered, "Bastard."

Rachel put a hand on her husband's arm. Chloe's eyes got wet seeing her dad so worked up. She'd never meant to put them in this position. If she'd just taken her birth control properly, none of this would have happened. It was her fault. She dug her nails into the skin of her arms, wishing she could take it all back.

Chloe sniffed. But then she wouldn't have Laina. The little human who'd been inside her all those months, moving and kicking and sharing life. Chloe looked to the baby again, an intense need to hold her close. "Hand her to me please?"

Rachel lifted Laina from the bassinet and placed her in Chloe's waiting arms.

"How could you go through with the pregnancy knowing this was a possible outcome?"

Chloe blanched. The question sliced her like a hot knife.

"You mean why didn't I have an abortion? How can you say that now when you're face to face with your granddaughter? I might have made a mistake, but I don't regret having her. Look at her! She's half of me."

Her parents stared. Rachel bit her lip. Aside from the brief transfer to Chloe, neither of them had even asked to hold Laina.

Chloe seethed. "If you guys can't support me, then you might as well go."

"Good," Chris said, spinning toward the door. "I was ready to fucking kill him the minute I found out, but your mother said I had to come see you first. With your permission, I'll just go grab my gun."

"Chris," Rachel snapped. "Don't even think about it. Get back here. It's five thirty in the morning." She turned to Chloe. "Honey, that's not what I meant."

"I don't give a shit what time it is—I'll go get him out of bed."

"I'm sure Monica's already taken care of that."

Monica's name sent a shock wave through Chloe. She winced. It was a whole different type of regret when it came to Monica. A physical pain. Different than the shame Chloe felt in front of her parents. Few people matched Monica in Chloe's eyes, and what Chloe had done felt like murder. She'd killed all Monica knew and loved.

"I need some air," Chris said.

Rachel stood her ground. "You're not going to their house."

"Don't tell me what the hell to do. The man crossed a major line and needs put in his place. No better person to do it than me."

"Chris, please. You're just going to make things worse."

"Worse?" His voice elevated, and Rachel shushed him to no avail. "So you're suggesting we don't say anything? Just accept that a grown-ass man, your best friend's husband, slept with our daughter? I don't think so."

Chloe watched the back and forth on the verge of vomiting. She'd caused this. And now her parents—who never fought—were fighting. Her mind went to dark places, where Laina's birth set off a chain reaction that fractured her entire family. Divorce. Estrangement. She choked on a sob.

"I'm saying just take a second to cool off," Rachel said.

"Fuck that," he mumbled with a furious swipe of the air and left the room without another word. Rachel dropped her head. Chloe clenched her teeth. A tear fell onto Laina's face, and Chloe gently wiped it away with the pad of her thumb.

Seconds later, a nurse entered. "Just need to check your uterus again." She pressed her fingers firmly into Chloe's abdomen, moving in a circular motion. Chloe held her breath with the pain.

"Sorry," the nurse said, "I know it's uncomfortable. This just helps the uterus shrink back down. How long has baby been sleeping? We'll want to keep her on the two-to-three hour feeding schedule." She went to the laptop and typed in Chloe's vitals.

Rachel moved closer; spoke in a low tone. Chloe could see red crisscrossed lines of bloodshot eyes. "I better go after your father. You just rest, okay?" She didn't look at Laina; didn't touch her velvety skin. Simply turned and disappeared from the room.

A cry caught in Chloe's throat. She held it. The door clicked shut. She let it out.

"There are a lot of emotions postpartum," the nurse said, ripping open a packet of pain pills and dropping two into Chloe's palm.

"I made such a mess," Chloe cried.

The nurse gave Chloe's leg a pat through the blanket. Chloe thought she saw her write the words *Watch for PPD* on the chart.

"Can I get you anything else?" the nurse asked. Chloe

shook her head. "All right. Press the call button if you do need something. I'll be back in a little while."

Alone again, Chloe tried to sleep, but her mind wouldn't still. Her body and brain felt like mush.

If only she could sleep for a bit. She let her lids close. But the second she teetered on unconsciousness, Laina gave a whimper that made Chloe's eyes fly open. She checked the nursing schedule written in blue marker. It was time to feed her baby.

There would be no rest. No time to slip away into fantasy. This was Chloe's punishment.

FORTY-SEVEN

MONICA

She would jump on him and use his face as a punching bag.

She would tell him Chloe's baby had arrived and wait for him to confess first.

She would grab a knife from the kitchen on the way up the stairs and stab his cheating heart.

On the drive home from the hospital, Monica went over different scenarios. Rage. Assault. Decapitation.

Castration.

She gripped the steering wheel so hard, her knuckles turned white. Her throat was thick, making it difficult to swallow.

No cars took to the roads at that hour, which only added to her heavy foot on the pedal. When she pulled into the driveway just before two thirty, the only illumination came from the spotlights dug along the front pathway. Monica parked in the garage and went inside, body loaded, ready to attack. It was dead quiet, and she knew she was about to break the silence in a big way but didn't care. The boys still used white noise machines. Even if they woke, she reasoned they had a right to know their father was an adulterous egomaniac. Let them see. *Boys, here is an example of what not to become.*

Up the stairs she crept, skipping the knife in the kitchen even though she understood now how easy it was for scorned wives to snap. At the bedroom door, she took a breath then pushed it open.

Roman lay on his side, a mound under the white comforter. She went to stand in front of him and studied his face. So calm, so unbothered in his sleep. It made her hate him even more. The fury grew inside her to the point she could hear her own exhales whistling through her teeth. Each second that passed, the wrath intensified. Eyes like thunder. Finally, she planted her feet, reached out with a flat hand, and slapped him square across the face.

Roman jolted up like a man struck by lightning. Only Monica's fire was hotter. She burned with something far more dangerous.

"Wha... wha...?" he blubbered, blinking in succession and cupping his cheek.

"You son of a bitch," she hissed.

"What are you doing? Monica, what is this? Are you fucking crazy?"

"I know about Chloe."

"Chloe?"

"Yes, Chloe. You know, the girl who's like a daughter to us? Or at least to me. The one you casually *slept* with and got *pregnant*?"

The room was dark, save for a bluish glow coming from the night light in the hall. Still, Monica saw his eyes go wide. His mouth clamped shut. She had him.

"Listen, it's not what you think," he said.

"How could it not be? Don't deny it. You had sex with her, didn't you?"

"Monica—"

Her voice rose. "Didn't you?" She leaned in as she said it, and he in turn pulled back.

"Yes."

There it was. The truth she already knew. It made her smolder. "Well, guess what? She just gave birth to your baby."

His eyes darted. "You don't know that."

"Oh yes I do. I was just at the hospital. She looks just like Logan. She has your ears. That's right, she. It's a girl. You have a daughter, you son of a bitch."

Monica lunged for him again, but he caught her wrists in the air. They tussled on the bed, grunting and panting. Her earlier sadness had turned to pure anger, and she wanted nothing more than to cause him as much pain as he'd caused her.

"Monica, stop!" he said over and over. Finally, size and strength won, and he pinned her. "You're going to wake the boys."

"Good," she snarled up at him. "Let them know what kind of man their father is." Then under her breath, "I knew it. I should have believed the stories."

He let go, pushing himself up from the bed. Their heavy breathing filled the room. He stood a few paces away, hands on his hips. Slowly, her body came down from its high. And with it came another wash of grief.

"How could you do this to me?" she asked, hoping for what —an apology? For him to beg? And then what? She'd forgive him?

Roman did neither.

His lack of response was the only response she needed. Monica's jaw set. "Get out of here. Get out of my sight."

"It's the middle of the night."

"I couldn't care less. You've never had a problem staying out late before."

He ran a hand through his hair. "I'll sleep on the couch. At least let me see the kids in the morning, okay? Then I'll pack a bag."

This time, Monica remained silent. He'd retreated so easily. Backed down at her first request. She didn't want it to end—she still had so much more to release. And yet, the sight of him made her sick. If she could throw him from the window right then, she would. But the boys. They hadn't asked for any of this. And so, the couch would have to suffice... for now. It was a compromise she was willing to make solely for the benefit of her sons.

Roman grabbed his pillow and left. A hush enveloped her again. The only sound the thumping in her ears—and dust resettling from the bomb she'd detonated. Outside, a lark chirped its morning chorus, and Monica hated its contentment. She reached for her own pillow, shoved her face into it, and screamed.

The sound of someone banging on the door woke her. The faintest hints of light coming through the curtains indicated it was near dawn. She'd somehow fallen asleep. Monica sat up, still in her clothes, on top of the comforter. Her neck was stiff, like she'd been slumped down into an uncomfortable position for hours.

Another quick succession of pounds. Hard, incessant. *What the...?* She got up from the bed and checked the clock. Almost six. The boys' alarm clocks would be going off in an hour if they weren't already up before then.

Monica slipped from the room. Her head throbbed, and she took the stairs carefully, not trusting her own balance. Coming through the living room, she caught sight of Roman, ahead of her, heading toward the door in pajama pants and T-shirt—the same thing she'd seen him in when he'd left their bedroom hours before. A quick glance toward the couch told her he'd pulled a sheet from the linen closet and spent the rest of the night there. An empty bottle of Chardonnay sat on the end table.

Roman opened the door mid-bang—and just as quickly stumbled backwards as Chris pummeled over the threshold, feet slapping on the tiled foyer.

"Motherfucker," Chris said, eyes black. Monica caught a vein bulging at his neck.

"Whoa, whoa," Roman said, backing up.

"How dare you touch my daughter!"

"Listen, Chris, she's an adult."

"Fuck you." He swung but missed.

Monica rushed them, jumping in the middle. "Stop it!" she yelled so loud the walls trembled. As much as she'd love to see Chris break Roman's nose, she didn't need it here in her entryway with a chance for the boys to show up at any moment.

"I want a paternity test," Roman said, still backing away. Chris followed, not letting Roman get far.

"Screw that—the baby looks exactly like you."

"She could have been with anyone."

Chris's face got redder than Monica knew possible. "Watch what you say," he warned with a pointed finger.

A second later, the door opened again, and Rachel entered without so much as a knock. "Chris," she said, as though she expected the sight.

The four of them stood in a highly charged circle. Four adults, one singular enemy.

Rachel was the first to speak. "How could you? You guys were like family to us. She's our daughter. She's... she's a *kid*."

"He has no response," Monica answered. "He's nothing but a coward."

"Even cowards deserve a black eye. And this guy has one coming," Chris said, lunging for Roman again.

Rachel caught him; pulled him back.

Monica got between them again, hands raised. "Listen, it's not going to do any good fighting. The baby is here. It's not like we can go back and change the past."

"Look at you being all levelheaded," Rachel said, placing her hands on her hips. "Like you're some innocent party in all this. Like you've never had a secret."

"What's that supposed to mean?"

"It means you knew about Chloe's pregnancy and never told me."

Monica's face flared. Here it was, the secret she thought would never be revealed. How had they found out? Chloe must have slipped. Dammit. She thought she'd been in the clear. "I— She— It wasn't for long."

Rachel's voice shook. "How could you keep a secret like that from me? You were supposed to be my best friend. What if Chloe had gotten rid of it? You would have just let me continue not knowing what was going on with my own daughter?"

"Of course not. I would have said something."

"Would you?"

"Eventually, yes."

"Eventually. Nice. This wasn't just some little, petty thing, Monica. This was huge. I never would have hidden something like that from you."

"Sort of like you didn't call me as soon as you found out about Roman's sexual harassment allegations?"

Rachel rose tall. "That's not the same and you know it."

"Well, if we're throwing around examples of withheld information..."

"I hardly think you can compare the two. This is my daughter we're talking about. A kid! Pregnant and you knew."

Monica's palms turned clammy. "She asked me not to tell. I told her I wouldn't."

"Don't you think better judgment trumps a promise to a teenager?"

Monica wavered. Hadn't she done the right thing? She'd thought so, but maybe she'd been wrong. Maybe Rachel had always deserved to know.

"Think about it," Rachel said. "Really, truly think about it."

Monica shrank. She felt defeated. Rachel's words rang true for the first time, and she knew she'd made a mistake. If the roles had been reversed, she'd have been furious if Rachel hadn't informed her of something so serious, so life-changing involving her boys.

"I'm sorry," Monica said. "I should have told you."

"A little late now."

Chris interjected. "I think the more important thing here is what this asshole did. He's the father of Chloe's baby." He turned to the accused. "You better be ready to pony up. You've got another child to provide for. Don't think you're going to sweep this under the rug."

"I don't want to hear this shit," Roman said. He turned on his heel and went for the stairs.

Monica imagined him haughtily tossing random things into an overnight bag. Minutes later, she was proven correct. Roman, changed into jeans and a ball cap and with a bag in hand, descended with a solemn look.

He passed by the rest of them but not without Chris hollering, "You're not off the hook. Just wait until this gets out. Your campaign is done."

The door slammed.

So much for saying good morning to the boys, Monica thought. She couldn't believe they hadn't woken up through all the commotion. A small miracle. Her pulse beat hard. The campaign. The media. How was Roman going to provide for the boys—and now a third child—without a job?

"Look," Monica said, lips trembling, "I'm as shocked as you guys. Can't we just figure this out between us?" It wasn't that she wanted to allow Roman any grace. Her thoughts centered solely on Lucas and Logan and the strong instinct to shelter them from any unnecessary attention.

No one said anything for a long moment. Was it a truce she was requesting? Was that even what she wanted?

"I can't speak for anyone else," Chris finally said. "but one thing I can say for sure is that I won't be stepping foot back into the office with him. I don't want to see his face ever again."

Monica let out an exasperated breath, though she couldn't fault Chris. She'd be happy not to see Roman either. It was just that her life was falling apart faster than any remedy could fix. Keeping this quiet or letting it out made little difference to the fact that her husband had slept with Chloe. That Chloe had slept with Roman. And that a baby now existed from their tryst.

"We need to get back to the hospital," Rachel said, speaking to no one in particular. She refused to make eye contact with Monica. "Chris, let's go. I think we're done here."

Monica didn't stop them. What else was there to say? The target of their collective bitterness was gone, leaving only three broken people facing a shocking new reality.

She stood in place long after they left, as though she could make time stand still. Each passing moment dragged her further into this mess she didn't know how to escape from. Only when the shrill beep of two alarm clocks from above echoed through the house did Monica move one heavy foot in front of the other. Right, left. Life didn't stop. There was no choice but to keep moving.

FORTY-EIGHT

RACHEL

October

It had been two weeks since Laina's birth. Fourteen whole days. Rachel was counting. Chloe's bedroom now functioned as a nursery rather than a teenage haven; a side sleeper attached to her bed—so Laina was always within arm's reach—and a changing table took up the corner where an oversized beanbag chair once sat.

"The baby can have my room," Savannah had offered a few months before Laina's birth. "I wouldn't mind sharing with Jacob. I've always wanted bunk beds."

But Chloe had refused. Her actions shouldn't upend her siblings' lives. So the bedroom was tight but functional, and Chloe spent a good deal of time there, napping when she could, feeding Laina every three hours. She'd venture downstairs to the living room for a change of scenery and had even taken the baby out for a couple walks, bundled under a blanket to protect Laina from the chill October air.

Their house had taken on a new yet familiar scent, one of powdery baby lotion and dirty diapers. Laundry piled up thanks to the endless spit up, soured burp cloths, and midday outfit changes—for both baby and adults. Laina spared no one.

Rachel, long since back to work after taking only two personal days, was awed at how Chloe had taken to motherhood. Things were far from perfect—plenty of tears on both sides, along with poor sleep and pesky hemorrhoids, meant Chloe was a shadow of her old self— yet Rachel couldn't deny the love that poured from her daughter. Rachel often caught herself falling back in time, remembering the early days of Chloe's life. Had Rachel been as enamored with Chloe as Chloe now was with Laina?

Yes. Of course she had.

The haze of unconditional love was enough to bolster Rachel through the storm they were currently weathering. Things might have seemed sunny from the outside—a new baby, how lovely!—but the truth was they were bunkered down. No one had seen the tornado coming, and now that the worst had passed, they were faced with the aftermath. The devastation. Rebuilding.

Rachel pulled into the driveway a little before four. Chris's car remained in the same spot it had been in for days, and Rachel got a little prick in her chest when she saw it there. Like something out of place. He shouldn't be at home; he should be at work. A sore reminder, bringing everything back to the forefront.

Rachel slung her tote over her shoulder and got out of the car. When her feet hit the ground, her knees buckled, and she took it as a cue to eat something. Chloe wasn't the only one dropping weight after Laina's arrival—Rachel's appetite had all but disappeared, causing her already-diminutive frame to shrink further. With no extra pounds to spare, she knew she had to be careful, but the stress had wreaked havoc on her body. Eating was the last thing on her mind.

Inside, Rachel nearly tripped over the shoes and backpacks

strewn across the floor. Their routine had gone out the window, taking with it the little kids' manners. She kicked a sneaker to the side. They were all in survival mode, and if it meant more frozen dinners and fewer rules for the time being, then so be it.

She dropped her stuff on the counter next to breast-pump flanges air-drying on a towel. The house was quiet, save for muffled music coming from the basement, which told her Savannah and Jacob were downstairs playing video games. Another broken rule—no screens until homework was complete. Whatever.

Rachel turned the corner to the living room and stopped. She wrapped her arms around herself, committing the scene to memory. On the couch lay Chris with baby Laina on his chest, both sound asleep—the baby's little body curled into a ball, knees tucked up under her, head turned to the side so her cheek smooshed against the flannel of his shirt. The sight never failed to stir something in Rachel. Chris as a grandfather was almost as good as Chris as a father. He relished his role, as though a new chamber of his heart had opened with each new family member.

Seeing her husband like that brought Rachel joy, but it also ignited lingering embers. The spark that burned for advancement, motivation, a better career. Rachel was busting her ass balancing work and kids and everything else that went into managing her home, and there Chris was, spending his days lounging with a newborn. She'd completely dismissed the idea of going back to school.

As much as she loved seeing his devotion to Laina and Chloe, the other half of her wanted to smack him. *Get up. Do something.* They couldn't survive on her preschool salary. Diapers weren't cheap.

Rachel sat on the couch just firmly enough to jostle him awake without seeming to be intentional. Chris's eyes bounced down to Laina and back up again, and he smiled.

"Look at this angel," he said softly.

"Mmmm. She really is."

Her initial hesitation toward the baby had been short-lived, and shame bubbled whenever Rachel thought of those first hours in the hospital. The shock had overtaken her. She couldn't make sense of anything. She hadn't been there for Chloe—for Laina—like she should have. But then they'd come home, they'd settled in, and the block on her emotions had vanished. Rachel couldn't get enough of the newborn, so much so that Chloe sometimes had to pry Laina from her hands.

Rachel traced Laina's eyebrow, desperate to pick her up but not wanting to disturb her sleep. The baby looked so peaceful. Rachel sat on her hands to keep from grabbing and chewed the inside of her cheek. Her old thought patterns threatened to destroy the sweet moment. They told her to nag her husband, to ask if he'd done anything but lie around all day. Any time she did bring up work, he said he was waiting to hear back from his old boss.

It felt like going backwards. The old Rachel would groan. She'd press Chris to reach for more. But so much had happened. They were no longer the same people they'd been a year ago. It had taken Laina to show her that. And so instead of berating him, Rachel did her best to smile and push away any lingering bitterness.

"I heard a bunch of Roman's staff quit," Chris said.

"Jump ship before it sinks."

"Yep."

It was true. Roman's campaign hadn't just hit a speed bump but a massive crater, one where the damage was too great to recover. It hadn't taken long for details to trickle out from the hospital. As much as they'd hoped for discretion within those walls, the story had simply been too good. Too juicy. Even medical professionals like to gossip.

It had started with a few texts from friends and even acquaintances who dared be so bold.

Is it true…?

We heard that…

On the third day, the same day Chloe and Laina had come home, the newspaper had uploaded a new article. First-hand account. Eyewitness sources. A delivery room in turmoil. The dots were easy enough to connect. The earlier allegations, paired with tips from inside the hospital, made the story hard to dispute.

"We'll sue their asses," Chris had said, but that had only made Chloe cry more.

"Please, can't we just drop it? I just want to forget and move on. I'm embarrassed enough."

In the end, her urging won out. It had been a major breach of confidentiality, but there was already so much dust in the air, tossing another grenade might break them completely. Rachel didn't want to see any of their names in the paper again.

The two families, once inseparable, hadn't spoken since the confrontation.

Rachel leaned back against the couch. She didn't want to pick a fight with Chris, but his stubbornness wore her thin. Why didn't he see the position they were in?

"Look, I feel like we're at a turning point," she told him. "We can go back to how things were, or we can really push for a new future. Don't forget, there's another little human in the picture. Another mouth to feed."

"Chloe's breastfeeding."

"You know what I mean."

Chris stabbed a finger at her. "And what about you?"

"What about me?"

"You're all preachy about new paths, but I don't see you going after what you were planning."

Rachel squinted, and Chris clarified, "Going back to school."

"I can't do that now!"

"Why not?"

"Because there's a baby here." She pointed to Laina, who made a few squeaks; twisted her body. Their conversation was disturbing her slumber.

"Not your baby."

Rachel rolled her eyes. "Someone has to help Chloe, and it's not like—"

"Don't say his name." Chris's jaw clenched. "I can barely get through the day without punching the wall. I hate him for what he did."

"I do too, but at some point, don't you think they'll need to be in contact? I mean, he should be supporting her."

"We don't need his help," Chris said firmly.

"Don't we?"

They eyed each other; they both knew damn well Rachel's job at the preschool wasn't enough. Even if Chris went back to his old position, they were no better than before, making ends meet but with little to no cushion. Chloe would have to work, but that wouldn't be for weeks at the soonest.

Chris looked away first, and Rachel followed, dropping her gaze to her lap. The silence made her retreat into her thoughts. It was in these quiet, still moments that Monica came to mind, and Rachel's heart hurt. Staying busy kept her distracted, but not enough to forget about the friend she'd lost and the abyss of sorrow she felt every single day. Not more than a few nights passed without Monica appearing in Rachel's dreams. Sometimes they were laughing, past versions of themselves, the way things used to be. But other times they were separated by a deep gorge, each on one side, arms out for each other but unable to reach. It was those dreams when Rachel woke crying.

She peered back at Chris. Tears crested her eyes, falling faster than anticipated. "I miss her so much," Rachel said, without further explanation. None was needed.

Chris's face softened. They took each other's hands.

Rachel leaned in to place a soft kiss on Laina's head. She couldn't imagine a life without Monica in it. For over twenty years, Monica had been her right-hand woman in all things good, bad, and ugly. Now, the ugly had divided them, and she didn't know if they'd ever make it back.

FORTY-NINE

MONICA

THE SOUND OF ANY INCOMING NOTIFICATION TO HER phone had become like nails on a chalkboard. Monica could never quite know for sure what to expect. Was it another bombshell? Or just a yearly reminder her car inspection was due?

This time it was the former.

She didn't think her stomach could plummet any further, but somehow it did. Part of her realized she should be almost used to surprises like this by now.

The news alert came from the *Pittsburgh Post Gazette*.

SECOND WOMAN COMES FORWARD WITH ALLEGATIONS AGAINST WEXFORD MAYORAL CANDIDATE ROMAN NASH.

Monica read, despite the sick feeling that overcame her. A former college student had written a blog post, wherein she claimed Roman had advanced on her. The *Gazette* called attention to the most damning part, directing readers to the full post for additional reading.

Dr. Nash was a creep. He always asked me to stay after class and had a habit of getting too close when he talked to you. Like in your personal space. Then one time he actually leaned in and kissed me. It was so quick because I immediately backed up, totally freaked out. It bothered me so much, I went to say something the next day and he acted like I was crazy, like I'd made the whole thing up. I knew if I went to the dean, they'd never believe me. I mean, it was Dr. Nash, the most charismatic professor on campus. When I heard he'd left, I was so relieved. Maybe he didn't get what he wanted with me, but I'm sure I wasn't the only one.

Monica couldn't make herself read the article in its entirety, but her eyes were drawn to the last paragraph:

This new allegation, stacked on top of the recent revelation of Nash's fathering a child out of wedlock with his campaign manager's daughter and speculation of mishandled funds, undoubtedly spells trouble for the once-respected politician. Outrage on social media has cast a shadow over the would-be hopeful, and with only three weeks until election day, Nash's favor in the polls has seen a massive hit.

She wanted to feel some sort of reaction, but all Monica could do was stare blankly into space. The first report—the female staffer—had turned out to be false. They knew that now. Katy Fischer denied ever having those interactions with Roman. Which meant it was all a ruse. There was no staffer, only a pregnant Chloe. The staffer was Chloe. But that didn't erase the painful truth of what Roman had done. Would it have been better if the woman had been real? If it were a stranger bearing Roman's child instead of Chloe? For outsiders, it was nothing but semantics. Roman had deceived her, broken her trust, and forever altered the rest of her and her boys' lives. But to Monica, the pain cut far deeper with Chloe's involvement. The infidelity cast a wide net, forever altering every important part of her life.

So now, with another allegation, Monica felt no need to search for credibility. Fool her once, shame on him, but Monica wouldn't be fooled a second time.

But despite what may have felt like passivity, Monica grieved for what she knew was happening—the dissolution of her marriage. There would be no coming back from this. Roman couldn't talk his way out of everything.

Monica placed her phone face down, feeling very much like a bear hibernating in its cave. Her office offered sanctuary from the turmoil outside. But even bears had to emerge sometime. Their very survival depended on it.

FIFTY

RACHEL

THE TODDLERS—ALL ELEVEN OF THEM—WERE ASLEEP IN their cots, which meant Rachel could finally sit for more than thirty seconds. She found the rocking chair in the corner of the classroom and slipped onto it, careful not to bump the tow-headed boy near her feet. This was one of her favorite times of the day, a stretch of quiet where there weren't children or errands, or responsibilities pulling her in a million directions. Sure, she'd have to wipe down the sticky table and chairs from lunch, but that could wait a little bit. The kids would sleep for a solid two hours. She needed a minute.

Seeing the latest headline about Roman had rattled her. More people were coming out of the woodwork, and Rachel could only imagine what might be waiting to be revealed next. All of it added up to one thing: Roman wasn't a good guy. She could list a handful of unbecoming adjectives to describe him now, but there was something else that couldn't be erased from the list: He was also her granddaughter's father.

Rachel closed her eyes and rested her head against the chair. It all felt surreal, so widely encompassing. And in those quiet moments, Rachel was able to put aside her own reality and think of someone who potentially had it worse: Monica. At the end of the day, both of their lives had been forever altered, only in different ways. Rachel's heart hurt for her friend, regardless of the events that had led them to this moment. Monica had no fault in the Roman and Chloe storyline. And for that reason alone, Rachel was able to separate her friend from the picture. She too was hurting.

With a small window of time ahead of her, Rachel drew her phone out and clicked the Favorites contact list, where Monica's name sat just under Chris's. She tapped it. As it rang, Rachel ran through what she would say: *I'm here for you. You're going to get through this. He doesn't deserve you.*

When Monica's voicemail picked up, Rachel was met with both disappointment and relief. It wasn't going to be an easy conversation. The awkwardness combined with heartbreak mixed into a weird cocktail Rachel hadn't tasted before. She hung up without leaving a message.

Rachel sighed. She let herself think back over the past few months, wondering where the problems between them had first begun. Was it really about a stupid cup? No, she determined. Those things were trivial. It was the secret that had tipped everything over the edge.

Rachel's heart rate accelerated just thinking about it. The hurt she'd felt at finding out Monica had withheld something so important. But the more she tossed it around, studied it from all angles, a new perspective emerged. Maybe Monica had done what she'd thought was right, which was being loyal to Chloe. Perhaps it was a reflection of her love. And while it didn't change everything, this context made it a bit more understandable.

Just as she was about to get up to distract herself with prepping a post-nap snack for the kids, her phone vibrated in her hand with an incoming text from Monica. A reply to Rachel's unanswered call.

Don't feel like talking.

Rachel's chest contracted. She pictured her friend, distraught, mascara caked under her eyes. Glued to her phone after the newest allegation.

Rachel let her mind wander, slicing apart the text in analysis. Did Monica not want to talk because she was crippled with sadness? Or was it something else: Did she not feel like talking to *Rachel*? Was she seeking solace elsewhere? In that moment, there on a wooden rocking chair in a room that held a permanent funky smell, Rachel welled up. She'd never felt more apart from the woman who'd been at her side for over twenty years. It was as though they were strangers living in the same town. Perhaps they'd never roomed together at all. Central Perk had never existed. No Rachel and Monica—no *Friends*.

A shiver made Rachel hug herself. She tried playing devil's advocate. What would she want if she'd discovered Chris was an adulterer? The answer came to her swifter than air: She'd crave the comfort of her best friend. Only it seemed Monica didn't want the same.

Her phone buzzed again, and Rachel all but jumped up from the chair. Monica must have changed her mind. Rachel's spirits lifted, predicting the text. *I was wrong. Call me. I need you.*

But when she looked to her phone, hope dashed. The message was from a number not saved to her phone.

Hi, it's Vienna! Got your number from Britt, Aaron's mom :) Just checking in. I'm sure you're feeling the effects of all this too. Hugs! How is Monica?

Rachel knew it was no more than snoopy gossip seeking, but Vienna had touched a nerve—Rachel *was* reeling. And for once, it felt good for someone to check on her. She may not be the scorned wife, but that didn't mean she wasn't affected.

So she replied despite the tug at her conscience that said to stay out of it, to keep all information between her and Monica—that is, if she ever talked to her friend again. There wasn't anything wrong with little tidbits here and there, she reasoned. After all, the school moms were simply concerned about their fellow parent and the ramifications to the children. Their hearts were in a good place. Hers too.

Rachel's thumbs hovered over the phone. She didn't want to admit she hadn't actually talked to Monica. What best friends wouldn't immediately confide in each other when shit hit the fan? She couldn't let Vienna know. She had to remain the informed source.

Rachel typed a quick response, saying Monica was going through a lot but hanging in there. Vienna's reply made her warm inside: **You're such a good friend.**

FIFTY-ONE

MONICA

Vacation rentals knew how to suck you in.

Book now for your next January getaway!

She usually liked these reminders. They'd booked their beach house around this time every year.

Until now.

Monica thought back to a little over a year ago when they'd been planning their Florida trip. How she'd been craving an escape. How much she'd looked forward to spending time with the people she loved most. She never could have expected that trip to be the catalyst for the greatest fallout of her life.

Monica clicked delete on the email. There would be no more beach trips with the Morelands.

She was in the parking lot, waiting for the boys to get out of school—a place she rarely inhabited. She'd had to cancel several appointments and leave work early, all of which had left her agitated. Her estrangement from Rachel had come with a voluntary dissolution of their routine, one in which Rachel had done most of the carpooling, even after things had become strained between them, for the sake of the children. They hadn't formally discussed it, but to Monica, it went without saying—the families needed a little separation. Now, it was up to Monica to deal with this professional hardship and figure out a new system.

Monica leaned against the car. She still wore her scrubs from a procedure earlier. She closed her eyes, breathing in the crisp fall air and letting it shock some energy back into her. Sleep had been hard to come by, and stress had made her clothes fit looser than before.

A voice made her eyes creak back open.

"It's Monica, right?" A woman with too-white teeth and perfect highlights approached.

Monica stood straight; gave a nod.

The woman extended her hand. "I'm Vienna Scott. I don't think we've formally met." A quick intake of Monica's outfit finished the rest of the sentence: *Because you're always working.* "Our boys play basketball together."

"Oh, right. Nice to meet you." Monica knew who Vienna was—who didn't?—but the two had never spoken. She wasn't in the business of befriending all the moms. Didn't have the time. And now didn't have the stamina.

"Lucas is a sweetheart," Vienna said. "We should totally get the kids together for a playdate or something."

"For sure." It was all she could muster.

Vienna must have picked up on the mood because she came a step closer, as though the two were longtime friends instead of just officially meeting. "Also, I just wanted to let you know that if you ever need anything... you know, with all that's been going on... I'm here. I'm sure it's been unimaginable. My sister actually went through something similar."

Monica's throat constricted. This woman had no idea how she felt. And yet, the offer came with a feeling of gratitude. She'd never felt more alone than she had in the past few weeks. After all, Roman had moved out, temporarily staying at a hotel until he could find a place to rent. Hearing the words "I'm here" was enough to make Monica want to jump into the woman's arms.

But this wasn't someone with whom to reveal her deepest thoughts. That person was someone else.

Like a twist of fate, something caught Monica's eye and she turned to see Rachel's car pull into the parking lot. She diverted, not wanting to be caught staring, but not before Vienna noticed.

"Her husband worked with yours, right? Oof, that's gotta be awkward."

"Just a little," Monica said, raising her eyebrows.

Across the lot, Rachel got out of her car, walked toward the school, and went through the door. There was no way she didn't see the other two women, yet Monica wrestled with whether to acknowledge her once-friend. It felt torturous not saying hello. But then, Rachel wasn't going out of her way to acknowledge her either. Monica kept her gaze square on Vienna.

"I mean, don't you think she should have said something? Her husband had to have seen stuff going on. Isn't that like basic friendship 101?"

Monica shrugged, feeling awkward with where the conversation had turned. Feeling watched with Rachel nearby. On one hand, Monica wholeheartedly agreed with Vienna. Chris *had* to have seen things. Rachel *most definitely* should have said something. Then again, who was she to talk about what friends were allowed to keep from each other? And what's more, how could she blame Chris for not seeing anything when she hadn't either?

"You guys went to college together, right?" Vienna said.

How did she know so much? "Duquesne."

"Ah. I was an Ohio State girl. Go, Buckeyes!"

Monica gave a pinched smile.

"You guys must have spent every minute together. College was the best, wasn't it?"

"Well, three years. Rachel didn't finish school."

"Oh, she didn't graduate?"

"No." The response came out like a breath of laughter. Why she'd said it—and why she'd said it like that—she didn't know. Almost a reflection of the absurdity of the conversation to begin with. It had just sort of tumbled out—more fact than mudsling. The exchange had simply pulled her along like a current, and frankly, her mind wasn't the clearest. That Rachel hadn't graduated meant nothing to Monica; had never been a topic within their friendship.

And yet at the same moment she chose to utter such an unimportant piece of information, Rachel was passing by again on her return to her car. Rachel stopped mid-stride, and even though she kept her head to the ground, Monica knew she'd heard.

FIFTY-TWO

RACHEL

November

RACHEL MADE A QUICK STOP TO PICK UP DIAPERS FOR Laina before work when a calendar reminder popped up on her phone: *L&L sleepover.*

A pang hit her chest. She remembered putting it on her schedule forever ago. Monica had some obligation—work? Campaign-related?—and Rachel had happily agreed to keep the boys overnight.

Only that was before.

Pre-scandal.

Pre-Laina.

Rachel's life had become a split existence of the time before everything fell apart and after. This was the longest stretch of time the two women had ever gone without speaking. She hadn't helped with the boys for weeks. That day in the parking lot, she couldn't believe what she'd heard. Monica had been gossiping about her. And bringing up one of Rachel's sorest spots to boot. She'd retreated to her car to wait for her body to stop shaking. An image of Monica and Vienna laughing behind her back had haunted Rachel for days.

Rachel deleted the calendar item, but even though it disappeared from the screen, it lingered in her mind. She and Monica might be on the outs, but now the drama was impacting the kids. She missed seeing Lucas and Logan almost as much as she did Monica. Surely the grown-ups could agree to put everything aside for the benefit of the little ones? It was the right thing to do.

Still, her breath quickened. Rachel tapped to open a new message. It would be their first communication in weeks. How did you start a text on the heels of such calamity? Hi? Hello? Hey, girl? By the way, don't worry about that insult?

Nothing felt right. So she skipped the greeting and got straight to the point.

Want me to just pick up the boys from school for the sleepover?

And then she waited, like she was texting with a blind date. A moment later, Monica's response appeared.

They don't need to stay over anymore.

Rachel drooped, feeling crushed by the declaration and its curtness. The boys didn't need a sitter. Did that mean Monica's plans had changed? Or had she got someone else to watch them? Someone who wasn't Rachel?

She stared at her phone, unsure whether and how to reply. In the end, she didn't. She was in a maze, a fun house where mirrors distorted everything and she didn't know how to find the exit.

. . .

The day passed in a blur. Rachel was loading Jacob and his backpack at the school when her son squealed in her ear.

"Lucas!" His arm flew up into a wave so fast it almost hit her in the face. Despite occasional passings in the hallway, the boys still got excited to see each other.

Rachel spun instinctively before her brain had time to register her new reality: *We're not friends with that family anymore. We don't say hi anymore.*

But, to her surprise, it wasn't Monica's vehicle Lucas and Logan were walking toward. It was Vienna Scott's.

Lucas detoured and ran over to Jacob. The boys clapped hands and began discussing Lucas's new shoes. Rachel recognized them as the same ones Jacob had pointed out at the store —she'd flinched at the price and moved them along.

From a few yards away, Vienna waved. "Hey, Rach!" It was too casual a reference, a shortening only Monica or Chris used. "The boys are having a sleepover tonight. Come on, kiddos!" She waved for Lucas, and he gave Jacob a quick *See ya* before skipping back and hopping into the SUV.

Rachel bristled at the sight of Vienna caring for Monica's boys. That was *her* role. She attempted a smile, but it felt false and probably came off as such. She couldn't help but take it as an insult. Someone—Vienna!—was a better choice than her. Rachel had been replaced. Spots flashed across her vision, her knees going weak.

Was this how it was going to be? Laina was over a month old already. Would there never be an attempt to fix things between them?

"Mom, are you okay? You look really pale," Jacob said.

Rachel glanced back to where Vienna pulled from the parking lot with Monica's kids.

"I'm fine," she said, placing both hands on the steering wheel. She took a gulp of air and let it out. She had to pull it together.

FIFTY-THREE

MONICA

When November seventh rolled around, Monica went to work instead of to the campaign headquarters. Her staff didn't question her presence, even though the day had been marked off on the calendar for a year. There was no *what are you doing here?*, only quiet nods and gentle smiles. She'd bought a new shift dress from Neiman Marcus, intending to wear it as a celebratory outfit when Roman won, but instead she walked through her office in scrubs and rubber shoes. Monica despised being treated like a porcelain doll, but if truth be told, she was liable to shatter at any moment, and so she accepted the extra baked goods in the break room and the fact that the nurses were on their A game.

The campaign had largely fallen apart, and despite Roman's best efforts to deflect and deny, his polling numbers shocked no one. He was a villain, a leper. But in line with his narcissistic personality, he didn't drop out. As election day went on and new reports filed in, his popularity dwindled. So much so, that around eight that evening, just as polls closed and without waiting to count ballots, Roman texted her.

Where are you? Need you here for concession speech.

She choked on laughter when she read it. Not only was he a cheater, he was a delusional cheater. Was he insane? They'd barely communicated beyond what was necessary for the children.

You couldn't pay me. Boys and I are at the movies.

We need to be a united front.

She turned the phone over on her lap.

Then twenty minutes later: **Monica, I'm serious. Are you coming?**

She read it and slipped the phone into her purse to buzz away. By the time the movie ended, there were seven missed calls and even more texts from Roman. If he thought she was going to stand behind him—a devoted wife in solidarity—he was sorely mistaken.

Instead, she took the boys home and put them immediately to bed—movie dates on a school night weren't the norm, but nothing was quite normal right now, so what did it matter?

With her little ones tucked into bed, Monica curled up on the couch. She flipped on the TV just in time to catch the local eleven o'clock news where her husband's face prominently took up the screen, looking tired, skin sallow. Along the bottom, the ticker tape read: NASH CONCEDES MAYORAL RACE AFTER BITTER DEFEAT.

"This is not the outcome we had hoped for," Roman addressed the camera. "But I have spoken with Haverty and congratulated him on his win. My team and I are disappointed, and I know many of our supporters feel the same. However, it's time to come together collectively as citizens of Wexford for the good of our community."

Monica's blood boiled just watching him. No mention of the scandals that surrounded him and undeniably led to his downfall. No public apology. Again, she found herself questioning everything. Who was this man she'd thought she knew?

But the rage quickly morphed into something else—sadness. Sadness for the life she'd thought she had, the husband who didn't live up to his end of the deal, and the future of her boys. She let the emotion wash over her, not resisting. She was alone in a room filled with beautiful things but no one to share them with. And that's when she registered a counterpart to sadness—loneliness. New friends—if she could even call them that—weren't the same as old ones. Her body ached for the true companionship she'd been missing for so long. Not only her husband, but a friend.

Rachel.

Maybe her longing traveled through the dark night to a house on the other side of town, because at the same moment she wiped her nose with the sleeve of her pajamas, her phone lit up. Monica's heart leaped into her throat. She read the text through blurry eyes.

Hi. I know a lot has happened, but I miss you. Can we talk soon?

She'd dismissed more than one attempt on Rachel's part, never mustering up whatever it took to mend such a wound. What was it—courage? But this time it felt different. It was as though a rope had been tossed across the crater of grief. An olive branch. One she hadn't had the courage to throw herself but was so eternally grateful for. Her cells tingled. She typed a quick response.

I miss you too.

Nerves made her fingers shake, as though it was a stranger she was texting rather than her best friend. Still, things were so very different now. Could she open herself to forgiveness? She heard her mother's wise voice in her head talking about releasing negativity. *Be like a tree and drop your leaves. That's the only way to start fresh.*

But it wasn't that simple. Rachel was now forever linked to Roman through Chloe and Laina. She couldn't be rid of one without associating with the other. It all tangled like a thick web in her brain, so much that she had to pinch her eyes shut. Could she be in Rachel's presence without thinking of Chloe? Could she see pictures of Laina without being reminded of Roman?

Monica let her mind drift back to college, to the shared room they'd coined Central Perk. The way two girls had clicked with such ease. Stumbling home from being out too late only to stay up even more to dissect Monica's crush over plates of day-old pizza. Standing next to Rachel on her wedding day then reversing roles a handful of years later. The Christmas they both got each other the same gift because that's how in sync their brains were. How Rachel read the eulogy at Monica's father's funeral because Monica simply couldn't.

So much history. Impossible to erase.

When the frenzy in her mind calmed, she sent a follow-up text.

I need a little time. But I'd like to try.

It was all she could give in that moment. The possibility of hope. And a promise to herself to accept a new day.

EPILOGUE

Ten months later

MONICA

The Prantl's box sat on the passenger seat while Monica drove. Normally, she'd be the one holding the box while Roman drove, but she hadn't been in a car with him in over a year, and now, with the boys too young to sit up front, the passenger seat was typically empty.

"Maybe LaLa will get a Power Wheels," Logan said from the back, referring to Laina with his chosen nickname.

"A baby can't drive a Power Wheels," Lucas sneered to his little brother. "It's going to be boring stuff like those buckets where you have to put the shapes through the holes."

"I like playing with those."

"That's because you're still a baby."

Logan whined. "Moooom, Lucas called me a baby."

"Boys, come on," Monica said. "Can't you just get along? We're going to Laina's birthday party." She peered at them in her rear-view mirror then took in her own reflection. New lines had formed between her brows over the last year. More gray hairs meant she'd had to book her coloring appointments closer together. She looked away, afraid of tumbling down into the thought that kept her up at night: *Who would want a middle-aged woman with two kids?*

The stress had peaked around the six-month mark, when it hit Monica that Laina—her sons' sister—was already half a year old. For the longest time, she'd buried her head in the sand, not wanting to face a world in which things hadn't turned out like she'd planned. She worked and went to bed, then worked and went to bed. Stay busy, head down. She'd blocked everything else out, even Vienna Scott, who, as it turned out, wasn't the type of friend Monica wanted. The divorce went through quickly, but even that didn't buoy her morale. It wasn't a fresh start; it was a bitter end—one she hadn't even caused.

It wasn't until that day in March when Chloe posted a picture of Laina with a big "6" on her onesie that something clicked. She'd stared at the picture, taking in every detail of Laina, marveling at how she'd grown. Time kept moving; the world kept spinning. Right then and there, Monica realized she was letting life pass her by. What good was it to hide away, letting anger turn her insides black? From that moment, she flipped a mental switch.

Or at least she tried. Maybe "flip" was too easy. Maybe it was more like a slow lift. Life hadn't handed her what she'd expected, but she was wasting what she did have by allowing resentment to win.

No more. Things had to change.

The following week, she spoke to the hospital administration about hiring another doctor into her practice. They interviewed several, ultimately landing on a talented woman not much older than Monica who fit into the office seamlessly. In turn, Monica's schedule relaxed. She was able to see patients, work on her research, *and* make it to her boys' functions without feeling the crippling guilt like before.

Lucas and Logan reveled in her presence. And Monica—well, she hung up the old thoughts of what it meant to be a mother and a woman in the world. Screw what others thought. Her life was hers and no one else's. She'd no longer let the pressure, the expectations, get to her.

Mostly.

It was a start.

As for Roman, with his political aspirations shot and the local colleges unwilling to risk hiring him, he'd turned to some sort of online consulting, which Monica didn't understand fully but had no need to so long as his work allowed him to keep up with their shared-custody agreement. In the end, the boys loved their father, and he was good to them. The rest—the undoubted questions that would arise—would shake out when they got older.

Closure would work its way into Monica's life, but not without first sitting down with two very important pieces to the puzzle. She'd begun with Chloe on a mild spring morning in the park. Monica had waited on a bench, and when she'd seen Chloe walking toward her pushing a stroller, she'd reminded herself of what she was doing; why she was there.

"Hi," Chloe had said meekly, stopping a few feet short.

Monica had taken in the scene. Chloe with a baby—not just any baby. She'd sucked in a deep breath and allowed the physical responses that came. The corners of her mouth had wanted to pull up. She'd let them. A gentle smile. "Come here, chickadee." She'd extended her arms, and Chloe had stepped into them.

"I'm sorry," Chloe had said, voice trembling.

"I know." Monica had planted her feet wide, feeling it all. "I know."

CHLOE

Chloe strung a happy birthday banner across the front of Laina's highchair. She couldn't believe her daughter was turning one—where had the year gone?—but was nowhere near as emotional about it as Rachel. Her mother had been walking around misty-eyed all morning, muttering things like "too fast" and "my sweet little baby."

Laina was still a baby in most senses of the word, but to the family, she'd grown leaps and bounds from the tiny infant with jerky limbs whom Chloe had worn in a carrier on her chest. Not yet walking unassisted, she cruised along furniture and crawled at the speed of light to get where she wanted. Curious and determined were the paramount adjectives to describe the little raven-haired girl.

It was nap time, and that meant Chloe had two hours to finish all her prep work for the party. She lined party hats along the counter to match the "ONEderland" theme. One for each guest—she fully expected everyone to be on board. A child only reached this milestone once, and Chloe wanted it to be special.

Her phone buzzed with a text, and Chloe pulled it from the back pocket of her jeans.

It was Ava.

On my way! Wait till you see what I got her.

Chloe recounted the triangle hats, making sure she had one for everyone. She was glad Ava was coming—she'd be the only other person Chloe's age at the party. As it turned out, having a baby at nineteen didn't exactly align with the rest of her peers, and friends had trickled off the map after Laina's birth for no reason aside from life's natural course. Chloe couldn't blame them. Her life went from beer pong to milk bottles. But Ava had been different. Ava stuck around, a token auntie who spoiled

Chloe's daughter and bought her books about influential women like Susan B. Anthony and Ruth Bader Ginsburg. Their friendship had saved Chloe, and she was eternally grateful, despite all that had happened, that she'd been able to forgive.

It wasn't easy at first. After Ava's media tip came to light, Chloe had been furious. What was Ava thinking? But emotional pain lessens over time, and Chloe simply couldn't find it in herself to hold on to hatred. Ava's persistent apologies didn't hurt either. She'd been filled with such self-reproach, going so far as to drive to the Morelands to repent to Rachel and Chris too.

In the end, Chloe came around. Ava's intentions had never been malicious. And the more thought Chloe placed on that forbidden afternoon at the beach house, the more she realized Ava was right. Roman *had* taken advantage of her. She couldn't blame Ava's fact-focused tendencies or her predisposition to uncover the truth. After all, it was what good journalists did.

Across the kitchen, Rachel cut tea sandwiches and arranged them on a platter.

"Okay," she said. "We've got these, and the fruit tray, and my grandma's famous macaroni salad."

"What's that empty tray for?" Chloe said.

"The cookies. Monica's bringing them."

The name fell from her mother's lips without a beat, and Chloe's insides warmed. A year ago, things had been so different. Tense and somber, like they were all tiptoeing around hidden landmines, afraid to set any off. If Chloe was changed, her mother had become a shell of her former self. As though losing Monica had ripped off a critical limb Rachel needed to function. The family had operated under a heavy layer of stress those first few weeks and months.

Then Monica called. Followed by a meeting in the park, cautious yet open. Then texts, check-ins. Not as often as before, but with a slow return. The baby steps made all the difference and eased much of Chloe's guilt. Never taking it fully away but allowing her to continue living for the people that needed her—most notably, Laina.

Chloe wasn't sure she'd ever forgive herself for the pain she'd caused Preston. The two had had no contact since shortly after Laina's birth, but young minds couldn't help but be curious, and so Chloe had, on more than one occasion, asked Ava if she ever ran into him on campus. He wasn't very active on social media, and Chloe wondered if he was happy, if he'd moved on. She'd been torn to hear that Preston had transferred schools, relocating closer to home. When she closed her eyes at night, she prayed he'd find it in himself to one day forgive her.

The thought of Preston came with a bittersweet pang. She often found herself falling down the rabbit hole of what ifs. How different would her life be if he'd been Laina's father? But those thoughts were useless. Laina had the father she had, and while Roman wasn't present in her life, he sent regular payments for Laina's upkeep. Thinking of explaining it all to her daughter someday did nothing but threaten to form an ulcer in Chloe's stomach, so she chose instead to lean into acceptance. It may not have been what she'd planned, but it was her reality. And at the end of the day, she gave silent thanks for all the good people Laina had around her.

RACHEL

Rachel fiddled with the piñata cord, then turned at the sound of someone coming into the kitchen.

"Hi," Monica said, placing the Prantl's box on the counter. Then, with a tentative point, "Do you need help with that?"

Rachel's throat tightened. Before, Monica wouldn't have asked; she'd just reach in to help. Now they tested all waters with each other, second-guessing instead of simply doing. "I'm good."

She wasn't. It was a two-person job, hanging the thing. But despite Chloe and Monica's gradual rekindling, things hadn't bounced back quite as easily for Rachel and her friend. As though a row of bricks had been removed from the street of their relationship, causing a hole deep enough to burst any tire that dared cross over.

When Chloe said she was inviting Monica and the boys to Laina's party, Rachel had had to bite her tongue from saying, *Are you sure?* In the handful of times they'd been in each other's presence over the last few months—kids' activities mostly—there had been a ghost in their company. A ghost of the past. They'd start on opposite sides of the room or field or court, moving slowly closer together each time, until the day they happened to be walking into the school at the same time, nearly knocking shoulders getting through the door. It had been the first time they'd touched in what felt like an eternity, the simple brush of skin all but taking Rachel's breath away.

Upstairs, the familiar sound of footfall reminded Rachel that nothing had changed between the little kids, and that made her heart happy.

Rachel pulled the twine, raising the piñata. She stood on a chair and reached to tie it off on a hook in the ceiling where a macramé plant holder usually hung. When she did, the twine slipped and the piñata crashed to the ground. "Dammit."

Monica stepped forward. "Let me help you." She lifted the piñata while Rachel again reached for the ceiling, securing it with a double knot. They stood close enough that Rachel could smell Monica's perfume. Calvin Klein's Eternity. The same one she'd worn for two decades. Rachel could detect it anywhere. A gush of nostalgia flooded her, like watching a favorite classic movie, wrapped in the comfort of home. She had to blink several times to refocus.

Satisfied, Rachel stepped down. "There. Perfect. Thanks." The friends locked eyes and exchanged quick smiles. Something in Rachel's tummy fluttered. A warmth fanning out from her core. "We always were a good team," she said softly.

Monica's lip shook. "We were."

A beat of silence hung between them before Rachel busied herself with a stack of bright pink paper plates. Monica cleared her throat.

"I stuffed this thing when I should have been working on a paper last night," Rachel said, feeling like the doors had somehow been opened for conversation beyond pleasantries.

"Chloe told me about your classes. That's amazing. How's it going?"

"Good, but exhausting. Night classes after work all day means I'm basically a zombie when I finally get home."

Chris had insisted that Rachel not let Laina's arrival thwart her school plans.

"Just give it a try," he'd said. "You still have to live your life."

After several talks, he'd convinced her to enroll. One class, that's all. Just to see how it went.

The following semester, she'd taken two.

She hadn't seen it at the time, but he'd been right. Laina was Chloe's responsibility, and while Rachel would always be there, her role was that of support. She was the grandmother, not the mother. Chloe would have to grow up and step up, which to this point, she'd done beautifully.

Monica gave a small smile. "I'm glad you're finally doing it. I'm really proud of you, Rach."

Rachel swelled. "Thanks."

"And Chloe?"

"She's thinking next fall. Part-time of course." It wouldn't be easy, but they'd spent plenty of time discussing options as a family. They'd make it work—somehow.

Monica stared at the floor for a long second then lifted her gaze. "I'd love to help," she said timidly. "I mean, if you need someone. I'm scaling back my work hours a bit. Shifting things around. I could take a day to watch Laina if you're at work and Chloe's at class."

Rachel's hands froze midway through fanning a stack of napkins. "Why would you want to do that?"

"I don't know. Guilt? Responsibility? Genuine desire?" Monica's face flushed as she talked. "I feel a connection to this baby even if I shouldn't. Even if it doesn't make sense. And Chloe's like a daughter to me. I really just want to help. Nothing more."

Rachel's stomach had flipped at that comment. *Like a daughter*. Hadn't that been part of the catalyst to begin with? The cause of the jealousy that had pulled them apart? And now Monica was swooping in again to save the day?

Rachel went to protest, but Monica was too eager and cut her off. She pressed her palms together as in prayer. "I know what you're thinking, Rach. But please. Understand that this comes only from a source of love. I could never replace you as Chloe's mom—Laina's grandma. The fact that I can hopefully still have a place in this family is enough for me. Listen, childcare is tough. I get it."

Rachel knew what that meant. "Tough" was code for expensive. She felt her defenses rising. Once again, it would be money that would separate them on different levels.

"I'm just saying it would help save a little," Monica said. "You wouldn't have to pay me. I wouldn't *want* you to pay me."

Rachel's eyes narrowed. "But how could you..."

Monica brought a hand to her brow with a laugh. "Who knows? Maybe I'm crazy." Her expression softened. "She's just a baby. A precious little thing. I guess my priorities have shifted. You've helped me so much with my boys over the years. I'm long overdue to return the favor."

An answer wasn't needed right then, which was good because Rachel wouldn't have been able to give one. Still, it felt like an offering rooted in goodness, grounded in support. And like the slow stitch-by-stitch repair of a rip that seems unmendable, Rachel felt something shift between them. Perhaps they could find their way back to each other, slow and steady.

A little later, Rachel watched Chloe walk back into the kitchen and pull a pale pink party hat on, letting the string snap under her chin.

"Where's Laina?" Monica asked.

"Still sleeping," Chloe said, hitting a button on the baby monitor to bring the screen to life. Just as she did, a gurgle came from the speaker, and they both watched as Laina stood up in her crib, grabbing hold of the rail. She babbled a string of sounds. "Or not," Chloe said with a chuckle. "I'll go get her."

As she left, she passed Chris, who entered the kitchen, greeted Monica, and planted a kiss on Rachel's cheek. Butterflies danced in Rachel's belly, just as they had all those years ago when their love was so new. For all the bumps in their road, they'd managed to hold on to each other.

After Roman's campaign collapsed and the dust settled, it took a little while for Chris to return to his old job, but when he did, it was with fresh zeal. Now in a management position, he was in talks with the owner about ways to continue moving up.

His paychecks were a little bigger, but that wasn't what made Rachel happy—it was the look of accomplishment and satisfaction on her husband's face when he returned home each day.

Laina's chatter reached the kitchen before Chloe rounded the corner with the baby in her arms.

"Well, didn't you have a nice, long nap," Rachel said, giving Laina's chubby thigh a squeeze.

"Hello, birthday girl," Monica said, to which Laina gave a wide grin. Two little teeth poked from her bottom gums. Then, surprising them all, Laina reached out a hand and then another toward Monica. Everyone turned their gazes.

Monica fumbled over her words. "You want... me?" She eyed the group as if asking for permission. *Can I hold this child?* Chloe gave a little nod, to which Monica extended her arms. "Okay, come here."

Chloe passed her daughter off to Monica, who bounced in place with Laina on her hip. Rachel sucked in a quiet breath. The scene was like something from a movie. One where scandal made it impossible for relationships to survive.

Only they had.

Mostly.

They weren't the old relationships but new ones.

Rachel pulled Chloe into her side and watched Monica. It couldn't be easy. Accepting, forgiving. The less complicated thing would be for them all to go their separate ways, to dodge the pain with distance. But then they would miss out on so much possibility, everyday moments like these where love surmounts hurt. Where even the biggest hurdles are matchless against well-built bonds.

For Rachel, much of the last year had been a lesson in contentment, a swift reminder that all that glitters isn't gold—when it came to work, family, and friend circles. Sometimes, the best things in life are the things you already had—the ones you had all along. And now, the things that make their way back.

An hour later, when the sandwiches were gone and the kids had creamed the piñata with a plastic baseball bat, showering candy across the tiled floor, Chloe sat in the living room with Laina on her lap. Surrounding her were bags exploding with tissue paper; boxes stacked like a pyramid. "You guys, this is too much," she said. By the third gift, Laina had lost interest and was too difficult to keep contained. She crawled to where the discarded wrapping paper lay in balls on the floor and played happily. Chloe opened the rest of the presents—light-up toys, outfits with bows, and the most adorable pair of little rubber rain boots.

When she got to Ava's gift, her friend clapped her hands together in anticipation. "I hope everyone can take a joke."

Chloe pulled from the bag a onesie with words screen-printed to the front: *Best Plot Twist Ever.* She held it up for the family to read. There was a beat of silence, followed by hysterics from all.

"Sorry, I couldn't pass it up," Ava said.

Chloe shook her head. "Only you, Av."

Rachel's mind spun with thoughts of the past two years—the peaks, the valleys, and the winding switchback road connecting the two. She'd almost fallen off the edge. But she didn't.

Gift opening complete, Chloe slipped Laina into her high-chair. They dimmed the lights and sang "Happy Birthday," as Rachel brought over a small, round smash cake topped with a single candle. Chloe held Laina's hands down so she wouldn't reach for the flame then helped her blow it out when the song concluded. Everyone cheered. Laina reached for the pink icing, smearing it over the bottom half of her face on the way to her mouth, sending sweet laughter through the kitchen.

Rachel looked around the room and saw nothing but smiles. Behind some of them, she knew, were souls still healing, lives still finding their way. Hers was one of them. But here in this moment, serenity was stronger. The day was bigger than all of them.

Rachel's eyes met Monica's. The two paused, holding on to each other's gaze, so many things passing between them. Wordless but received. Seasons, she understood, were very much one day at a time. And while there would be rain, there'd also be rainbows.

A LETTER FROM JEN

Dear reader,

Thank you so much for reading *Her Daughter*. I hope you enjoyed it! If so, and if you want to keep up to date with all my latest releases, just sign up at the following link.

https://www.bookouture.com/jen-craven

Your email address will never be shared, and you can unsubscribe at any time. I would also be very grateful if you could leave a brief review of your thoughts—reviews are so helpful for increasing a book's visibility and also make a difference in helping new readers discover one of my books. Hearing from readers makes my job all the more enjoyable—you can get in touch with me on Instagram, Facebook, or through my website. Again, thank you for your support. You had endless book choices, and I'm very appreciative you chose to read mine.

Jen Craven

https://www.jencraven.com

facebook.com/JenniferCravenAuthor

instagram.com/jencravenauthor

BOOK CLUB DISCUSSION QUESTIONS

Her Daughter, as with Jen Craven's other novels, lends itself well to book clubs as it's rife with meaty discussion points, juicy plot twists, and plenty of room for insightful conversation. If you're interested in selecting Jen's books for your book club, please reach out at www.jencraven.com. Jen regularly meets with book club groups and would love to join yours!

Here are some discussion questions to consider:

1. Rachel experiences jealousy when it comes to her daughter's relationship with Monica. Do you think her reactions were justified? Do you believe underneath even the closest friendships lies some level of envy?

2. Both women withheld information from each other throughout the book. Which did you agree with, and which (if any) did you find unforgiveable? How would you have handled these situations?

3. One of Rachel's worst fears was history repeating itself. How do you think this belief influenced Rachel's actions both toward Monica and Chloe?

4. A theme throughout the book is accepting what you have, along with the lesson, "the grass isn't always greener on the other side." Do you believe Rachel and Monica reached a point of contentment?

5. Monica brushes off several red flags in her marriage. What does her storyline say about intuition? What does it say about modern motherhood?

6. Part of Chloe's story is a coming-of-age journey. Have you ever had a time in your past where you made decisions you wish you could take back? How did those choices impact your future?

ACKNOWLEDGMENTS

At the heart of this novel is a story of friendship, and therefore it feels only right to start out by thanking the people I'm lucky enough to call my friends. Whether I've known them for twenty years or two years, I feel fortunate to have such supportive people in my corner. If I've ever cried on your shoulder, or if we've ever sang into hairbrushes, shared bad fashion trends, or if we can read each other's minds with just a look—you're one of my people. To the friends I see regularly, and the ones I don't, but who are still just as important as ever: You know who you are, and I thank you.

Among these friends are fellow authors, some I've never even met in person. The writing community has been invaluable to me, providing endless inspiration and encouragement. To the women of my author collective, The Eleventh Chapter, I so value your friendship and the vision we share. Our conversations never fail to make me laugh and think, and I've learned so much from all of you.

Thank you to my early readers, Kerry Chaput and Caitlin Weaver—my OG betas!—for your insight and guidance in getting my manuscripts where they need to be. I love that I can email you something like, "This is a hot mess, but would you mind taking a look?" and the answer is always yes.

Books go through countless rounds of editing, and so I'm eternally thankful to my editor Billi-Dee Jones, along with Harriet Wade, who had eyes on an early draft. Thank you for guiding the story in the right direction while letting me stay true to my vision. The "fabulous Lauras," Laura Kincaid and Laura Gerrard did the most detailed copyedit and proofread. I'm grateful to the entire Bookouture team for providing a top-notch, enjoyable publishing experience.

My Instagram followers helped name baby Laina, and I think it was the perfect choice. Thank you for playing along and having fun with me.

Thank you to the booksellers and indie bookstores who have supported me through book launches and beyond. Hometowns are something special, and mine is always eager to support me, whether it's through displaying flyers, promoting my books on social, or inviting me to community events.

To my family who are endlessly supportive and enthusiastic about every new book I publish: thank you from the bottom of my heart. Lastly, to my kids' teachers who have to hear about my books on repeat: thank you for humoring three small kiddos who are proud of their mama.

PUBLISHING TEAM

Turning a manuscript into a book requires the efforts of many people. The publishing team at Bookouture would like to acknowledge everyone who contributed to this publication.

Audio
Alba Proko
Sinead O'Connor
Melissa Tran

Commercial
Lauren Morrissette
Jil Thielen
Imogen Allport

Cover design
Emma Graves

Data and analysis
Mark Alder
Mohamed Bussuri

Editorial
Billi-Dee Jones
Nadia Michael

Copyeditor
Laura Gerrard

Proofreader
Laura Kincaid

Marketing
Alex Crow
Melanie Price
Occy Carr
Cíara Rosney

Operations and distribution
Marina Valles
Stephanie Straub

Production
Hannah Snetsinger
Mandy Kullar
Jen Shannon

Publicity
Kim Nash
Noelle Holten
Myrto Kalavrezou
Jess Readett
Sarah Hardy

Rights and contracts
Peta Nightingale
Richard King
Saidah Graham

Printed in Great Britain
by Amazon